Return this item by the last date shown.
Items may be renewedby telephone or at
www.ercultureandleisure.org/libraries

east renfrewshire
**CULTURE
andLEISURE**

| Barrhead | 0141 577 3518 | Mearns | 0141 577 4979 |
| Busby | 0141 577 4971 | Neilston | 0141 577 4981 |
| Clarkston | 0141 577 4972 | Netherlee | 0141 637 5102 |
| Eaglesham | 0141 577 3932 | Thornliebank | 0141 577 4983 |
| Giffnock | 0141 577 4976 | Uplawmoor | 01505 850564 |

# THE NARROWBOAT GIRLS

Elsie Barker is desperate for a new start after her husband leaves her. When her friend Izzy – who needs to escape her abusive boyfriend – tells her about the jobs going for women as narrowboat crew on the canals between London and Coventry, she jumps at the chance. Their new boss, Dorothy, is kind and fair, but it's clear she has a secret of her own. The crew is completed by Tolly, searching for a new vocation. The work is hard, but the girls forge close friendships that will see them through the darkest times. They could never have predicted how much the canals could change their lives...

# THE NARROWBOAT GIRLS

# THE NARROWBOAT GIRLS

*by*

Rosie Archer

**Magna Large Print Books**
Gargrave, North Yorkshire,
BD23 3SE, England.

British Library Cataloguing in Publication Data.

A catalogue record of this book is
available from the British Library

ISBN   978-0-7505-4734-5

First published in Great Britain in 2018 by Quercus Editions Ltd.

Copyright © 2018 Rosie Archer

Cover illustration © Woman by Head Design: Background © Topfoto
by arrangement with www.headdesign.co.uk

Published in Large Print 2019 by arrangement with
Quercus Editions Ltd.

Magna Large Print is an imprint of Library Magna Books Ltd.

Printed and bound in Great Britain by
T.J. (International) Ltd., Cornwall, PL28 8RW

For Dee Williams, my friend for over thirty years. A London saga novelist par excellence who has taught me much about writing.

## Chapter One

'I couldn't help it. Now she's having my baby, what can I do?'

'You could have kept it in your trousers!'

Elsie Barker turned away from her husband of ten years. She wasn't going to allow him to see her fall to pieces. No matter what she felt on the inside, outside she would show him she could handle things.

'Who is the woman who's carrying your child?' She was finding it difficult to keep calm.

'Just someone from my office.'

Unanswered questions began hurling themselves around her brain. 'Does this "just someone" have a name?'

'Hmm.' He coughed. 'Sandra. But it's not her fault that...'

For someone usually so articulate her husband was having difficulty in answering.

Sandra? Even the name sounded more glamorous than her own, thought Elsie. Then came his second blow.

'I'm happier now than I've ever been so I'm putting the house on the market. There should be enough money for you to buy somewhere in Gosport.' He screwed on the lid of the home-made marmalade and the scent of the oranges

11

faded as he calmly picked up the newspaper. Fleetingly she remembered cutting the rind into chunky pieces just the way Geoffrey liked and marvelled that he could even think about reading and eating after telling her she should be the one to leave their home.

'Why can't I stay here? My severance pay from teaching helped buy the house!' Tears were pricking at the back of her eyes. How could he do this awful thing to her? She thought suddenly of the early days, the fun they'd had searching antiques shops for just the right pieces of furniture to fit into the five-bedroom Western Way house in Alverstoke. This was her dream home, backing on to Stanley Park, a house with a considerable garden on which she lavished care and attention.

Geoffrey put down the paper and adjusted his cuffs beneath the sleeves of his dark pin-striped jacket. At forty years of age he liked his highly polished shoes to complement the colour of his suits and ties, to add just that little something extra to inspire confidence in his clients. He eyed her speculatively.

'This house is too big for one person. When I bought it we were going to fill it with children but you—'

'Don't you dare make it out to be my fault! Our doctor says infertility can happen to couples who want children too much...'

Elsie longed to hold a baby of her own in her arms. She blinked back the tears.

'It's no one's fault,' Geoffrey said quietly, with surprising gentleness. 'But you must surely understand why I need to buy another house, and I can't afford it until this one is sold.' His eyes met hers. 'You'll be happier in a small place of your own.'

The silence that followed was almost palpable. Elsie found she was staring at him as though she'd never seen him before in her life. So many questions needed answers but every reply might split her heart into pieces.

Then, despite everything, she could see his logic. The house, after all, belonged to him, Geoffrey Barker of Barker and Knowle, Solicitors, of the high street, Gosport in Hampshire. He was nothing if not logical and his quick brain was what made the partnership so successful. Even the terrible war years had been profitable for the firm.

'Will you leave me now?' Elsie asked. 'I need to think about this carefully.' She looked past him to the conservatory where the honeysuckle she had lovingly planted a couple of years ago was beginning to climb the glass to give shade during the hot days of summer.

Geoffrey folded his newspaper methodically. He was a very tidy man. For a while he simply stared at her, then asked, as he laid the newspaper by the side of his plate, 'Will you be all right?'

'I'll be as all right as any woman whose husband tells her over the breakfast toast and marmalade that he's fallen in love with a tart from his office.' Her anger was rising again.

'Stop it, Elsie. Sarcasm doesn't become you.'

And suddenly she could hold herself back no longer. 'Go!' she yelled, leaping up and shaking her fist. 'Get out! Get away from me!'

He beat a hasty retreat from the kitchen. Presently she heard the front door slam and his car start up. Then there was the crunch of tyres on the gravel in the driveway and he was gone.

Of course she hadn't wanted him to leave.

What her heart desired was for him to take her into his arms, beg her forgiveness and say they would get through this together. Tell her there was no Sandra from his office, no baby, and that he would always love her. But that was as impossible as him suddenly swinging her around in his arms, high off the floor and telling her he adored her. The spontaneous part of their marriage, despite her own efforts, had died long ago.

Elsie sat down at the kitchen table, put her head in her hands and gave way to her grief. Her marriage was over. Her home was shortly to be sold. Her life was in pieces.

She wanted to curl up in bed and die.

But in less than an hour she'd be standing on the line in Priddy's Hard munitions factory where she worked part-time filling shells with gunpowder, helping the war effort in the fight against Adolf Hitler.

Tonight after work she was to attend a farewell get-together. Her friend Izzy was off to do another job left vacant by a man who'd gone to fight. Elsie couldn't possibly put her own feelings first and not meet Izzy at the Fox public house in Gosport town. Could she put on a brave face and pretend everything was fine with her, Geoffrey and their marriage so Izzy wouldn't have to worry about her?

She realized she'd been a fool for never questioning Geoffrey's tales of working late. She'd tolerated his stories of weekend conferences at Brighton,

Worthing and other seaside places – there had been quite a few, these past months. Excuses for meetings with Sandra?

Had she been too occupied with the house, her job, the garden to wonder about Geoffrey's frequent disappearances? It had honestly never entered her mind that Geoffrey was straying further and further away from her. She'd accepted her marriage for what it was, and she had trusted him.

Elsie picked up the teapot to pour herself more tea and saw that she hadn't touched the first cup but allowed it to go cold. She stared at the beautiful blue creation in her hand. She and Geoffrey had discovered it in an antiques shop in Winchester on a wonderful summer's day just before the war had started.

'Damn you!' Elsie cried and flung it towards the wall. The pot smashed. Brown tea streamed down the pale wallpaper in rivulets, then dripped onto the cream rug. For a moment she felt triumphant, then distressed. Her outburst had changed nothing.

She could dig in her heels and refuse to budge from her home. But what good would that do?

Her mother had told her many years ago, 'You catch more flies with honey, than with vinegar.' She had been a wise woman. Did she really want to hang on to a man who had so callously cast her aside?

Elsie would take the new home offered her. Better to do that than pursue a long-drawn-out fight over property that she couldn't win. Geoffrey's name was on the deeds and his profession meant he would already have covered all aspects of a possible divorce, including any maintenance claims she might make.

Geoffrey's job didn't stop him enlisting but he'd had rheumatic fever as a child and it had left him with a heart murmur. There was no way Fate in the form of call-up papers would intervene and leave her in the house she loved.

She would not dwell on her husband sleeping with another woman – why waste mental anguish on something she couldn't change?

She stared across the table at herself in the mirror. She was thirty years old, still slim and by no means stupid. Then it hit her like a ton of bricks: losing her husband wasn't as painful as thinking about him impregnating another woman. That hurt. Like a knife twisting in an open wound.

It might be wise to remove herself from Gosport.

The thought of bumping into pregnant Sandra on Geoffrey's arm in the small town was too much for her to think about.

She would get ready for work. The chatter of the factory girls on the line was enough to brighten anyone's day. She would decide where she could go to get on with her life while her affairs were put in order.

That would pose a problem. How long would it take Geoffrey to find a house buyer? Where could she go to lick her wounds until she was ready to buy a place of her own? Elsie had no relatives. Her mother had died earlier in the war. She had very little money of her own. Could she rely on Geoffrey to fund her? Probably not if he needed to sell the house: his excuse would be that his new family must come first.

Automatically Elsie began to clear up the mess she'd made. When she had swept up the broken china and tea leaves, she took the dustpan outside, then slid the pieces of her beloved teapot into the dustbin, with the rest of her broken dreams.

## *Chapter Two*

Elsie propped her bicycle beneath the shelter among the long line of other bikes. With petrol rationed, most of the staff cycled to work. She liked riding along leafy Green Lane, down Whitworth Road then Weevil Lane to the munitions factory, even though due to the incessant bombing Gosport's roads frequently changed shape and were sometimes difficult to negotiate. Heaps of rubble that had once been homes and shops were piled like gapped teeth. The stink of dust and cordite seemed ever present.

Izzy caught up with her at the main gate to Priddy's.

'You are coming tonight, aren't you?' Isabel Baker, whom everyone called Izzy, looked worried. She reminded Elsie of a mischievous pixie, with her cloud of red hair framing a heart-shaped face. Her black eye, courtesy of her boyfriend, had changed colour today and the thick Pan Stik foundation almost, but not quite, disguised it.

'Wouldn't miss it,' said Elsie. She really liked the nineteen-year-old girl who was quick and nimble-fingered at her job, always ready with a

17

smart retort.

Already the pair had begun shrugging off their coats ready to hang up when they entered the locker room. All the women starting their shifts would remove their everyday clothes and put on the navy-blue dungarees and turbans in different colours depending on the area in which they worked. They would be searched for contraband. Hair grips, jewellery, cigarettes and matches: anything that could cause a spark was a fire hazard. Safety at all times was paramount.

Elsie asked, 'Is your Charlie coming back late tonight or tomorrow?'

She saw the flash of fear in Izzy's eyes before the girl whispered, so that only she might hear, 'He's due back tomorrow afternoon from his business in Southampton. By then I hope to be arriving in the countryside. Mum won't say a dickie-bird. She's been telling me for ages to get away from Charlie Osborne.'

'You keep it that way. That brute doesn't deserve a nice girl like you. And, rest assured, when I get hold of an address to write to you, Charlie won't worm it out of me.'

Elsie was aware that Charlie was obsessed with Izzy and needed to know where she was at all times. But his jealousy caused him to be cruel. Convinced he couldn't trust her, he frequently lashed out at her. Gunpowder in cuts and grazes stung like hell. In Elsie's locker in the changing room she kept a small brown bottle of iodine to dab on Izzy's skin when Izzy refused to see the nurse at Priddy's.

The temper that Charlie couldn't control was

what Izzy's mum called being Highly Strung. One day he would be happy, almost over-excitable, and the next so down in the dumps that once Izzy had caught him crying over a newspaper account of the discovery of Hitler's concentration camps. Not that the atrocities weren't horrendous, they were, but on another day Charlie could read the same story and gloss over it as though it was simply part and parcel of war.

Charlie was generous but Izzy told Elsie that he seemed to imagine he owned her. He had been married when he was younger – he was now thirty – but his wife had left him and he'd taken a long time to get over the shock and the shame. Izzy thought Charlie was terrified the same thing might happen again, so he hardly let her out of his sight. It wasn't as if she could look forward to the possibility of Charlie being called up because forged medical papers meant he would never fight for his country. Charlie dabbled in the black market, courtesy of the American stores at Southampton, lent money at exorbitant interest rates and often went to extraordinary lengths to make sure the money was repaid. At present he was working on a project, he'd told Izzy, that would make him exceedingly rich. A small band of his faithful satellites shone about their star leader.

Izzy had been flattered when the curly-haired, good-looking young man had asked her to dance with him at the Connaught Hall. She'd been sixteen, naïve, and now rued that fateful night.

'If the only way I can get out of his clutches is to leave Gosport, I have to take this job. I'm frightened of making a new start but more scared that one day Charlie might do me some proper damage,' she added.

Weeks previously Izzy had gone for the job interview. She hadn't said a word to anyone at the factory except Elsie. She'd asked for the day off, telling her line manager a fib about a hospital appointment.

Charlie had been waiting as usual outside the main gate when her shift had ended. Izzy had run from Hutfield's coach station in Forton Road to arrive at the munitions factory only minutes before Charlie had arrived to collect her.

Elsie knew Izzy hated deceiving anyone, but with Charlie it was sometimes a necessity to stretch the truth a little. 'I heard of a woman once whose husband was like Charlie,' Elsie said. Sometimes Geoffrey offered her morsels from his cases. 'She was too frightened to tell the hospital what was happening to her when she had to return time and time again with injuries. Kept saying she was walking into doors and falling downstairs. She was too scared not to keep taking him back every time he walked out on her and the kids after he'd given her a beating. Each time he told her things would change.'

As her friend tucked her hair beneath her turban, Elsie saw the blue marks of new bruising around her wrists and knew she'd touched a nerve.

'Was it ever different for her?'

Elsie shook her head. She watched Izzy pull on the special boots they all had to wear. She wouldn't tell her that the woman had died by her own hand. She'd had every shred of her confidence knocked out of her and sooner than strike out on her own, away from her awful husband, she'd ended it all with a rope in the shed.

Her two little girls were being cared for in a children's home. Izzy didn't need to be aware of that either, thought Elsie, not when she had the chance and the courage to run from her own abusive relationship.

Inside Priddy's the air smelt of sulphur, saltpetre and charcoal. Gunpowder clung to every surface and Elsie hated it. The dust turned skin yellow, and although the turbans protected the women's hair, fringes that hadn't been tucked in properly went orange. The cordite was also responsible for most of the respiratory difficulties to which the women succumbed. Itchy skin and kidney problems featured a great deal in the workers' lives.

Though the women, and men, were aware of the health risks, they felt they were serving their country.

Yesterday Elsie had heard on the wireless that the Allies had taken back Florence in Italy from the Germans. But the news reader had also spoken of the dreadful V-1s that had fallen on London and along what was known as Buzz Bomb Alley, the strip of England running across the south coast. Adolf Hitler was concentrating the showers of bombs on where he knew airfields, factories, munition yards and ship builders abounded.

Children were being evacuated again: a hundred to a hundred and fifty V-1s were aimed daily towards the area and had caused, so far, almost three thousand deaths and serious injuries.

Elsie tucked her arm through Izzy's. Working together and sharing secrets had made the two firm friends, despite the difference in their ages. Today Elsie was determined she wouldn't spoil Izzy's pleasure in her new job by telling her about Geoffrey's infidelity.

Izzy mustn't be allowed to leave Gosport worrying about her.

'Come here,' said Elsie. She swung Izzy round to face her and poked into the turban the ginger curls that had already strayed out. 'Red hair goes green! You've got to remember that!' Izzy laughed.

After being searched and checked by Petunia Yates, the overseer, the two women crossed the stone floor and walked down to their workroom. Their rubber-soled boots were silent as they moved. Leather soles were forbidden, as were the metal toe and heel clips called Blakey's that prolonged shoes' wear but caused sparks.

'Just you think yourself lucky the wedding never happened.' Elsie stared at Izzy. 'You'd find it more difficult to get away from him if you were married.'

'Some angel must have been looking after me when Charlie got into a fight on his stag night and ended up in hospital.'

Elsie squeezed Izzy's arm. 'I know you were too scared to tell him you didn't want to get married.'

'He'd spent a fortune on the reception.' Izzy tried to make light of the wedding that hadn't happened at Fareham register office.

'And he's never let you forget it.' Elsie knew Charlie was angry with himself for messing things up and took it out on Izzy. 'Thank goodness you never went to live with him,' she added.

Izzy still lived with her mum in Albert Street. Of course Charlie wasn't happy about that but Izzy could hardly cohabit without the advantage of a wedding ring, so for the sake of propriety, Charlie had had to abide by her decision. Gossipmongers were rife in Gosport.

Elsie remembered when Izzy had broken off their engagement and thrown the ring at him. Charlie had scared her mother half to death by hammering on their front door in an effort to get Izzy to speak to him. After the door knocker had broken and Charlie had shattered the front-room window, Izzy had given in and opened up to see him, tears streaming from his eyes.

Apologizing, he was soon on his knees, in front of all the neighbours. To save further embarrassment Izzy had taken back the ring that Charlie had searched for and found in the gutter.

Everything had gone well for a while. Until Charlie had taken her to a dance at Bury Hall in Gosport and a sailor on leave had spoken to her. Horror of horrors, she'd answered him. Izzy had said then, 'The only way I can escape from Charlie's clutches is to leave Gosport and pray he doesn't find me.'

Now she confided to Elsie, 'These few days have been so nice without Charlie driving me to and from work. It's been lovely being on my own.'

'You've got it all to come again after tomorrow, don't forget,' Elsie said, patting Izzy's arm.

Izzy gripped Elsie's hand. 'Charlie's due back from Southampton around four. Promise me, no matter how much he goes on, you won't tell him anything? He's bound to be waiting outside the gates, and when I don't turn up he'll make a bee-line for you.'

Elsie tried to make light of her friend's fears. 'It won't be a smack from your feller you'll get, but one from me if you ever think I'd tell anyone.'

The two women had reached the long workroom where the huge machines and conveyor-belts sent along the shell cases to be filled. On the line, concentration on the job was of the utmost importance. Whatever Elsie was feeling about Geoffrey's ultimatum, she dared not allow it to interfere with her work. Lives depended on steady hands. Already the wireless was playing the music that helped to keep the girls' spirits up. Vera Lynn with her patriotic songs, to which they all sang along, and the latest heart-throb Frank Sinatra, the skinny Italian boy with the wonderful voice.

The munitions factory, hidden in woodland but set on the banks of Forton Creek, had easy access for ships to carry the shells across the harbour. It had its own railway line that connected to another munitions factory on the outskirts of Fareham. Wages were high, but Elsie spent most of what she earned on the garden and the house.

'I'll be getting bed and board,' Izzy began, then became quiet as two chatting workers passed them. 'The pay isn't good but I can't see what I'd need to spend it on.'

Elsie nodded. 'You're so much more relaxed when Charlie's not about,' she said. She didn't want to think of her own unhappiness.

'He's doing a deal on drink and cigarettes at the American base. Those black-market schemes are extremely profitable for him,' confessed Izzy.

'Won't you miss some of the perks? Stockings, perfume, make-up?' Elsie asked.

Charlie liked to shower Izzy with little gifts. The war had been going on for such a long time that the Americans were the only people with decent food.

'I don't care about that. Having my freedom is much more important.'

'Ssh!' More women were filing into the workshop. Elsie didn't want anyone to overhear the two of them talking. Izzy had never told her exactly where she was going so Charlie wouldn't be able to force her destination from her.

Elsie rubbed her eyes. 'You're doing the right thing, you know.' She smiled at Izzy.

If only she knew what her own next step would be.

### Chapter Three

At seven o'clock Elsie pushed open the side door to the Fox in North Cross Street and was engulfed by a cloud of cigarette smoke. Wearing her second-best grey two-piece suit and a cream blouse, a sober outfit befitting a solicitor's wife, she stared shyly around the noisy bar. Izzy jumped up from the worn velvet bench in the corner and came to meet her with a broad smile.

'I've saved you a seat,' she said excitedly, pulling her inside. 'Want a gin and orange?'

Sam, the landlord, heard Izzy call to him and

began pouring gin into the measure then tipping it into glasses. Elsie made herself comfortable next to Izzy, and when genial Sam brought over the drinks, the red-haired girl waved money at him and told him to take a drink for himself.

The wireless was blaring big-band music, the once white paint in the bar was yellowed by nicotine, but the pub was a haven for locals.

Elsie soon forgot she'd stood outside for a long time plucking up the courage to enter because she wasn't used to going inside licensed premises without Geoffrey. Before the war only women of ill-repute had gone into pubs alone. But now so many women were in the workplace doing men's jobs and the young had grown brave.

Elsie took a sip of her drink, then stared about her, nodding at a couple of old men in cloth caps playing dominoes in the corner. A crowd of sailors in their bell-bottoms and tight vests gathered about the dartboard, and a couple of middle-aged women with over-painted faces sat smoking and chatting with Sam, who had returned to his place behind the counter. His barmaid, lolling with her elbows on the counter, was whispering to an airman.

The grubby little backstreet pub had an air of friendliness that eased Elsie's sadness. Needless to say, she hadn't set eyes on Geoffrey since that morning.

She had a fleeting thought that he might be appalled if he saw her now, his prim and proper wife contentedly drinking gin and orange among overflowing ashtrays full of dog-ends.

Suddenly she didn't care. This was the happiest

she'd been all day and she had a scrap of a girl with bright green eyes to thank for it. She took a deep breath and said to Izzy, 'I'm going to miss you. And I mean every word of that.'

Izzy brushed strands of curly hair from her eyes and said quietly, 'I'll miss you an' all. Drink up. You need another.' Then she looked keenly at Elsie and asked, 'I think it's time you told me what's been making you miserable all day.'

Elsie stared at her. She was saved her explanation by Pat and Connie, two workers from Priddy's, who had risen from their chairs and needed to squeeze past.

'Excuse us!'

They wanted to dance on the postage stamp space of floor to the Glenn Miller music. Elsie, her heart beating fast, stood up. Once the giggling girls had passed them, Izzy held Elsie's gaze and said softly, 'You can't fool me. I know something's wrong.'

Elsie's happy mood slithered away. Despite her good intentions, she could no longer hold back her emotions. The kindness in Izzy's voice opened the floodgates and, through hiccups and tears, Elsie blurted out her story.

'He also wants to sell the house and there's nothing I can do about that.'

'There's no point in causing yourself more grief by not going along with his wishes.' Izzy put a hand over Elsie's fingers to stop them worrying at a loose thread in her skirt. She lifted Elsie's glass. 'Finish this.'

Wordlessly Elsie obeyed. She used her hand to wipe her eyes, then delved into her bag for a ten-shilling note. 'You get some more drinks.' She sniffed.

Izzy was foraging in her handbag. She came up with a worn newspaper cutting. 'Don't let anyone else see this,' she said, pressing the paper into Elsie's hand.

Elsie smoothed it and focused on it as best she could through the smoky atmosphere and the remnants of her tears.

## THE GRAND UNION
## CARRYING COMPANY
### requires women to work boats

**How would you like to transport a boat carrying valuable supplies along England's waterways? You'll be doing essential war work.**

**Full training given.
Telephone...**

Elsie stared at her. 'So this is where you're going?' She took another look at the telephone number as though she could gain more information from it if it was imprinted on her brain.

Izzy nodded. 'You know I had a day off work to go for an interview. I waited for them to write to me and I was accepted. What can you lose by doing the same? Let me know what you think when I come back.' Izzy swept up the two empty glasses. Elsie again scrutinized the advertisement. 'It would be a completely new start,' Izzy said, moving away.

A bubble of excitement rose in Elsie's breast. Could she? Would she have confidence enough to apply for a job like this? Full training given, it said.

Apart from her war effort at Priddy's, Elsie hadn't worked outside the home since she had given up teaching to marry Geoffrey.

Again she looked at the newspaper article. No address, only the telephone number.

'What d'you think, then?' Izzy, back again, put down the two drinks on the table. 'I don't have to beg you to keep this under your hat, do I? This is our secret, yours and mine.' Izzy's eyes were shining. 'We might even end up working together!'

'But I don't know what they'll expect of me.'

'Neither did I until I went for the interview. There was a woman who explained everything. She asked me loads of questions and I never thought I'd hear from her again but, well...' She shrugged. 'The rest is history. Just be honest and be yourself.'

Elsie knew nothing about boats. In fact the only vessel she'd ever sailed on was the ferry that ran between Gosport and Portsmouth. And what did she know of the canals? She was sure somewhere at home there was a book on their history. Later tonight she might hunt it out.

In that moment Elsie knew she would telephone the number on the piece of paper tomorrow morning as soon as Geoffrey had left for work – assuming, of course, that he returned home this evening.

'Put it away,' hissed Izzy. Pat and Connie had returned to the table, talking loudly about their dancing partners. Elsie slipped the piece of paper into her handbag.

Both women worked on the line alongside Elsie and Izzy. Of course they knew nothing of Izzy leaving Priddy's.

Connie, who was dark-haired and looked a little like Vivien Leigh, said, with a giggle, 'I think we've clicked with those two sailors.'

Soon the four girls were chatting. Then Connie was telling them about her sister's friend. 'She's bagged herself a business bloke.' Connie gulped at her gin and orange. 'Mind you, even at school Sandra was a tart. It's a wonder she didn't find herself in the Pudding Club long ago. Of course he's married. Not that she'd let that stop her.'

Elsie realized they were discussing her husband's affair. She listened silently.

Apparently, gushed Pat, Sandra Eaton had bleached her mousy hair blonde and gone after anything in trousers since she'd left school. The opposite sex were fascinated by her large bosom. After a series of jobs she'd ended up as a typist in a Gosport office.

'Sandra usually gets what she wants,' Connie assured them, drinking the last of her gin. The two sailors had returned to take Pat and Connie onto the floor again. When the girls had swept away Izzy said, 'I'm sorry you had to hear that. They didn't know that awful Sandra had set out to take your man. You know how the girls at the factory love a good gossip.'

Elsie squeezed Izzy's hand. She had no intention of dissolving into tears again to give Pat and Connie even more to talk about. But neither did she want to stay any longer in the little pub that had become a den of torture. 'I have to go,' she said. 'Write to me. You have no idea how much I'm going to miss you, Izzy. Stay safe.'

Elsie hugged Izzy, waved to Pat and Connie in the sailors' arms and then fought her way outside. It wasn't long before she was hurrying up the high street towards the bus station.

Arriving home to an empty house she discovered a note on the kitchen table telling her that Geoffrey would be staying with Sandra because he didn't want any more distress. Elsie tore it up. She hadn't wanted any distress at all.

Looking in the wardrobe and drawers, she found he had taken sufficient clothing to last a few days. In the bathroom there was a space where his razor and shaving brush had been. Staring at the gaps on the shelf brought fresh tears.

'He's not worth crying over,' Elsie tried to assure herself. 'Think of all the times you might just as well not have been in the same room for all the notice he took of you. It was as if you were invisible.' She curled up in bed but, unable to sleep, she eventually went downstairs to forage through bookshelves, finally returning to the bedroom with a cup of tea, a book about the English canals, some notepaper and a pencil.

Sipping the tea and reading about the birth of the canals in the 1790s was soothing and distracting. She was amazed by what she learned. A two-thousand-mile network of waterways stretched across the country, providing not only access to rural idylls but also an efficient transport route.

She felt cheered by the pictures of charming brick bridges, stretches of water intersected by wooden lift bridges and deep locks to change water levels. There were aqueducts and tunnels and, above all, the sheer beauty of the countryside through which the network ran. Within stepping distance of the canals there were lock cottages, pubs and quaint villages.

Pictures of the vessels intrigued her. Long craft painted with bright gypsy-like designs of castles and roses. Brass-covered boats and barges, the metal polished to a high shine, and lace curtains at round windows.

Feeling herself sliding into sleep, despite Geoffrey's devastating news, Elsie closed the book and tried to decide on her next step.

It would be to write on the notepaper exactly what she intended to say to whoever answered the telephone when she rang tomorrow about the job.

It was important that she asked for an interview, where and when and what would be expected of her. She needed to know about accommodation, wages, food, uniforms, the boats, the training, the routes...

When eventually Elsie dropped off to sleep, the pencil still clutched in her fingers, her last thought was of a narrowboat gently cruising along a leafy waterway with ripples of water nudging against the craft's wooden sides.

## Chapter Four

Tallulah Whitehead threaded the damp tea-towel through the metal handle of the range in the kitchen of the Currant Bun café and sighed.

This was her last afternoon in the village of Titchfield, working in the tiny café for Mrs Simmonds, who had taken her on as a chubby girl of fourteen to be a waitress and helper, and had taught her all she knew about baking cakes, buns, pastries and pies. If it wasn't for the dreadful decision that the café had to close, Tolly would be happily making tea there for ever more.

However, the war – or, rather, the difficulty of obtaining sufficient sugar, flour, butter and all the necessities needed for baking quality food – had caused seventy-year-old Edith Simmonds to decide to shut up shop.

'You can buy the premises off me, Tolly,' Edith said. 'I'm in no hurry for payment.' The older woman sat down heavily on an upright chair next to a table and added, 'There's no one I'd rather see carry on here than you.'

Everyone called Tallulah Tolly. She had been named after the actress Tallulah Bankhead, a great success in the play *The Little Foxes*. Tolly's mother had been so taken with Miss Bankhead's performance that the following year when Tolly's sister was born, the new baby girl was named Regina after Tallulah Bankhead's character. Regina had soon

33

become Reggie.

'We can come to a mutual arrangement about the price,' Edith offered. She had once baked at the Savoy Hotel in London. She stared at Tolly expectantly.

'If you can't afford to keep open then it doesn't matter who owns the Currant Bun café. There'll be no profits without good food,' returned Tolly, as she looked sadly around the pristine interior she loved.

Everything had been cleared away. But Tolly was reluctant to leave. A last cup of tea had been the answer for both women.

If it wasn't for the war, Tolly would have gone on bended knees to beg, steal or borrow the money to own the bow-windowed café. It was everything she desired as premises and as a job.

Set in Titchfield's picturesque square, the street door opened straight into the café with six tables seating four customers each. The highly polished counter, with its glass shelving, normally displayed cakes and sandwiches, and was home to the till and crockery. It separated the café from the kitchen. Alongside the kitchen a passageway led out to a wildflower garden overlooking fields with cows. A glass conservatory was furnished with tables and chairs. Potted plants abounded and another door led on to a lawn where, in the height of summer, several iron tables and chairs were set out; they overlooked the little stream at the very bottom of the property.

Opening at one in the afternoon, the mornings were reserved for baking, or had been until the exceptionally busy café's popularity had dwindled without its usual mouthwatering offerings for sale.

Edith lived in the small flat above the café. Once the premises had been sold she was going to move to share her sister's bungalow in nearby Lee-on-the-Solent.

Tolly had been a fast learner and now, at nineteen, she had developed into a rounded woman with an even more rounded and happy disposition. Her father, a part-time fireman and Titchfield tomato nurseryman, and her sister Reggie, who worked in the village hat shop, understood that Tolly wouldn't be able to cope with the pain of passing the closed-down café each day. Tolly knew if her dad had had money to lend her he'd have done so willingly.

'Are you going to be happy leaving the village?' Edith began pouring fresh tea for herself and Tolly. On the white tablecloth gleaming china cups and saucers sat next to a plate of fresh scones. Edith was aware that Tolly had already applied for another job: she'd seen an advertisement in the newspaper. To their surprise, her application had resulted in a successful interview.

'Not really.' Tolly shrugged. 'It's been explained to me that there will be two women assigned to each narrowboat. We'll live and sleep aboard.'

'They're quite long, the boats, aren't they?' Edith asked. She poured milk into the cups.

'They're also barely seven feet wide. I was given a tour,' Tolly explained. 'I hope I won't get in my partner's way. I'd be happier if the boats were wider!'

'I expect the other girl is feeling just as apprehensive,' Edith said, to pacify her.

'What if she has annoying habits? What if I irritate her?' Oh, dear, it was all becoming very complicated, thought Tolly.

'Best to take each day as it comes,' said Edith, splitting a sweet-smelling floury scone and spreading it with margarine. 'This should be served with home-made jam and lots of cream,' she grumbled. Tolly knew there wasn't any and Edith's mouth had now set in a hard thin line of disgust.

Tolly thought about Dorothy Trent, the woman who had interviewed her and who had asked, 'Won't you miss the village dances? A young girl like you might find life dull on the waterways.'

Tolly had stared at the neat woman in grey slacks and a pink puff-sleeved jumper. She'd decided that if Dorothy Trent hadn't worn her dark hair pulled back in such a severe bun she would have looked much prettier. 'When my sister and I go to dances she's always the one on the floor and I'm the wallflower. So I don't think the lack of dancing will bother me.' Tolly didn't share with her a conversation she'd overheard in the local hall at the last dance she'd attended.

'There's no way that fat bitch is Reggie's sister. She must be adopted,' said one of the boys, a sweet-looking blond lad that Tolly had hoped might ask her to dance. She knew then that they all saw her as a blob. The ugly sister of the very pretty Reggie.

Dorothy Trent had smiled at her. After a while she'd said, 'I think that's all I need to know. I'll be in touch.'

And in less than a week her acceptance had come by post.

Tolly thought it was a good thing the woman hadn't asked her about boyfriends. There had been one man Tolly had been interested in, and Norman had started out as a penfriend. They'd written to each other for six months. When Norman had asked for a photograph Tolly had sent him a head-and-shoulders print. The one from Norman had showed him with some army friends. He was the taller man with fine fair hair, his hand resting on a pal's shoulder. They'd arranged to meet when he next had leave.

Excitedly Tolly had caught the bus into Fareham where she was supposed to meet him outside the Embassy cinema. She tried to imagine she hadn't seen the disappointment on his face. During the interval he bought her an ice cream but their chatter gradually tailed off to silence. When the film ended and they stood together in the foyer, Norman said he had to go and meet a friend.

He walked her to the bus station and waited until the Titchfield bus arrived. Tolly knew then she wouldn't see him again. He hadn't exactly told her the reason but she knew it was because of her size.

Once she was home again she shut herself in her bedroom and cried, but eventually had to let Regina in. 'I'm too big. It put him off. But you know I've tried to diet and nothing seems to work. Sometimes, I think, the only way I can make a man care for me is if I throw myself at him.'

Reggie had put her arms around her sister. 'And what kind of a man would allow you to do that? Anyone would think by the way you're talking that you're enormous and you're not – well-padded, maybe. I think Norman wasn't the right person for you. If he'd bothered to see deep inside you he'd have found a kind, sensitive girl.' Then she'd made Tolly laugh when she said, 'He's not the only cake on the shelf!'

When the letter came accepting her as a narrow-boat woman, Tolly was overjoyed. She was nimble on her feet, hardworking and she knew how to cook so, if nothing else, she'd make sure everyone's belly was filled.

Dorothy had explained that many of the men working the canal boats on the Inland Waterways had joined up and were now away fighting. The scheme to ask women to take over the men's jobs hadn't been as widely advertised as the need for land-girls and women to join the services and munitions factories.

However, it was a necessary job. Timber, coal, iron, cement and steel had to be moved from London to Birmingham and surrounding areas, and it was considered safer, due to the bombing, to tow materials by boat than to drive vehicles on the roads.

'Thank you.' Tolly accepted the scone from Edith. 'I shall miss you. You've taught me a great deal,' she said, then bit into the crumbling softness.

At least, working away from Titchfield, she wouldn't see her beloved workplace sold and turned into something quite different. 'I've no idea what the future will bring but I actually feel as though a new chapter is beginning,' Tolly said, determined to make the best of a bad job.

## Chapter Five

The following morning it was raining when Elsie set off on her bike for the munitions factory. She'd thought about taking her car, a small black Austin, but after making the phone call to the number on the advertisement and talking to a woman called Dorothy Trent, she had decided to save her petrol ration for the journey to Lower Heyford in a few days' time.

'I've had a cancellation and can fit you in for an interview if you're willing to come here?' Dorothy's educated voice and the reassuring way she answered each of her queries swayed Elsie immediately.

The agreed time for the interview was three o'clock. Elsie explained she needed to plan her route and allow time for the possibility of losing her way. She decided as she returned the phone to its cradle that she would take an overnight case and stay at an inn or bed-and-breakfast. She was due two days off from Priddy's and it might be fun to look around the area, whether the interview went favourably or not.

That morning the exacting work at the factory went slowly. The wireless cheered the workers and the chatter was just as loud but, without Izzy, Elsie felt alone and lost. That morning, she'd felt something similar, getting up to an empty house and making breakfast for herself that she hadn't wanted to eat. There was no word from Geoffrey. Elsie refused to cry again.

When her shift finished for the day, Elsie half expected Charlie to be outside the main gate waiting for her to wheedle information from her of Izzy's whereabouts. When she didn't see him she cycled home, relieved, and spent the evening deciding what to wear on Thursday and charting her way to Oxfordshire on a road map.

However, on Wednesday morning, Charlie was outside the factory. He got out of his Chrysler and barred her way. Dark-haired and brown-eyed, the good-looking man's easy smile didn't reach his eyes as he said, 'Izzy isn't at home. Her mother won't answer the door but a neighbour told me she'd left in a taxi.'

'What makes you think I know where she is?' said Elsie. She sensed he was keeping his temper in check.

'You're mates, aren't you?' He stared hard at her.

She took a deep breath. 'Depends what you mean by that. We work together. She didn't turn up yesterday.' Elsie hated lies and was determined to keep to the truth where possible.

'So you expected her to come into work?'

'It wasn't her day off. Have you asked our boss?'

Charlie was very close to Elsie and she could smell his musky scent. Her heart was thumping but she knew it was to her advantage to act as though she knew nothing. The difficulty was that she was aware this calm, cold man could change in an instant to someone to be scared of. But she'd made a promise to Izzy and she would keep her friend's secret at all costs.

'Why would I ask your boss?' His eyes had narrowed.

'He might know the reason she's not in work.'

Elsie barely got those words out before the wail of the siren cut through the air. Charlie uttered an oath. Never before had Elsie been glad to hear Moaning Minnie. Without a further glance at Charlie she threw her bicycle against the wall and ran through the main gate to the workers' shelter. Jock, the gate manager, waved her inside, recognizing her as a regular worker. Charlie, not being an employee, couldn't follow so the last Elsie saw of him was his dash to his motor to start it up.

She breathed a sigh of relief as the car turned and sped back down Weevil Lane.

The brick-built shelter was already full of people. One of the men from the packing department made space for her on the bench inside the doorway and said, 'Won't it be marvellous when all this is over?'

He then foraged in his work bag and took out a flask. Elsie knew he would offer the first drink to her and she would accept gratefully. Not just because she was parched but because she was relieved Charlie had gone, for now.

She thought of Charlie's good looks, which were enough to ensnare any woman. Trouble was, you never knew what any husband or boyfriend was capable of until it happened. Look at Geoffrey and his Sandra. Who would have thought Elsie's life could change in such a way? Actually, the more she thought about it, it seemed incredible that a woman like Sandra should fall in love with a fuddy-duddy like Geoffrey, with his sober way of dressing and his narrow outlook on life. Yes, he had a brilliant legal brain but he didn't always live in the real world. Elsie pushed him from her mind as she sipped the hot sweet tea. Her neighbour had pressed a mug into her hands with a gruff 'Here you are, love.'

She was sitting near the open doorway of the below-ground shelter. Eventually she passed back the mug, then watched the area of sky that was visible to her. She saw a sinister black shape with a pointed nose and fins. A huge gush of air, flame red, spurted from its rear end, like some majestic tail. Even with the noise from the people around her in the shelter, the whine it made was fearsome.

Mesmerized, she watched and the ear-splitting sound cut out.

Then the machine seemed to hover before it nose-dived to earth. The explosion that followed was terrifying. Spirals of thick black smoke hurled themselves into the air. Elsie had no idea where the self-propelled V-1 had landed but the morning sky was now filled with a dirty black and grey mist too thick to see through. She shuddered.

The man beside her, sensing her disquiet, said softly, 'Try not to think about it, love.'

Elsie looked into his face. He was kind. He probably had a wife and family somewhere and was praying they were safe. She gave him a small smile.

She had no idea how long she sat there, sandwiched between people she didn't know. The one thing she was aware of was that if a V-1 hit the factory, with all the munitions stored there, within seconds she would be no more.

A cheer went up as the all-clear sounded, followed by the bells and horns of emergency vehicles approaching the black dust cloud.

Employees began trickling from their hiding places. Work would go on as normal now at the factory. Elsie ventured out and walked through the crowds of people to retrieve her bicycle and put it away.

Afterwards the day progressed as any other. She doubted she'd seen the last of Charlie but the future would take care of itself. Tomorrow she was driving to Lower Heyford for her interview.

Elsie had still had no word from Geoffrey but she was beginning to find peace in the silence around the house. Her own company suited her, and although it had been only a couple of days since Geoffrey had left, she relished being able to eat when and what she wanted, even though her appetite had deserted her. She could also listen to wireless programmes that Geoffrey had decried as 'silly'. And reading in bed without him huffing and puffing about the light being kept on too long was liberating.

She had decided to wear her grey costume with a white blouse and large bow at the neck. She felt the costume to be a lucky article of clothing. With her black court shoes and matching black handbag she felt ready to face Dorothy Trent, who had sounded so positive on the telephone.

Lower Heyford was a small place, containing a steepled church with fine stained-glass windows. The village looked deserted, except for three children sitting by the roadside taking down car numbers. A watermill stood on the banks of the Cherwell. A clapboarded building partly hidden by trees looked over the river.

It didn't take her long to find the Bull, a public house near the canal. She had been advised to turn down a small lane to reach the boatyard. Elsie had gauged the time well for she was only half an hour early and, after parking the car, decided she would take a short walk alongside the canal before she knocked on the door of the boatyard's office. An elderly man waved to her from a moored boat. Just like the village, the yard seemed practically deserted.

Elsie looked with interest at the canal boats moored along wooden jetties. Each was named after a bird. They were much longer than she'd envisaged and seemed to be moored in pairs. A work boat was coupled with another that looked as though its space was possibly habitable. Elsie hoped she'd be shown over one.

'Hello.' The voice made her jump, for she was deep in thought. When she turned to face its owner, she was surprised to see a woman of a similar age to herself. Her dark hair was pulled into a tight bun that made her face look severe but the tone of her voice and her smiling eyes suggested otherwise.

'Are you Dorothy Trent?'

The woman nodded. 'And you must be Elsie.' She turned and walked, with a slight limp, towards the clapboard building, Elsie following. At the door, she twisted the handle and stepped aside so Elsie could enter the tidy office.

'Sit down,' Dorothy said, and busied herself

with a Primus stove that stood on the side. 'Did you have a good journey up from Gosport?'

Elsie immediately felt at ease. 'Yes, I did.' She took a chair in front of the desk and watched as Dorothy, who was slim, and wore navy slacks with a pale blue jumper, prepared tea.

Within ten minutes, she had blurted out her real reason for wanting to escape from Gosport. Half an hour later Dorothy had explained that the job vacancies had not been widely advertised but that trips from Limehouse, in London, to Birmingham, via Coventry and other routes, delivered goods to factories. There were no extra coupons for work clothing, no uniform given. The pay was two pounds a week, with food and accommodation included. Two women were needed for each vessel.

'One's a diesel-powered boat, the other's a butty, an engineless craft towed by the one with the engine. To live in close proximity with someone you've never met before can be quite eye-opening. Mentally and physically it's hard work. Probably like nothing you've ever tackled in your life.' She paused. Elsie knew Dorothy hadn't meant to sound patronizing. 'Normally I'm on the boats but I hurt my foot so I'm recuperating. I'm back aboard on Monday. I've taken over interviewing trainees to give the other woman who usually does this job a much-needed break. Although working on the narrowboats is a reserved occupation, many of the men have joined the services so we need all the help we can get.'

Elsie could sense the strength in Dorothy's mind and body. It was easy to imagine her in charge of one of the long narrowboats. A seed of doubt entered Elsie's head. The romantic notion she'd had from reading the advertisement was nothing like the actual work involved. Could she do it? Could she learn something different in entirely new surroundings?

If she was offered the chance, she'd take it. One thing was certain: she wouldn't have time to dwell on Geoffrey and Sandra and their baby. Living and working on a boat wouldn't give her time to mourn the loss of her beloved house and garden either. As she sipped at the strong tea she listened eagerly to all that Dorothy had to say.

## Chapter Six

'Have you ever been on a boat before?'

Elsie walked swiftly to keep up with Dorothy. 'Only to cross on the ferry from Gosport to Portsmouth,' she said. 'It's a very short trip.'

Deftly Dorothy slid herself into the moored narrowboat, waited for Elsie to join her, smiling as Elsie had to hoist her skirt to climb in awkwardly over the side. Dorothy pushed back the hatch and went down the small steps into the cabin.

'Bring as few belongings as possible. As you can see, there's little room for your things,' said Dorothy. 'It gets very hot in here so we keep the hatch open most of the time.'

Elsie could smell coal dust and something sharp that made her want to sneeze. A small black-leaded stove was obviously used for heating and cooking. Dorothy slid back a small partition to reveal cups and plates stacked neatly. Next to it another cupboard held canisters marked 'Tea' and 'Sugar'. 'The larder,' Dorothy said. There were also some tins of condensed milk. 'You'll soon get used to tea with that in it – we can't always get fresh milk,' she added. 'Don't forget to bring your ration book with you.'

Elsie nodded.

'There's not a lot more to show you, except your bed and the engine, and I don't want to frighten you off with that.' Dorothy swung back a curtain revealing a small square of wood barely two foot wide. 'During the day it's a table, but at night it converts into bed-space.' Dorothy put her hand on a cupboard beneath the table, 'Inside here are extra blankets. Most girls bring their own sleeping-bags. Space is at a premium so everything has a double use.'

'I thought two people were needed on each boat.'

'You want to know where the other bed's hidden?'

'Yes, please.'

On the far side of the boat there was another long cupboard. Let down, the plywood door revealed a space barely wide enough for a person to sleep, stuffed with a pillow, sleeping-bag and blanket. 'My quarters,' said Dorothy. 'Don't worry, some nights you'll be so tired and cold that when you come in you'd willingly sleep on the floor and find it comfortable!'

Elsie liked the woman's honesty, her directness,

but sensed she was hiding something. Not about the job and its requirements, for anything Elsie asked she replied to quickly, with precision. She was just sure there was more to Dorothy than she was letting on.

A thought struck Elsie. 'Who looks after the engines?'

Dorothy turned to her and Elsie caught a whiff of floral perfume. 'We do!'

Elsie's face must have showed amazement for Dorothy laughed. 'It's not so bad. Anything we can't cope with as a team, we get in touch with the office here and they'll send out someone. But we're doing men's jobs and there's not much we can't do that they can.' Dorothy stamped on the floor. 'The engine room's below. The diesel Lister engine uses a very high cylinder compression to start the ignition process, unlike the petrol engine, which needs a spark. Regular servicing is recommended, and we'll take turns, you included.'

Elsie had begun to think she'd like the challenge of something new when Dorothy added, 'The first trip will be to Limehouse in London. You're travelling on this boat with me. We'll be empty on the way there but collect materials to deliver on the return trip, the exact route I'm not sure of yet. It could be coal from a coalfield near Coventry or wood, possibly metal bars. The round trip normally takes three or four weeks. We'll check in at various points along the way. An experienced crew would do it quicker but beginners need a lunch break and regular hours. Look...' she paused 'if you're agreeable the next step is a medical. I can tell you straight away I think you and I will get along fine. We leave here on Monday and I'd like you to join me. I can arrange for Dr Wells to do the medical tomorrow morning before his surgery hours. If you pass that, the job's yours and later you'll receive official notification, but on Monday morning we leave at six. How about it?'

The pay was well below what Elsie was earning at Priddy's, but on the plus side the job was away from Gosport. She would need to tell Geoffrey she was leaving the house. Without having to pay for her keep, she might even be able to save her wages. 'Monday?'

Dorothy nodded. 'Twisting this stupid ankle has kept me out of action so I'm behind with deliveries. I've also had to put up a young woman at a nearby hostelry while I recovered. I'd like to tell her to come on Monday, too.'

'I understand,' Elsie said, making up her mind. 'How about letters?'

'You can have them redirected here – that's what the girls do. There are also collection points at post offices along the waterways.' Anything else she needed to know, she would be taught. Elsie thought she and Dorothy would get along fine together, though she wondered what the girls in the butty-boat would be like. She had no doubt she would pass the medical in the morning and she was glad she'd brought an overnight case. She decided she would return to Gosport after she'd seen the doctor, then come back and spend a few days before departure looking around the area.

'Will the Bull put me up?'

'They'll be glad to have you. The other girl arrived when they were fully booked for a local wedding so she's staying a few miles away. I suggest you book in now and ask for your bill to be charged to this base.'

'Oh, that sounds good,' Elsie said.

'If you don't pass the medical at least you'll leave with the memory of a little luxury,' said Dorothy. 'The Bull's meals are top notch. Of course, you won't have much time to sort out your affairs back in Gosport.'

Elsie thought of her empty house, the few clothes she wanted to pack and the letter she would leave for Geoffrey. 'I won't need much,' she said.

Elsie drove fast back to Gosport. She'd booked into the Bull until Monday morning. The doctor had assured her she was as fit as a fiddle.

As she turned down Western Way her heart dropped as she spied the Chrysler parked on the road outside her house. She drove straight into her driveway, but before she'd turned her key in the lock, a figure loomed menacingly beside her. The man was so tall. Dark curls fell across his forehead from beneath his trilby. He leaned with an easy grace against the door frame. 'Enjoy your trip? You didn't come home last night.'

Elsie's heart was pounding against her ribs. What right had he to comment on her whereabouts? 'How did you know where I live?' Now she was angry. 'I don't have to report my comings and goings to you.'

'Of course not, except if you'd gone to visit Izzy.'

'Don't be stupid! I told you I don't know where she is.' This at least was the truth.

Charlie put his hand on her arm. Immediately he touched her, Elsie shrank away from him.

'Not scared of me, are you?' He leaned in closer and she could smell his sandalwood cologne. Her heart beat even faster. He still hadn't told her how he'd known where to find her. He was towering over her. One of his hands rose towards her cheek and, with exaggerated gentleness, he tucked a strand of her fair hair behind her ear. Remembering the bruises and welts she'd seen on Izzy's skin, she tried hard not to show her fear. She looked out into the street. Of course it was deserted.

'Why should I be scared of you?' She tried a laugh. Then she took a deep breath and repeated, 'Izzy isn't here with me. I have no idea where she is.'

'I know she's not living with you,' he snapped. 'But I think you know more than you're saying.' He let his hand fall. Elsie was relieved when he took a step away from her. 'Don't think you've seen the last of me.' He leaned forward again, his breath hot against her ear as he spoke. 'It didn't take me long to find you, and I always get what I want.' Then he turned and walked back down the driveway towards his car.

Once she was inside, Elsie slammed the front door and leaned against the wood. Her hands were sweaty with fear. She made herself take deep breaths and when she finally felt easier she went into the front room and stared out of the window until the Chrysler had gone.

After a cup of tea she felt better and switched

51

on the wireless to listen to the news.

The Germans were leaving the Channel Islands, occupied since 1940. Elsie was happy to hear the good news but the bad news was the Germans had perfected the V-2 rocket, which was even deadlier than the V-1. She had asked Dorothy whether many bombs had fallen on the villages alongside the canals. She'd been told that sometimes German pilots saved fuel by jettisoning bombs they hadn't dropped on targets. A fortnight ago one had landed in Farmer Wilkes's field. Elsie had smiled inwardly, remembering her fear in the air-raid shelter at Priddy's. The countryside certainly wasn't Hitler's priority.

Dance music now filled the rooms as she packed a holdall.

Winter trousers and as many jumpers as she could fit in, along with her thick nighties, her toiletries and underwear. None of her clothes matched, but they were warm and serviceable and that was what mattered. She jammed in the black wellingtons she wore in the garden and a pair of white canvas flat shoes. Remembering the difficulty her skirt had caused when she was stepping onto the boat, she dispensed with her suit, hanging it in her wardrobe, and packed a cotton skirt, just in case.

Deciding she would eat when she returned to the Bull, Elsie ran a bath, remembering to be careful with the water, in accordance with wartime regulations. While she bathed she thought of the words she would use to explain her disappearance to Geoffrey. She must also write to her boss at Priddy's, apologizing for her decision to leave. Her job would soon be filled by someone else because it paid well but, still, it wasn't in her nature to let people down without an explanation.

She had a stamp so she could post that letter. The one to her husband she decided to leave on the kitchen table. Sooner or later he would return to raid his wardrobe again. She would also have to give him the address of the boatyard. Geoffrey would no doubt be happy she had decided to leave Gosport. He had offered her money for another property when the sale of the house went through and she didn't want him to forget that promise.

Elsie came down from the bathroom swathed in her dressing-gown. She went out into the back garden for a last look around. It was still light and warm, a lovely summer's evening.

She would miss the garden, miss sitting out on the lawn beneath the trees, reading. Quickly she dismissed the thoughts that were making her feel sad. She turned to go back inside. A flowerpot, containing a geranium, lay broken in the border near the back door. She stared at it. It had fallen or been knocked from the sill. Had someone tried to enter the back of the house while she'd been away?

Elsie pushed away the thought.

Back inside she sat at the table and wrote the two letters. Then she dressed in dark green slacks and a light green jumper. She decided on her gabardine raincoat and sensible flat shoes. Twisting her hair up and jamming in grips, she finished her tea while she made sure she had everything she needed, including a couple of books to read, an Agatha Christie she had already started and James

Hilton's *Random Harvest*. As an afterthought she packed the canal book. She went towards the front door.

A thought struck her. She sped back to the kitchen and searched in the drawer for the packet of candles she kept in case of emergencies, and found a space for them, with a box of matches, in the corner of her holdall.

It was dusk as she closed the door behind her, telling herself that she mustn't cry. 'This,' she said softly, 'is a new beginning.'

## Chapter Seven

Geoffrey rolled over in Sandra's small bed. The air in the room tasted of stale sweat and sex. He longed to open the window but Sandra couldn't abide draughts. He didn't want to wake her but he needed to get comfortable. His face met fur that crept into his eyes, up his nose and into his mouth.

'Get off.' His hand made contact with Sandra's cantankerous Persian cat and he swept it from the pillow. He heard a flop and a disgruntled miaow as the cat landed on the lino, then felt the bounce as it jumped onto Sandra's side of the bed.

Sandra idolized Fluffy and Geoffrey hated the orange devil. Of course he was aware that, cats being cats and clever creatures, Fluffy understood this, so she slept on his suits until he had found space to hang them up. She had been sick in his shoes. He'd also found deep gouges and scratch marks where she had sharpened her claws on his Italian leather briefcase. When Geoffrey was standing up, the feline wove in and out of his ankles, purring, as though she knew how much he disliked the long orange hairs that clung to his trouser turn-ups and socks.

Geoffrey looked at the clock on the bedside table. It was too early to get up and too late to go back to sleep. Sandra slept as though she were dead.

He remembered that in the galley kitchen the sink was still full of last night's dirty crockery. He thought of the frying pan covered with grease and shuddered. Sandra wasn't as house-proud as Elsie. Still, he couldn't have everything, could he?

So far she had never refused him when he felt like making love. And he enjoyed the feel of her silky thighs across his legs, and the large breasts he could bury his face in. But she was very untidy. She never thought to put things away, so when he wanted something, anything, he usually had to burrow among piles of clothing to find what he was looking for. She'd said that if she had a bigger house things wouldn't get lost so easily. He couldn't argue with that.

Sandra also ate at unconventional times, and often forgot about supper, which was his main meal of the day. Except for the previous night when she had provided him with a blackened and greasy fry-up. Different smells made her nauseous; she said it was her pregnancy. Sometimes he cooked for her, the idea alien to him when he was living with Elsie. It was much cheaper than eating out, which was one of Sandra's pleasures.

55

Another of her pleasures was dressing him up. So far he'd managed to get away with not wearing the pork-pie hat or the wide, bright ties he thought made him look like an out-of-work comedian. God only knew where she managed to obtain fashionable clothing for herself and him without coupons. Sandra said she 'knew people'.

'For goodness' sake, forty isn't old! Those dark suits make you look like an undertaker!'

Perhaps he shouldn't have been so hasty in agreeing to move into the small basement flat in The Crescent. Though it hadn't seemed so small when Sandra, with the estate agent, had shown him around it. Geoffrey certainly didn't think the mortgage was low and he should know: he'd been paying it for the last few months.

Sandra put out her arm, momentarily trapping him in the bed. He could hear the cat purring. Any moment now the blasted thing would come over to his side and plump itself down again on his pillow.

Perhaps he'd get up and have a quick cup of tea. Then he could return to his house in Western Way and collect more clothes, which would be hair-free. Of course he had other things at Sandra's flat but they weren't suitable for work. There was a funny-looking suit hanging on the back of the door that Sandra had cadged from an African-American marine one night in the Swan. She said she'd won it in a bet. Geoffrey didn't ask questions. Sandra insisted he try it on. He didn't like it at all. The jacket made him feel as though his arms were too long, and the gathered trouser hems reminded him of Aladdin's outfits in the pantomime. Geoffrey didn't know how to refuse her.

'I don't want people to think I'm living with my granddad,' she'd wailed. 'That's the latest fashion in America.'

Five minutes later Geoffrey was in the minuscule kitchen and, with the door closed on the sleeping woman and her cat, he was tying his shoelaces. Or he would have been, if one lace and insole hadn't felt damp. He left it to dangle. Ten minutes later, tea forgotten, he opened the front door to a sunny late-August morning.

Geoffrey breathed a sigh of relief. As he walked to his car he looked back at the flat. Those living quarters were definitely not for him. Bought for Sandra so she could live away from her family in Old Road, he'd thought the love nest perfect for visits when she'd told him gleefully of the pregnancy. So overjoyed was he that at last he was to become a father, he would have bought Buckingham Palace if it had been available.

He wondered about the possibility of Elsie agreeing to a straight swap while they waited for a house buyer. Elsie in the flat, himself and Sandra in the larger property: that would be ideal. Alas, Elsie definitely wouldn't like that. Oh, well, he'd have to advertise to sell the marital home.

The Gosport roads were quiet, the warmth of the new day already cheering him as he entered leafy Western Way.

Geoffrey drove into the driveway and parked. Out of the car, he stood for a moment, looking at the house on which he and Elsie had lavished care and money. It was a pretty place, with its gabled walls and thatched roof. The diamond-shaped glass in the leaded windows winked in the bright sunshine. He breathed in the scents from the climbers Elsie had planted, flowering along the walls. He'd definitely be sorry to leave this house.

He'd worked hard for it, and Elsie had contributed the pay-out she'd been given on finishing her teaching career. Of course, she hadn't been happy to give up her job, but the house and its garden had become her salvation.

He'd had no say in the matter a year ago when she'd started part-time at the munitions factory, but his partner had praised his patriotism in allowing her to help the country in its hour of need.

Geoffrey had no living relations, other than a brother in Australia. He didn't think about Cecil very often and they communicated even less. Since Cecil had served a term of imprisonment for embezzlement before he'd left England, Geoffrey had no wish to be reminded of him. What Geoffrey desired more than anything was to found a new dynasty of his own family, hopefully starting with a son. After all those years of childless marriage, he had thought that was impossible.

Until now. With Sandra.

He could smell the polish, lavender as usual, immediately he stepped into the hall and went straight upstairs to run a bath before he ransacked his wardrobe. In the bedroom he looked at the clock, then at the bed, which hadn't been slept in. His first thought was that Elsie had taken on an early turn at the factory. Then he noticed her open wardrobe.

Nothing much seemed to be missing. She hadn't taken her best clothes so there was no man involved. He smiled at that absurd thought.

Geoffrey reached on top of the wardrobe for the large suitcase. Something was missing. Usually the small leather holdall sat next to the case. He shrugged and began to fold underwear and shirts.

Later, after an invigorating bath and a change of clothes, Geoffrey went downstairs, left the suitcase by the front door and drifted into the kitchen. The change in the atmosphere drew his attention to the open back door.

'Stupid woman,' he muttered, and went to close it. That was when he saw the lock was broken.

Geoffrey searched every room in the large rambling house. As far as he could make out, nothing was missing, except his wife and a small holdall. Had someone broken in? Had Elsie forgotten her key and broken the glass in the back door to gain entry? Wouldn't she have closed the door? And he felt sure she would have employed a locksmith to make good the door before she left.

While Geoffrey was still searching for clues he spotted the letter addressed to him on the table. It looked as if she had resealed the envelope.

After reading the single page he sat down at the kitchen table to get over the shock. Elsie had told him she was leaving and had given an address where he could forward letters. It was the first time she had simply 'told' him she was doing anything! She'd not mentioned the broken door lock.

He telephoned for a locksmith.

Then he rang his office in Gosport and said he wouldn't arrive until later in the day. His new secretary, a replacement for Sandra, a grey-haired middle-aged woman named Nellie, was to rearrange all his appointments.

It occurred to Geoffrey that the only way to make sure his house in Western Way wasn't broken into again, if indeed Elsie had had to break in, was for him, and possibly Sandra, though she should follow later, to live in it.

He picked up Elsie's letter.

He would write and explain it would be easier to show prospective buyers over the property if it was lived in. Surely she couldn't argue with that.

## Chapter Eight

Izzy stretched her arms above her head as she looked out of the window across the flower-filled gardens tumbling down towards the canal. She couldn't remember when last she had felt such happiness, such freedom as she had while living at the Black Cow Inn. And she was being paid for this! She took a deep breath of the warm morning air, tinged with the scent of roses, listened to the comforting noise of cutlery being used in the kitchen below and sighed as the smell of fried bread rose and enveloped her. Breakfast was cooking, and she was starving.

A movement on the black-painted narrowboat caught her eye and she realized she was staring at a dark-clad figure who was clearly watching her. Izzy shivered. It's not Charlie, she told herself. It's not. She shook as fingers of fear crept up her spine. The figure put his hand to his cap, a signal that he was acknowledging her presence, then turned and disappeared into the bowels of the boat.

After a while Izzy's breathing became normal as she realized the man she had seen was Nelson Smith, or Sonny, as he was known to the canal folk.

'Five minutes!'

The shouted words, with a knock on her bedroom door, brought Izzy out of her reverie. 'Coming,' she called back, and immediately chased away her terrified thoughts. She washed her face and hands quickly in the small corner sink, dressed, and went down to eat with the pub's employees.

The kitchen was warm and the chatter rose to greet her as she hurried into the big old-fashioned room to find Esme had saved her a seat. She smiled her thanks as she sat down next to the young barmaid and helped herself to food from the sizzling dish. Fried tomatoes, an egg and a slice of fried bread washed down with a mug of strong dark tea was a treat after the meagre rationing back home in war-torn Gosport. Here in the countryside Izzy relished mealtimes. Customers sometimes, in lieu of payment, brought in a few farm fresh eggs, poultry or ham. Soon she'd be helping cook her own food and that of the other three women on the narrowboats and eking out the meagre rations.

Almost as if reading her thoughts Esme said, 'So you'll be leaving us on Monday?'

Izzy swallowed. 'Yes. Dorothy's ankle is strong enough for her to put weight on it now, and she's ready to supervise the two boats travelling to London.'

'You'll like working with Dorothy. She's a grand lass.' This from Bert Sellers, the owner of the Black Cow, a corpulent man spreading himself at the head of the table.

'I think I will,' replied Izzy. 'I thought when I arrived in Lower Heyford I'd be starting work straight away, but I've enjoyed being here with you, even though it's a fair distance from the boatyard. I'm glad the Bull was fully booked with that wedding party.' Izzy smiled at the young girl next to her. 'I've loved every minute of helping out around here.'

Izzy had received wages from Dorothy: it hadn't been her fault she'd been unable to fulfil her contract.

'You've changed such a lot in the short time we've known you,' said Esme, her bobbed dark hair falling across her eyes. 'You were like a frit rabbit!'

'What on earth is that?'

Esme laughed. 'A rabbit that's scared of traps and headlamps,' she said. 'You were forever looking about you and staring into darkened corners. I thought you were afraid you'd see a ghost.'

Izzy grinned back at her. 'Perhaps I was,' she said. 'Maybe I still am.'

It had taken her a while to realize how much trust she'd placed in her mother and her friend Elsie not to give away her whereabouts to Charlie Osborne. Just a glimpse of a tall man staring at her made her panic.

Remembering earlier how seeing Sonny had

jolted her, she said, 'Sonny acknowledged me this morning from his boat.'

Esme spluttered into her teacup. 'Acknowledged? Like, he waved or something?' She used her fingers to wipe her chin where the tea had spurted.

'Well, he tipped his cap.'

Esme's eyes grew dreamy. 'I wish he'd known I was here.'

Izzy had already gathered that the gypsy boatman with the reddest hair she'd ever seen, even brighter than her own, was considered quite a catch.

'You keep away from Sonny Smith. There's many a lass wishes she'd never met him.' Bert Sellers glared at his breakfast, as if it was about to rear up and bite him.

'Just because you own this pub doesn't mean you know how young girls feel when a handsome man looks their way. Eat your breakfast,' Josie, his wife of many years said.

'I know what's in that devil's heart,' Bert said. 'Wasn't too long ago I was like him!'

'Ah, but I tamed you, didn't I, pet?'

Al, the cellar man, laughed and pretty soon the five of them were giggling and chatting happily.

After breakfast, Izzy and Esme elected to wash up in the stone sink while Bert and Josie readied the pub for opening time. Al disappeared down some stone steps muttering about changing barrels.

'I served him in the bar last night.' Izzy knew Esme would guess who she was talking about.

'What did he say, apart from asking for a drink?'

63

Esme was wiping a plate with a frayed tea-cloth.

'Just wanted a drink, he barely looked at me.' Izzy didn't want to say he had managed to make her feel like a fifteen-year-old. As she had turned from the till in the busy bar and handed him his change it was as though a lightning bolt had passed through her. Then she'd experienced the awful feeling she'd got every time she'd left the factory at Gosport to find Charlie waiting for her.

Sonny had turned towards the dart-board and challenged another local man to a game. She had watched his muscles flex beneath his pale green shirt with the sleeves rolled high on his bronzed arms. He'd thrown the arrows so confidently. She was aware he knew his worth. He also understood the effect he was having on the women in the bar. Young and old alike couldn't tear their eyes off him. It wasn't just his height or the breadth of his shoulders: there was a boldness about him that put other men in the shade. Yet last night Izzy had averted her gaze. He reminded her too much of Charlie and she'd had enough of Charlie to last her a lifetime.

Elsie walked alongside the canal. Tomorrow morning at six she'd be taking this path carrying her sleeping-bag and holdall to embark on a new life, one she was looking forward to. The work would be exhausting, Dorothy had told her, so she would have little time or energy to dwell on what was going on back in Gosport with her husband and his new love.

A sudden movement at the side of the canal, and she was just in time to see a rat disappear into the undergrowth below the purple rosebay growing along the towpath. In her thoughts the canals had been filled with glistening clear water, but in reality it was a murky grey, and floating rubbish threatened to ensnare boat propellers.

In the boatyard Elsie could see the two boats tied side by side, *Mallard,* the one she would be sleeping on, and *Bunting,* the butty-boat. Both were canvas covered. *Mallard* was the one with the engine. Elsie shuddered. What did she know about engines? Come to think of it, what did she know about narrowboats or hauling coal and other goods? Nothing except what she'd read in her trusty canal book brought from home, and the conversation she'd had with Dorothy.

Elsie knew she would tackle the job and try to make a success of it. To give in and run home to Gosport with her tail between her legs would be to admit defeat and it wasn't in her nature to give up without a struggle. Why, then, wasn't she making more of an effort to hold on to Geoffrey? Because, deep down, she knew he was a lost cause.

Through the cottage window Dorothy watched Elsie turn and make her way back towards the Bull. Should she knock on the window, run out into the garden and call her in for a cup of tea? Neighbourliness told her she should, but she turned away, the much-read letter clutched in her hand.

Tomorrow would be time enough to remind the women how hard the work would be. They could also experience at first hand the wrath of the real canal folk who mostly disliked the chits

65

of girls who had taken over the work of their men, away fighting for the country.

The true water gypsies were paid by the trip, travelling with their wives and children on the waterways they had always travelled, and as a working unit. All were savvy individuals, though few could read or write. Where did they find the time for such niceties when they were always on the move? To keep the peace on the canals, the girls were paid significantly less than the water gypsies. Of course, the girls were allowed paid days off, which the canal folk were not, and because Dorothy had twisted her ankle and taken time off, she had elected to pay the girls' board and lodging herself on the understanding that the proprietors of the two pubs kept it secret. She had the feeling that this time the girls she had chosen would take to each other and to canal life. It was important to her that she had a good crew and that the girls found her to be beyond reproach.

During the years she had worked for the company she had sometimes despaired of the childishness shown by grown women who had been told what to expect from the job and what they needed to put in to gain limited success.

But there had also been successful women who had gone on to take out further teams of narrowboat women, nicknamed 'Idle Women' as their badges proclaimed 'IW' for Inland Waterways. Idle they were most certainly not. Dorothy was proud of her crews on the commercial waterway of the Grand Union Canal.

It wasn't her chosen profession. Her past had dictated it.

She reread the words she had stared at so many times. The letter was dated 21 May 1942. It was the last communication she had received from the man she loved.

*Darling Dorothy*
*Please excuse this writing but I'm in a lorry only a few miles from Dover. A dispatch rider caught up with us on our way back to Camberley. We have orders not to return to camp. I can only think we are on our way to France or Belgium. I will write again as soon I can. I'll ask someone to put this in the post for me. At least you'll have some idea where I've gone if you don't hear from me soon.*
*Love Jakub*
*PS You mean all the world to me.*

## Chapter Nine

'If you need anything, write.'

With Regina's words ringing in her ears, Tolly watched the coach with its barely glowing head-lights disappear round the corner of the lane.

Fearing there'd be no room on the boat for a suitcase she had jammed all her belongings, in-cluding a sleeping-bag, into four brown carrier bags with string handles that now cut into her hands as she walked purposefully towards the boatyard.

At first she'd had mixed feelings about Regina accompanying her on the long coach journey. Her sister knew how apprehensive she was at leaving Titchfield, and wanted to satisfy herself that Tolly wasn't falling into a den of iniquity.

It was half past five and the birds were chirpily calling to each other. Already she was out of breath. On the top of the bridge Tolly paused to look about her.

Four ducks paddled towards the opposite bank of the canal. The air was still and clear without the ever-present stink of destruction that Hitler's bombs had wreaked over the south coast. She breathed in deeply. A tiny well of excitement opened deep inside her. She picked up her bags again and strode purposefully towards the boat-yard's entrance.

Dorothy was in the office, mug in hand, chatting to a fair-haired woman of about Dorothy's age. They fell silent as Tolly let go of her bags and knocked on the open door. She was rewarded by wide smiles from the two of them.

'Nice and early, I see. Welcome, Tolly. This is Elsie. She'll be bunking with me in *Mallard*. Your shipmate should be waiting canalside near the Black Cow. Both of you will live aboard *Bunting*. Did you have a good journey up?'

Tolly felt at ease immediately, especially when Elsie grinned at her and poured tea into a mug, then set it in front of her. A spoon was poised over the condensed milk tin and Elsie looked en-quiringly at her.

'Yes, please.'

'I thought we'd cook breakfast on the boat later,' Dorothy said, 'but there's a loaf of bread and some marge here if you're hungry now. We were looking at the map showing our route. I know where we're going but sometimes it looks easier on the page.' She pushed the crumpled paper across her desk and Tolly picked it up.

'I never was any good at maps. I thought we'd get on the canal and stay there until we got where we're going,' she said.

'Well, in theory that's correct,' said Dorothy, 'but the map shows locks and bridges and waterways, called arms, that may not be navigable. Should we accidentally stray along one we could run aground, and as all the signposts have been taken out in case of German invasion, maps are about the only tool we have for navigation.'

Tolly was blushing at her own ignorance.

'Once we've done the first run you'll know exactly what I mean. Don't be afraid to ask about anything you're not sure of.'

Tolly felt easier at Dorothy's words and sipped her tea. She'd not experienced condensed milk as a whitener and sweetener before, although of course she'd used it in cake-making. She remembered Dorothy explaining that cow's milk was sometimes difficult to obtain.

Dorothy grabbed a jacket from the back of her chair. 'We'll go when everyone's ready,' she said.

Tolly asked, 'Is your ankle better now?'

'Much,' Dorothy said. 'Don't either of you do the silly thing I did and think there's room for you to jump from the boat if there clearly isn't. It was stupid of me. Too many injuries occur leaping on and off boats, especially in the locks and approaching tunnels. I should also warn you against sitting on top of the boats facing the steerer.

Lovely and comfortable but remember your back is towards the cut and you can't possibly see overhanging branches or bridges with your back to them.'

Elsie made a face at Tolly, who could no more see herself leaping on and off a narrowboat than flying to the moon.

Shepherded by Dorothy, Tolly and Elsie left the office, along with their luggage. Tolly found herself being led to two craft lying one behind the other in the basin. Other narrowboats bobbed in the water, tied together like sardines in a can.

'Get aboard the second boat and stow away your things,' advised Dorothy.

Izzy's short spell at the Black Cow had ended but she would return to visit her new friends at some time in the future. Yesterday everyone had insisted she take it easy because she'd be starting work today so she'd spent the afternoon in the pub gardens, reading, in the sunshine.

Out of the corner of her eye she'd noticed an elderly man in a wicker bath chair, quickly turning the pages of a book. He seemed to be more interested in looking for pictures than actually reading the words. After a while when Izzy saw he'd flicked through the chapters, come to the end and started again, she got up and went over to him.

He looked up at her as her shadow fell across him.

'What are you reading?' She spoke softly as she didn't want to startle him. The man gave her a gap-toothed smile and passed her the book. Izzy saw it was a recent edition of Alexandre Dumas'

*The Man in the Iron Mask.*

The effort of moving caused him to have a coughing fit. Izzy felt guilty for disturbing him. He finally wiped his mouth with a grubby handkerchief, bright red, like his neckerchief. Before he managed to tuck it into his waistcoat pocket Izzy had noticed the spots of dark blood. Her heart went out to him. She decided no good would come of her mentioning his illness so said instead, 'I'm not doing anything for a while, except enjoying the sun.' She flicked through the book's closely printed pages. 'Would you like me to read a little to you?' She didn't wait for him to answer. 'I've noticed you're not wearing spectacles. This print is very tiny. I used to read to my grandmother–'

This time he interrupted her. 'I'd like that very much.' His voice crackled with phlegm. 'If you're sure you can spare the time?'

Izzy had looked at his clean collarless shirt and corduroy trousers, brown shoes peeping out from below the turn-ups, and grinned. 'I'd be glad to,' she said. 'My name's Izzy.'

'And I'm Stefan but I'm known as Stevo.' He had a wicked glint in his dark eyes. His remaining teeth were very white, his skin dark and lined.

'Right then, Stevo, shall I begin?'

He nodded. Izzy had realized that speaking was difficult for him. She turned to the beginning of the book and began.

Although the story seemed ponderous she went on, immersed in what she was doing. Stevo seemed engrossed in the story. After a while she turned another page, then chanced a look and saw he was asleep. There was a woven blanket on the handles of the chair so she put down the book, got up, gathered the covering, and draped it gently over him.

Izzy was dying to go to the lavatory. Stevo looked so comfortable she decided to leave for a little while and carry on reading upon her return, when he might wake.

She had been gone only a few minutes, but when she returned, the bath chair and Stevo had disappeared. The book was on the table. Children were still playing on the wooden swings. Boats were moored on the canal and customers still enjoying their drinks in the gardens.

She'd picked up the book and wandered around, looking to see if Stevo had magically wheeled himself away. Then she'd gone to her room to begin packing for tomorrow. Izzy hadn't had time to dwell on Stevo's disappearance until now. She'd almost decided one of his family had reclaimed him and then they'd left the pub. Still asleep, he wouldn't have been able to say goodbye to her. Izzy decided she would keep the book until she saw him again, if she saw him.

Now Izzy smiled to herself. Sitting on her coat on the damp grass she was waiting for Dorothy to pick her up. Her bags were spread about her. The day promised to be sunny and warm. She listened to the murmur of insects in the grass and thanked God she'd escaped from Gosport and Charlie Osborne.

The two boats were moored by ropes to rings along the concrete wharf. They were each about seventy feet long, Tolly reckoned. *Mallard* and

*Bunting* were painted black, and both were covered with long tarpaulins, tethered firmly to keep out the weather.

'*Bunting's* the butty so has no engine. I suggest you claim your sleeping area,' Dorothy reminded Tolly. 'Both boats have been idle for a while so that's given our staff a chance to do some cleaning, but in future that's up to us. The holds have to be kept scrupulously clean, especially after we've transported coal or cement. When you've familiarized yourself with the space come over to us. I think it's a good idea to collect and greet our last crew member together, don't you?'

Tolly nodded in agreement.

The initials 'GUCC' were painted along the sides of the boat, with the craft's number and its name. Tolly lifted over her bags, then took a while deciding the best way for herself to climb aboard. The small ladder, a plank with cross strips nailed sideways to stop slippage, was still on the boat. Not that she required the ladder because the craft was moored tightly against the towpath and the water level of the canal made it relatively easy to step in, as long as she held on to the side of the boat. Going down the steps into the cabin backwards seemed her safest option. She cursed herself for her size – at least the butty had more space, due to the lack of an engine, than *Mallard*. She heaved her bags down, looked about her and sneezed.

A white coating of dust had settled everywhere, not enough for Tolly to want to clean immediately but she sneezed again, then blew her nose.

Cupboards and shelves lined the varnished

walls of the small space, which was barely five foot high. Someone had used a sharp instrument to comb the varnish so it looked wood-like. Mugs, jugs and anything with a handle dangled from hooks that jutted from shelves. Heat was coming from a small stove with a flat top and she stepped away from it. Of course, she thought, the stove doubled as a cooker, so even though the weather was warm it had to be alight. Where was her bed? There should be space for two, shouldn't there? She sat down on what appeared to be a long seat and pulled a knob that opened a cupboard to reveal tins of food and condensed milk. To the side there was another cupboard, empty this time, so she filled it with stuff from her bags. Then she spotted a hinged pull-down cupboard running along the opposite side of the cabin.

Lifting the wooden plank she saw she could erect a table by placing it along cut-outs in the shelving. Pleased with herself, Tolly saw that if she fitted the plank into similar slots lower down, the table became a bunk running diagonally across from the seat she was sitting on.

'Of course,' she said to herself. She had been sitting on the second bed. Deciding it wasn't possible that her cabin-mate could be larger than her, Tolly tumbled her sleeping-bag into the space below the seat to nestle with a pillow and a folded blanket. She sneezed again, disturbing more of the powdery substance. Sitting there in the small space, she decided it was quite cosy. How it would feel containing another person as well as herself, time would tell.

'Tolly?'

Dorothy's voice was loud and clear. Moment-arily Tolly had forgotten the other two women were eager to be off to collect the fourth member of their party.

Tolly poked her head out of the hatch and yelled, 'Coming!'

## Chapter Ten

Elsie handed Tolly a mug of tea and Dorothy started the diesel engine that powered *Mallard*. Then, with her hand on the tiller, she eased the seven-foot-wide narrowboat out of the basin and into the main canal. *Bunting*, tied closely to *Mallard*, bobbed behind.

'*Bunting* has a tiller but it's a little different from this one. All the time the boat is on the move, you must be in front of the tiller.'

Elsie saw Tolly stare at Dorothy, her forehead creased. Dorothy had called her from *Bunting* onto *Mallard* leaving the butty-boat without any-one at the helm. 'But–'

'We're only going a short distance,' Dorothy said, 'we're carrying no cargo, and I need to show you both how to use the tiller and the gear lever. Never do as I do, do as I tell you. Come here and take over, Tolly.'

Dorothy motioned towards a handle. 'There are no brakes on a narrowboat and it doesn't steer like a car.' She pointed to an R on the lever. 'Reverse,' she explained. 'Even if you put the boat's engine in reverse, momentum will keep it travelling forward so you must be aware well in advance of any manoeuvre you need to make.' Elsie saw Tolly nod, understanding Dorothy. 'When our fourth worker is picked up,' said Dorothy, 'I expect the two of you to guide the engineless butty safely behind us. You'll show our new girl all you've learned.'

'But–'

'You'll be surprised at how much you can gain from doing it yourself.' Not allowing Tolly to remonstrate, Dorothy moved forward and Tolly, her face white, grabbed the swan-necked tiller from her, standing in the position Dorothy had just vacated. 'I can't stand beside you, there's no room. If you have to swing the tiller sideways, I could end up in the canal, or "cut", as it's called. As you can see, there's very little room for us all to stand on the stern of the boat.'

Elsie could see Tolly was trying not to show how petrified she was.

'Because this boat's engine pulls the butty-boat, you'll soon see that the turn on the tiller causes the boat to move in a different direction. Take it easy. There's no need to go more than four miles an hour because if you do we'll be washing the sides of the canal away, causing the earth to fall into the water, and the cut's in a poor state as it is.'

Tolly took her eyes briefly from the front of the boat. Its position in the centre of the cut shifted sideways towards the bank. Elsie watched as, hastily, Tolly corrected its course.

'Using the tiller should become automatic, not

something you have to think about. The boat must become part of you. Sometimes it helps you relax if you chat instead of looking and feeling terrified. Did you put your stuff away?' Dorothy asked.

'Yes, and when I get a chance I might give the boat a good clean to get rid of the white dust I found everywhere.'

'Oh, that's nothing to worry about.' Dorothy smiled. 'It's Keating's Powder, sprinkled lavishly to get rid of the fleas.'

The sudden silence that followed caused Tolly to take her eyes from the boat's progress to gape at Dorothy. Suddenly they were heading towards the towpath. 'Tolly! The boat!' Elsie cried. The bank loomed precariously close.

Tolly stepped quickly forward and pulled the gear lever into reverse. The boat struggled against the command but checked. Elsie breathed a sigh of relief as the water churned beneath the long vessel and its path was corrected.

'Well done!' Dorothy was ecstatic in her praise. 'Excellent reflexes! I knew you'd soon get the hang of it.'

Tolly put the motor switch into an upright position that signalled she was giving it no more commands and the boat found its own impetus in the water. The butty-boat bumped *Mallard's* rear bollards but no damage was done. The plump white rope fenders hanging from both boats had softened the impact.

'Which is why a person needs to steer on a boat that has no engine!' Dorothy's face was wreathed in smiles. 'I knew I'd picked a good team,' she said.

'Fleas? What did you mean?' Tolly shouted.

'In the warm weather the boats often get an infestation of fleas, and they're absolute buggers to get rid of,' answered Dorothy. 'Keating's Powder's the best there is.'

Elsie could think of no words to explain how she felt about the possibility of the unwelcome passengers on the boat.

Dorothy moved the motor into a forward position and said to Tolly, 'Get the boats back on course. Not far now before we pick up our fourth.'

In a remarkably short while both boats were sailing in a straight line up the middle of the canal and the talk had turned back to fleas.

Dorothy said to Elsie, 'You don't seem too shocked at the prospect of fleas.'

'The last time I slept in an air-raid shelter all night I found I was covered in flea bites in the morning. Thank God for Keating's Powder! I did notice it was dusted liberally in this boat as well. One of the hazards of living in a confined space where there's plenty of heat, I suppose.'

Dorothy nodded. 'Don't worry, you two, we manage to keep the pests at bay. Mostly.'

Elsie made a face at Tolly. Then she sat with her back to the water allowing the early sun to warm her face. Soon they would be picking up the final member of their team. She hoped she'd take to her – she'd already warmed to the plump girl holding the tiller. She smiled at Dorothy, who had now pulled a shapeless knitted hat over her hair.

The three of them looked as though they'd dressed from a rag-bag, Elsie thought. All in mismatched but warm clothing. Dorothy had stressed that it could be cold on the cut early in the mornings so keeping warm was a number-one priority.

'Is it true the water gypsies resent us being on the cut?' Elsie couldn't help herself. She looked across at the vista before her. Fields and flowers and trees blended into the sunshine, so beautiful that she didn't want anyone to harbour bad feelings.

'Why shouldn't they? I'll give you a few tips. Don't call them bargees. Don't be overly familiar with the menfolk – the women won't like it and you'll not do yourselves any favours with the men as they'll think you're easy. And always ask permission to board their boats even when we've had to tie up alongside to get off the cut and on to the towpath.' Dorothy paused. 'You have to remember, we're the newcomers, they've lived all their lives and in many cases their ancestors before them, on the waterways.'

Tolly gasped. 'They live on these barges?'

'Yes, and have brought up families here. The women take great pride in furnishing the cabins with brasses, china and lace. They're very proud people,' Dorothy answered. 'And they're boats, not barges,' she admonished.

'I never saw a tap or a sink,' Tolly said. Elsie realized she was referring to the cabin.

'You probably didn't notice the pail of fresh water,' said Dorothy, 'which must be refilled from water points along the way. Be sparing with the fresh water and use water from the cut for cleaning. And before you ask, no, there's no lavatory on board. Use a different bucket for that and tip it over the side in the mornings.'

Elsie saw Tolly wrinkle her nose. Dorothy had already chatted to her about life on board so had also explained that there were several towns they would pass through where they could pay at the slipper baths for hot water to bathe.

'There's a store of coal on *Mallard* that we refresh from points along the way,' added Dorothy. 'The stoves take wood and anything that'll burn. We often pick up logs and such in the countryside.'

God, thought Elsie, there was so much to learn, but it would be such hard work that she wouldn't have time to think about Gosport.

She wondered about Tolly and why she'd joined the narrowboats. She looked forward to the girly chats they'd no doubt have when they got to know each other better. Dorothy was the deep one, the enigma, she thought. For although Dorothy seldom stopped talking it was all about the work, not herself.

Elsie looked towards her – she was keeping her eyes on Tolly with the tiller.

'It won't be long before we pick up our new friend,' Dorothy said. 'I've already spoken to her about locks but I think I'd better explain to you how they work.

'Because the land isn't flat the canals need locks to allow the water to become a levelling point for the boats. Normal depth of a canal can be as little as three feet, and you'll notice how low the boats are when fully loaded. Narrowboats need to go up and down hills and this is where the locks come in. We trap the boats in a lock then let the water run in or out so the boat can be raised or lowered.

Locks are easy to manoeuvre as long as you abide by the rules. We have windlasses, or lock keys, to open or shut the gates. These lock keys you must guard with your lives. Never leave one behind or let one fall into the canal. The canal folk usually tuck theirs into their leather belts.'

Dorothy lifted a wooden cover from a box-like contraption at the rear near the tiller and took out an L-shaped piece of metal. 'All the canal mechanisms should have safety ratchets on them. You must slip the ratchet down. If you don't bother, the lock key can fly off and injure you.' She held up the metal object. 'This is a lock key or windlass. There are four on this boat, one for each of us.'

Dorothy thought she'd given Tolly and Elsie enough information to worry about, so after returning the windlass to its home she perched on the stern rail and began to enjoy the sunshine that promised to become warmer as the day went on. It wouldn't be many minutes before the Black Cow came into sight. She hoped Elsie and Tolly would take to the new girl as easily as she had.

Two horses stood in a field, watching the boats pass, and the chugging of the engine was soothing her frustration at being unable to do the things she most wanted to do. Like other people during this hateful war, Dorothy was having to make do with second best.

She spied the lone figure sitting in the grass. 'That's her, up ahead. When you get closer, pull in towards the towpath.'

Tolly began slowing the engine. As the figure rose to a standing position Dorothy was surprised to see a smile light Elsie's face, and she began waving frantically. Tolly brought the narrowboat as close to the bank as she dared. Dorothy was so busy checking Tolly's movements that she almost missed the excited squeal Elsie gave before she jumped from the boat, landed in front of the girl and threw her arms about her, almost knocking her off her feet.

'Why didn't you let my mum know you were following me?' The new girl was jumping up and down with joy.

'I thought you'd be on another boat and long gone!' Elsie said.

'Dorothy hurt her foot and I've been boarded out while a crew was formed.' The girl smiled at Dorothy, then to Elsie she said, 'Oh, it's lovely to see you!'

The two women hugged and laughed.

Of course, Dorothy thought. Both came from Gosport, both had worked in the munitions factory there, so it was likely they knew each other.

'Had I known you were friends I could have put you on the same boat,' said Dorothy. 'Never mind. I'm sure we'll all get on together fine.' She began introductions. 'Tolly, this is Izzy, Izzy, Tolly. And before we go any further I trust you've all brought your gas masks?' Nods all round.

Izzy unwound herself from Elsie's clutches. 'Elsie, I've got loads to tell you,' she said. 'And I'm happy to start work. I'm on the butty, aren't I?'

'Correct,' said Dorothy. She turned to Tolly. 'Now I know how good a steerer you are, it's your job on *Bunting* to show Izzy what you know.' She gestured towards the second craft bobbing against the side of the canal. 'Izzy, get your stuff on board, we'll all chat later. Tolly, how d'you feel about cooking breakfast? I lit the stove early this morning and there's bread, plenty of groceries and water on board. Don't forget, everyone, to hand me your ration books for shopping. You won't need to pay me. It's only the coupons I'll need.'

Elsie climbed back on board and Dorothy watched as Tolly helped Izzy carry her bags to *Bunting*. She allowed them time to sort themselves out, and when Tolly and Izzy appeared from the cabin, their faces wreathed in smiles, she waved to let them know she was ready for the off again.

As Elsie took the tiller, looking apprehensive, Dorothy engaged the engine for her and thought how brilliant it was that both girls had managed to keep secret that they knew each other until the last moment. The government was fond of its slogans proclaiming, 'Be Like Dad and Keep Mum', and 'Loose Lips Sink Ships', and now she had, in her care, two women she hoped she could trust ... perhaps even with her own secret if it leaked out.

### *Chapter Eleven*

'Isn't it a beautiful morning?' Elsie grinned at Dorothy. 'And what a lovely smell!'

'Tolly's obviously got the hang of cooking on that small stove,' said Dorothy.

Elsie felt ridiculously happy, one hand on the

tiller as she watched the front of the boat sailing midstream down the leafy channel of water. She realized she was at peace, probably for the first time since Geoffrey had dropped his bombshell about his affair and the baby.

She and Izzy had a lot of catching up to do. She was looking forward to telling her all her news. A lot had happened in such a short while. Unless Izzy asked she decided she wouldn't volunteer the information regarding Charlie's visit to her home. Izzy seemed happy – let her stay that way.

'This work's not popular with the girls,' said Dorothy, breaking into Elsie's thoughts. 'It hasn't the glamour of the services and doesn't pay as well as the factories but after your first trip the money will rise by a pound a week.'

'That's good,' said Elsie. She took a deep breath of the cooking smell. 'I'm really looking forward to breakfast.'

'Narrowboat ahead,' said Dorothy.

As the boat approached Elsie knew she must slow down. Her heart was beating fast – did she pass on the left or the right? It was difficult to re-member when she was so new to steering a seventy-foot-long boat pulling another craft.

She slowed, steered to allow the other boat to pass, and as the elderly fellow in cap, shirtsleeves and a jaunty yellow waistcoat also slowed down, she remembered to hail him and thank him for his consideration. Out of the corner of her eye, she saw Dorothy checking behind to make sure *Bunting* was giving the boat clearance.

'Good morning!' Elsie cried.

She was rewarded with a glare, an 'Argh' and a

gobbet of spit that fell into the water as his boat passed.

'Did you see that?' Elsie was shocked.

'Not everyone likes to see young women working the cut,' Dorothy said. 'Take no notice. You behaved impeccably, and I certainly liked the way you handled this boat, but you can speed up again now. We'll stop for breakfast before we reach the bridge and lock.' Then Elsie was startled to hear Dorothy sing, '"Spit me goodnight, Sergeant Major..."' She'd changed the first word, 'kiss', of the well-known song. Elsie giggled, then joined in with Dorothy's lusty tones, their voices carrying on the still air. Singing was a wonderful tonic, Elsie thought.

Eventually Dorothy paused. '"Laugh and the world laughs with you..."'

'"Cry and you cry alone!"' finished Elsie. They laughed. How smashing it was to feel so happy, she thought. The throb of the engine and the faint whiff of diesel obviously agreed with her, but she thought it would be lovely to stop and enjoy a good breakfast in these wonderful surroundings. She didn't want to think about the bridge and the lock, though.

Eventually Dorothy supervised both boats mooring up. This time metal spikes were driven into the earth and the boats tied close to the towpath to stop them drifting. Dorothy and Elsie were presented with breakfast carried from *Bunting* to *Mallard*.

Scrambled eggs and a huge pile of pancakes adorned each plate. It smelt delicious and Elsie licked her lips.

'I hope you like pancakes. I know we normally only have them on Shrove Tuesday but I took a chance,' said Tolly, producing salt and pepper from her trouser pockets after she'd handed Dorothy her plateful. 'There's jam to go on them, if you want. Sorry the egg is powdered but I hope you'll like it. I thought at first I'd not be able to cook on that stove but it's easy once you get the hang of it.'

'Yum-yum! I've never had pancakes for breakfast,' said Dorothy. 'What made you decide to cook them?'

Tolly said, 'I saw the flour and the egg powder and thought, Why not?'

Elsie couldn't say a word for her mouth was full of pancake. Eventually she found her voice. 'I wish you'd always cook for us.'

'I wouldn't mind,' said Tolly. 'I can make a delicious bacon and egg tart and there's plenty of dried egg powder left...'

'Sadly, we have to take our turns at all the tasks ahead of us,' said Dorothy. 'But I'll happily allow you to carry on doing more of the work you decide you like most.'

'Isn't this heaven?' Izzy turned her face to the sun. Elsie thought she looked so much more relaxed than when last she'd seen her that night in the Fox.

After their plates had been wiped clean, with chunks of bread certainly seeming more tasty than the grey loaves Elsie had been buying in Gosport, Dorothy allowed them to chat and get to know each other until it was time to go.

Elsie and Izzy had taken a walk along the

towpath. 'Oh, I have missed you,' Izzy said.

'Well, it's lovely we're together now,' Elsie answered. 'It would have been even better to share the butty with you. How is it with Tolly?'

'She's a good sort,' said Izzy. 'Quiet at first, now won't shut up about what she'd do if she owned that café she worked in, but I really like her.'

'That's just as well as you'll be sharing with her for a few weeks. I like Dorothy.'

Izzy nodded. 'I'm so glad you decided to come on the narrowboats.'

'Getting away from Charlie's done wonders for you,' Elsie said, stopping and staring at Izzy. 'You look so rested and happy.'

'I think this experience is going to be the making of both of us,' Izzy said, giving her a big grin. Their conversation was cut short by a shout from Dorothy.

'I think that means we're wanted back on board,' said Elsie, turning and waving at the others. Arm in arm they walked towards the moored boats. As Elsie neared *Mallard* she heard Dorothy and Tolly talking about chores.

'I vote that whoever cooks a meal also washes up,' said Tolly. 'That way the cook'll make sure there are fewer used plates and pans.'

'Good idea,' chorused Elsie and Izzy, as they stepped on board.

'That seems a good solution, unless anyone feels like helping wash up the dishes?' said Dorothy. 'Unanimous vote?'

Everyone shouted, 'Yes!' Tolly and Izzy began collecting up the dirty crockery.

'You'll be all right if I go below and get on with

some paperwork, won't you?'

Elsie nodded, trying to look more confident than she felt about handling the narrowboat alone.

'Won't you find it too dark in the cabin?' She hoped Dorothy might suggest she'd prefer to sit up top and work. At least then she'd be able to keep an eye on her.

'Papers fly away in the breeze,' answered Dorothy. 'Give us a call when the lock's in sight. There's a bridge ahead but as long as you keep to the middle of the cut and remember to slow down as you pass beneath, you'll be fine.'

Sure enough, Elsie passed through the ivy-covered red-brick bridge with inches to spare on each side of the boat. She even managed to turn to Tolly and Izzy, giving them a warning wave.

So far there had been little traffic on the water but the nearer they got to London the more there would be. Elsie wondered what Oxford would be like. Dorothy had explained that they would stay overnight in Oxford, then go down part of the Thames to Limehouse where they would pick up materials that they would then drop off at Birmingham, via the Grand Union Canal. There they would be loaded with coal that would be unloaded, possibly at Coventry, and perhaps pick up another cargo to discharge at Banbury, or thereabouts, on the Oxford canal. From there it was a short distance to Lower Heyford where they'd clean the boats and refuel, then start all over again, this time with different orders to fulfil. Dorothy said they'd be more than ready after that to go home to their families for a few days.

As far as Elsie could guess, Izzy would prefer

not to return to Gosport where no doubt Charlie Osborne would find her. She thought she might suggest Izzy accompany her to Western Way; she doubted the house would have been sold in that short time. It was highly unlikely that Geoffrey would discover a buyer so quickly.

Tolly would be going home to Titchfield, which was not far from Gosport. Dorothy had already told her she intended visiting her mother in South-ampton before she returned to the cottage she rented from Rousham Cruisers in Lower Heyford. Elsie had left her car in the boatyard and one of the staff had thrown a tarpaulin over it to stop the birds messing on it. Elsie rarely used her car, pre-ferring at home to ride her bicycle, but she would offer to drive them all south to save them paying for train tickets as there was still plenty of petrol in the car's tank.

So deep in thought was Elsie that the lock was suddenly ahead of her, looming like a castle to be conquered.

She slowed the engine. Dorothy poked her head out of the cabin and shouted back to *Bunting,* 'Lock ahead.' To Elsie she said, 'Move in towards the bank so you can get off the boat. I'll take the tiller.'

Panic took over. Was she supposed to open those huge black wooden lock gates by herself? What had Dorothy said about pushing or pulling the balance beams, the long square wooden arms? Lock key? She'd need one from the box.

Despite the roiling of her stomach she couldn't help but notice a very pretty cottage within a white-painted fence and a path leading to the open front door. Tea roses, creamy and full, were growing practically as high as the diamond-paned windows below the thatched roof. Looking at the house was a small distraction until panic consumed her.

Could she remember all that Dorothy had told her about locks? As she looked now at the huge wooden gates, she couldn't be at all sure.

Tolly had already jumped from *Bunting* and was moving quickly, puffing and panting, across a small high iron bridge to the other side of the lock.

'The gates won't open themselves.' Startled by Dorothy's voice, Elsie stepped from the boat, after making sure the vessel's rope was loosely hooked round a nearby bollard. The boat needed to be raised to the next water level. Windlass in hand, she followed Tolly's example and ran to the lock gates.

Ha! The lock was empty so the boats needed to enter. Water had to flood inside the chamber so the boats could rise to the level of the water on the other side of the lock. Well, Elsie thought, that much she'd worked out, so now the gates had to be opened to allow the boats to move in. She pushed against the balance beam, saw that Tolly was doing the same on the other side, and put her lock key on top of the beam. With her full weight against the wood, she was happy to see and feel it move.

And move it did until it came to a juddering stop and she looked in horror as her lock key jumped into the air, fell into the water and disappeared.

'Why the hell didn't you call for the lock-keeper

if you've no idea what you're doing?'

Elsie whirled around and found herself face to chest with a tall man who, she saw, as her eyes travelled upwards, had hair the colour of tow rope and eyes as blue as the sky, encased in dark-rimmed spectacles. He was frowning at her. 'You shouldn't be let loose on the cut!' he bellowed, so loudly she felt his warm breath on her face.

Elsie's knees buckled at the shock and she staggered backwards. He grabbed hold of her before she fell into the lock, pulling her forward and against him. Momentarily she was caught in his arms.

It was like nothing she'd experienced before, that feeling of being cocooned.

Oh, God, she thought, as her stomach knotted and her breath became strangled. Heat ran through her like molten metal. For a moment he was motionless. A peculiar look had entered his eyes. It shook Elsie to her core. With great difficulty she pushed him away.

There was a need there, unspoken, not that Elsie was going to admit it. That look was something so rare and unexpected that it had taken her only a moment to recognize he yearned for her, body and soul. He stared at her, the moment of eye contact seeming unending, then said grudgingly, 'I'll give you my windlass. You can return it when you're back this way.'

'What makes you think I'll come here again?' She sounded as though her mouth was full of treacle. Her mind was still on the unexplained look in his eyes. Perhaps she should feel outraged at his audacity. But she didn't, not at all.

Suddenly he smiled at her. 'You're from the boatyard at Lower Heyford. You'll be back. Maybe by then I'll have fished your lock key from the water.' He put a finger to the bridge of his nose and pushed his spectacles higher.

Elsie, pulling herself together, allowed her eyes to dwell on his tanned skin. He wore corduroy trousers and a grey waistcoat open over a white shirt. She noticed as he moved he had a slight limp. It didn't seem to affect his quick skill at unwinding the rack and pinion. Elsie looked across the lock at Tolly, who was now attempting a similar job on the other side. Elsie wondered if she had seen her clutched in the man's arms.

Both boats were now nestled side by side in the empty lock with Izzy at the tiller of *Bunting* and Dorothy in charge of *Mallard.* Dorothy was staring up at her, a bemused look on her face. Obviously she had witnessed everything.

'Now we close the gates, allow the water in and the boats will rise to the next level,' he said. 'Then we open the gates and off you go.'

The anger had left his voice. Elsie knew instantly that whatever she had felt just now he had experienced it too. She looked back towards the cottage and suddenly it came to her. 'Are you the lock-keeper?'

He nodded. 'And this one's a deep lock. I'm here to help, and you're supposed to wait for me if you're unsure of the procedure.'

'I didn't know.' Her excuse sounded feeble. She knew she was blushing. She had no idea what to say to him, this man who had unleashed something inside her with no warning.

'Well, you do now. Your mate,' he inclined his head towards Tolly, 'seems to know what she's doing.'

The water level floating the two boats was now almost equal to the depth of water outside the lock. He began winding down the rack and pinion, making sure the ratchet was on safely, then put his windlass on the grass. 'Leave the gates to me and your mate. You'd better get back on the boat. It's a long walk to the next lock.' He smiled, showing even white teeth. 'I'll finish up here.'

For some obscure reason Elsie didn't want to leave him. Together they pushed against the balance arm, opening the lock gate. Tolly was making her way to the side of the bank ready to board *Bunting* as it came out of the lock. Elsie knew she ought to get back on board. Reluctantly she turned from him.

'Don't forget the windlass.' He bent, picked up the lock key and handed it to her. Again she noticed his slight awkwardness when he bent his knee.

Her tongue felt too large for her mouth, as she managed, 'Thank you,' and dazedly walked away.

A sadness settled over her but was immediately dispelled when he yelled, 'I don't know your name!'

'Elsie,' she called back.

'Jack,' he shouted, and grinned. For the first time she noticed a small white dog at his heels. She liked dogs. She couldn't wait to tell Izzy about all the feelings the man had unleashed in her.

As Elsie climbed aboard *Mallard*, Dorothy said, 'Well, that's a turn-up for the books! I thought I was going to have to tell you off for losing a precious windlass, instead you've charmed the lock-keeper.'

## Chapter Twelve

'I'm happy with the progress we've made so far,' Dorothy said. The smell of cooking hung in the air as they huddled in *Mallard's* cabin. They'd eaten a simple evening meal that, again, Tolly had prepared: potatoes, carrots and a tin of corned beef, with gravy. 'I don't know how you manage it but even this humble meal tastes special,' she added.

Tolly beamed with pleasure. 'Wait till you try my Woolton Pie,' she said.

'Wasn't that created by a chef at the Savoy Hotel in London?' asked Izzy.

'It was,' said Tolly, 'and the woman who taught me to bake worked there.'

'Well, I can't wait,' said Izzy.

The light was boosted by candles, provided by Elsie, despite Dorothy's warning that she should save them as they weren't easy to get hold of. All the tiny windows had been covered as blackout restrictions were still in force.

Dorothy said, 'I see you made a friend of Jack Lumley.' She raised her eyebrows. 'Quite a feat as he doesn't like us girls on the cut. Thinks we're more trouble than we're worth.'

Tolly giggled. 'He didn't think she was bothersome! I wish it was me he'd held in his arms.'

'A bit of all right, if you ask me,' added Izzy, pushing a hand through her red curls.

Elsie put her plate on the floor. 'He seems nice. Well, he gave me his windlass after mine fell in the lock.'

'He's not normally so kind,' Dorothy said. 'Usually any of my girls who put a foot out of line get the sharp end of Jack's tongue. He's taken a fancy to you.'

Elsie spluttered into her tea. 'But I'm a married woman!' She waved her left hand with the tell-tale wedding ring.

Tolly and Izzy laughed. 'I don't suppose he noticed that,' Izzy said. 'Anyway, being nice to you doesn't mean anything more than ... well, that he was being kind, but it was rather a particular look.'

'He's taciturn at the best of times–' Dorothy began.

'Why isn't he in the forces?' Elsie interrupted.

'He was. Air Force, shot down and lost part of his leg.' Dorothy didn't usually gossip but Elsie had asked. 'He prefers a solitary life. He's lived in that cottage working as a lock-keeper for a couple of years now. Got quite a reputation for being grumpy.'

Dorothy was aware that Elsie's husband had strayed and that she had left her home town so she could think about the future. Elsie was far too sensible to be swept off her feet by another man so soon ... wasn't she?

She couldn't help herself, Dorothy yawned. Pretty soon Tolly was complaining that she was sleepy, too.

'You're not used to being out in the fresh air and I'm so tired I could sleep on a line,' Dorothy said. Nevertheless the women sat and chatted, until Dorothy advised Izzy and Tolly to return to *Bunting*. 'An early start tomorrow,' she said, as she began clearing the plates and picking up the empty cups. 'I'll leave you to get ready for bed, Elsie. Give you a little privacy while I help Tolly and Izzy take these dishes back to the other boat. Don't worry about the Keating's Powder. It'll do more good than harm.'

She knew how difficult it could be undressing and washing in a confined space with a virtual stranger present. She also knew the shyness would soon wear off – it always did.

On *Bunting* Dorothy chatted amiably with Tolly and Izzy, and dried a few pots as the girls washed up.

The sky was clouding over as she walked back to *Mallard*. She was glad the two in *Bunting* seemed to be easy in each other's company.

Elsie was in bed when Dorothy pushed open the door and entered the snug cabin. All she could see of her was the top of her head peeping up from the sleeping-bag. The dry smell of the Keating's Powder hung in the air. Tomorrow, hopefully, they could dust it away.

'Are you warm enough?' Dorothy asked. 'Luckily the stove keeps the temperature up.' A grunt came from Elsie's bunk.

She poured water from the bucket into a bowl, then undressed. Quickly she scrubbed her face and neck, cleaned her teeth and put on a pair of flannelette pyjamas. Then she climbed the steps, opened the door and threw the used water over the side of the boat. Within moments she had bolted the cabin door and was in her own bunk. She had no idea how long she'd been asleep but she was woken by Elsie leaning over and shaking her.

'Shouldn't we find an air-raid shelter?'

'Don't worry, they're ours.' Dorothy spoke sleepily but her voice was drowned by the heavy growl of planes overhead. The deafening roar took her words away, like leaves in the wind. She extracted a hand from the warmth of her sleeping-bag and laid it on Elsie's shoulder. The rumble of aircraft seemed to have fled into the distance.

Dorothy sat up. She could see Elsie was scared. 'Upper Heyford's RAF station for Bomber Command is close by. The Wellingtons fly from the training unit on night manoeuvres. If it had been a raid, you'd have heard Moaning Minnie same as back in Gosport.'

She saw relief spread across Elsie's face. 'I'm sorry. I'm so used to the boys' night flying I forgot to warn you all. Actually, this is where your lock-keeper trained.'

Elsie said crossly, 'He's not my lock-keeper!'

Dorothy smiled to herself. 'I ought to go and warn the other two. I don't want them frightened out of their wits.'

Elsie, calmer now, said, 'I think they'd have been knocking on this boat by now if they were worried. I'm getting back into bed. It seems to have quietened down now out there. Besides, it's raining.'

Dorothy's head fell back on her feather pillow.

The rain reminded her of needles being thrown against a window.

'Night.' The small voice came from Elsie.

Dorothy mumbled back to her. She hoped the girls had all brought sensible footwear and clothing to keep out the rain. She feared it would last all of tomorrow.

Elsie lay warm and still. She didn't want to disturb Dorothy again, especially now her fears about the bombers had been dealt with. She could hear the even breathing that signalled Dorothy was asleep again.

She thought of Geoffrey and how they'd longed for a child. Now he'd dashed any hope of her becoming a mother. She willed herself not to cry, not to make a sound. The thought of becoming a childless, wrinkled spinster wasn't something Elsie looked forward to. Never had she envisaged her marriage becoming so shaky that Geoffrey would look elsewhere. But he had.

She thought of the feelings that had coursed through her body that afternoon. She'd known immediately her eyes had held Jack's that he had felt it too. The sudden look of bewilderment on his face before he'd taken her in his arms had confirmed it. And he had been so eager to know her name. The whole scenario was very puzzling. Elsie knew she would soon be asking a lot of questions about Jack Lumley.

Tolly was happy with her sleeping-bag covering her. She had opened it out flat, deciding she didn't want to be confined within its limited space. She hoped with all her heart that Izzy was soundly asleep and comfortable on the smaller bunk.

She didn't know when she had last enjoyed a day as much as she had today. Out in the sunshine, in the fresh air, then showing off her cooking prowess to her new friends. At least, she hoped they looked upon her as a friend. She'd tried so hard not to get in the way when the many boating jobs had had to be carried out. Already she had so much to write and tell Reggie.

Her body felt ridiculously tired. She suspected the extra exercise had made her use muscles she'd never known she had. Several times Dorothy had sent her on ahead, walking along the towpath to set the locks so they could go straight into the chambers. If other boats were already lined up she'd had to wait her turn until they'd passed through, then reset the locks. It had been hard work, harder than making tea and serving customers. Her arms felt now as if they were falling off!

She wasn't stupid, though. As it had been only their first day together no one had really talked about themselves, but she was sure there was more to her three companions than they were letting on. Elsie and Izzy obviously knew each other and were firm friends. She gathered they'd worked together at the munitions factory in Gosport. What had happened to make them leave their home town? In Izzy, Tolly could sense fear. It showed in the way she constantly looked about her as though she expected to find something or someone she didn't want to see. Elsie wore a wedding ring. Had her husband died, been killed? And that look from the lock-keeper! Oh, how Tolly wished she could inspire a man to look at her like that.

Dorothy was the strangest of the three. For all her authority there was vulnerability. No, Dorothy might pretend to be the strongest – after all, she was their boss and knew the job and the canals in a way they never could – but Tolly believed she was hiding a sorrow far greater than any of them could possibly imagine.

## Chapter Thirteen

Jack Lumley pushed away his cocoa mug and sighed. What on earth had happened today? A woman he'd never before set eyes on had thrown him into turmoil.

'Move over, Matey,' he said companionably, to the white Jack Russell curled up at his side, trying for the lion's share of the armchair. The dog opened one eye and Jack lovingly scratched the rough hair behind its ears.

Elsie had felt it, too. Whatever 'it' had been that had coursed through him with such power and sent him reeling.

Oxford would be the first real stop on the canal-boat girls' journey to Limehouse. It usually was. They needed to be able to walk on pavements, see shops and buy a few bits and pieces, if they could in wartorn England, to keep up their morale after they'd been on the alien territory of the cut. There wasn't much that went on in the village or on the canals that he wasn't privy to.

A sharp twinge in his leg made him grit his teeth. He was due a hospital appointment in Oxford very soon. Sensing his discomfort, Matey stared at him with large, moist eyes.

'I'll get someone to look after you for a couple of days – you'll not be left on your own.' He remembered the little dog cowering against the hedge trying to shield himself from the stones thrown at him by several village boys. Jack had brought the frightened, snarling and bloodied animal into his home after he'd chased the lads away. He'd inserted a notice in the post-office window, saying he had the dog, but no one claimed him. A good thing too, for now, a year later, Jack and Matey were inseparable.

Jack smiled at the little dog, then gazed around the home he had made for himself. A low fire burned, warming the comfortable room. A letter on the mantelpiece from the Inland Waterways, his employer, was tucked behind the clock and needed no reply. The hospital appointment ditto. Books lined a shelf running along the top of all four walls, just below ceiling height. Books were his friends.

'Damn leg,' grumbled Jack. The dog licked his hand sympathetically.

'Suppose she finds she can't cope with life on the cut and Oxford is the end of the line for her?' If he expected a reply from his canine friend he didn't get it.

He'd noticed the wedding ring on her left hand. 'Means very little nowadays, Matey,' he said. 'If she had a loving partner I doubt she'd be working for Dorothy and the canal company.' Unless, he thought, the man was abroad and likely to be so for the unforeseeable future. If that was the case, he'd not force himself between them. He'd bow out gracefully. But he had been able to tell that Elsie, although shocked, had felt the same as he had. 'A woman in a loving marriage would have slapped my face for holding her like that,' he said to Matey. The dog's tongue lolled in agreement. A further twinge caused him to rub the ankle he no longer had. He coped with the prosthetic limb well. The Dutch surgeon had done a fine job.

Outside, rain flung itself against the windows. His thoughts went back to that cold, overcast February night in 1942 when he had been returning in the Wellington from a successful mission. He believed he was on course but he was unable to see clearly for the ice on the Perspex.

The ferocity of the freezing weather had caused the iced-up port engine to stall, then part of the propeller had broken off, forcing itself through the side of the aircraft.

Fear had filled the plane but the men's cries were tempered by the wind and extreme cold. With the hydraulics damaged they had come down in the freezing sea. He had managed to pull himself onto the floating carcass of the plane and alongside the damaged controls. The water had flushed him away so fiercely that he had no recollection of why part of his foot was missing. When he saw he was struggling for safety with one booted foot and a leg that ended in shredded trousers at the ankle, it surprised him that there was so little pain. The blood streaming from him made him realize he stood little chance of survival unless he could stem the flow quickly. The answer to that had been the ripped sleeve of his shirt tied as a tourniquet. Then he had lost consciousness.

He knew he was not the only survivor when, retching up the seawater he'd swallowed, he was pulled into a dinghy that already contained three men. Although they stayed near the scene, using their hands as paddles while they continued to search, no more of the seven-man crew were found.

Flight Lieutenant Danson had suffered a chest wound but was conscious. William Deveraux was in shock. Edward Luston was quiet, and quieter still when it was discovered he had died, slipping away silently. Hypothermia was a killer. Shivering and wet, apart from Luston, they had survived the first night. Jack was determined to keep everyone from falling asleep.

There were no oars so the dinghy drifted. No water, except the sea around them. Deveraux rallied briefly. On the second morning he told them about his first day at infant school, then slipped into unconsciousness and simply drifted away. Jack shook him but he had gone peacefully. The water was as flat as a millpond but Jack could hear seabirds. His body felt as though it no longer belonged to him. He was too cold to feel pain.

'You've done your best, Jack,' said Danson.

Jack thought he was dreaming when a Netherlands fishing boat hauled them aboard. They left the bodies in the dinghy to be towed behind. The Dutch Resistance brought them safely home. But not until 1943 because the Germans were heavily defending the coastline and covering Dutch airspace with their radar. Jack still woke crying for his crew.

Since then, living beside the canal had suited him. His parents had died in a London bomb blast and his wife had written to him to say that she couldn't cope with an invalid and intended to live alone in London. He doubted she would stay alone long: it wasn't in her nature. All he'd needed was complete peace and quiet. Lower Heyford suited him and Matey fine.

Until today: that woman had made him feel he wanted to live again. Never before had he given in to an impulse, so... He couldn't think of another word to fit his actions except impulsively.

'Maybe she'll despise me for what I'm about to do, Matey. After all, it's completely alien to me. But if it means seeing Elsie again, if only for a moment, it's a chance I have to take. Move over,' he said, standing up and going towards the telephone. 'I'm going to reserve a hotel room in Oxford, and this time I'll take a walk along the canal.'

Elsie opened her eyes to the sound of Dorothy breathing steadily, despite the noise of the rain on the wood and canvas roof of the narrowboat. For a moment she lay thinking of the lock-keeper and the dreams of him that had haunted her sleep. She wished she was sharing a boat with Izzy instead of Dorothy. It would be so easy to voice her thoughts to her friend.

Elsie crawled from her bunk, in her flannelette pyjamas, and put fresh kindling, then some small pieces of coal on the still glowing embers in the stove. She soon had a kettle of water heating for tea. By the time Dorothy was awake Elsie had cleaned her teeth and was wearing the clothes she'd taken off last night. She raked through her hair with a comb and decided there was little point in applying any make-up as the teeming rain would spoil any effort she made to look nice.

'How did you sleep?'

'Surprisingly well,' answered Elsie. She handed Dorothy a mug of tea. 'And I've examined myself for flea bites and found none so I'll not be too hasty in dusting away that powder.'

Dorothy smiled. Elsie pulled back the small covering from the round window. 'It's getting light out there.' She remembered that Dorothy had told her the boats tied up when darkness fell. The boat's headlight was used only in a tunnel: everyone on the cut observed the blackout. 'Pity it's such a filthy day.' She thought about the previous evening and how the four of them had sat out in the fresh air. It had been decided that Izzy would cook today but Elsie couldn't see them eating breakfast outside. Dorothy was pulling on her clothes and Elsie was pushing bedding into the recess when they heard frantic voices, then thumps on the locked door of the boat.

'C'mon, let us in! We're getting cold and wet!' Dorothy unlocked the cabin's door and the two girls from *Bunting* almost fell down the steps, bringing with them rivulets of rain that pooled on the floor and a covered tray.

'Take this!' Izzy pushed the piled tray at Elsie and shrugged herself out of an enormous oilskin that she left to lie on the floor at the bottom of the steps, dripping and steaming in the heat.

Tolly thrust a surprisingly dry bag at Dorothy from beneath her coat and said, 'Move up, we've brought breakfast. That's bread in there.'

Elsie set down the tray and helped Tolly off with her coat, which now also lay beside the steps, water running into the coir mat.

'We must eat it while it's hot,' Tolly added. 'Everyone find somewhere to sit.'

No one needed second bidding, and within moments the four women were sitting around the stove each with a breakfast of scrambled dried egg, beans and fried bread.

Dorothy was smiling at her charges while the cabin steamed with the wet clothing. Tolly was first to break the contented atmosphere. 'I brought a pack of cards so we won't get despondent with nothing to do until this downpour stops.'

Dorothy almost choked. 'Sorry, girls,' she said. 'But the schedule doesn't make allowances for the weather. We have to be at Limehouse on the due date. It's my fault we've not already picked up a cargo,' she glanced down at her ankle, 'and, like the other workers on the cut, we ignore the rain.' As if to reinforce her words a particularly heavy gust sent raindrops clattering against the roof. 'Our next official stop is near Oxford. You two,' she nodded at Tolly and Izzy, 'have already proved this rain doesn't stop you supplying breakfast so it won't stop us getting to our destination on time. We're going to move off shortly.' She gazed at each of them in turn, then looked at the kettle on the stove. 'But not before I've made us all a good strong cup of tea.'

## Chapter Fourteen

Elsie had never felt so tired in her life. She'd tumbled into bed after tearing off her damp clothes, which she'd spread, along with Dorothy's, over every available space to dry out in the warmth from the stove. The stale aroma of fish and chips in vinegar-soaked newspaper added to the smell of damp clothing.

'What happened to your crew before us?' she asked. Even her bedding felt damp.

'They left.'

'Why?'

'Because they couldn't handle the hardship.'

'From what I've experienced today, my job in the munitions factory was child's play.' Elsie was thinking that working on the narrowboats hadn't been a good idea after all. She propped herself up on one elbow and watched Dorothy brushing her long hair. 'You look younger with your hair down,' she said.

Dorothy smiled. 'Someone else used to say that.' There was a faraway look in her eyes.

'Tell me about him,' urged Elsie. Perhaps he was the writer of the letter Dorothy had tucked beneath her pillow. She didn't like to pry.

'What makes you think it was a man?'

'Because there's always a man,' said Elsie.

'Do you think you'll like working on the boats?' Dorothy hadn't answered the question, clearly not wanting to carry on with that particular conversation.

'Don't know. I'll give it a fair try.'

'Well, you can't be more honest than that,' said Dorothy. 'It looks like I've got a good crew this time.' She crawled into her sleeping-bag. 'Damp gets everywhere,' she added.

Elsie was too tired to read either of her novels. Dorothy had turned down the oil lamp but the glow from the stove gave plenty of light. She looked at her slacks, steaming above the coal bucket. No one cared how they dressed on the cut. Today had been all about keeping dry until it had become pointless to worry about being wet through. They'd travelled through nine locks and countless lift bridges and she'd had enough excitement for one day. She was so looking forward to Oxford where they would be able to bathe and wash their hair at the public baths. Until then, as long as she cleaned her teeth regularly, Elsie didn't care how she looked.

She'd learned a great deal about the boats. Today the battery had died. It had had to be dragged out and a charged one installed in its place. It had also been her job to grease the couplings, the devices used to join the engine parts, which meant the cover in the cabin's floorboards had had to be removed, the shaft checked for loose nuts and bolts and re-greased with stuff that looked like thick margarine. She'd done that after clearing out the mud box and the bilge pumps. Water was filtered from the canal to cool the engine, and the muck that came in with it had to be cleared by hand and thrown back into the canal. Then, of course, there were the daily housekeeping chores. Keeping the fires going. Making sure the water and coal buckets were topped up. And today, because of the rain, the everlasting wringing out of mops used to swab the wet floors. She wondered how whole families managed to live on the boats and keep themselves and the craft shining with cleanliness.

A smile touched the corners of her mouth. While waiting to enter a lock, with a gypsy boat ahead of them, Elsie hadn't been able to stop herself peering in through its open door. Her eyes had widened at the cosy scene before her. She'd even spotted a baby asleep in a rush cot, the quilt white and lovingly embroidered. The wife was helping her man open the lock and Elsie had ceased spying before she was discovered.

Today, Izzy had fallen into the cut. She'd hopped off at a bridge to run along the towpath to prepare the lock but when she'd jumped back on the boat in the rain her foot had slipped on the wet surface and she'd gone down and under.

At first Elsie had feared she might be dragged beneath *Mallard* but Tolly had hauled her out of the muddy water and Izzy had been more frightened than hurt. It had taken mugs of cocoa and a plate of corned-beef sandwiches all round before Izzy was back to normal, wearing borrowed dry clothes, her own rinsed in the canal.

The rain had finally exhausted itself by seven that evening when Dorothy had suggested tying up for the night alongside several other boats moored near a pub. 'There's a pathway through a field that leads into a village and I vote we walk in and buy fish and chips for tea,' she'd said.

Fish wasn't on ration, thank goodness.

'Suppose anyone sees me looking like this?' wailed Tolly.

'Well, it won't be anyone you know, will it?' Izzy said.

After they'd roped the boats to the iron rings in the side of the concrete footpath they set off. To reach the field they'd had to trek through the gardens of the Jolly Boatman. Wooden tables and stools were positioned outside for those who preferred not to enter the pub. They were used mostly by canal folk. The women were seldom to be found inside licensed premises, that domain belonging to the men. A couple of dogs chased each other around on the grass. A thin sun had broken through to end the day and warmed them, making the trek to the village more enjoyable and less wet than Elsie had envisaged.

Elsie remembered the seductive smell of the fish and chips wrapped in newspaper she'd clutched as she walked back through the Jolly Boatman's garden.

'Why don't we have a drink and eat here?' Izzy had suggested.

'Good idea. But it means one of us has to go inside to buy drinks,' Elsie had said. She'd glanced around the gardens and her eyes had fallen on an apple tree. 'Wouldn't mind one of those for afters,' she said.

Dorothy had scolded her. 'I'm not coming to haul you out of the local nick for scrumping.'

'I'll go,' said Izzy. 'I went in the Fox on my own, when I could.'

'That's settled, then.' Dorothy handed over a

110

ten-shilling note. Izzy left her parcel of food on a table and trotted off towards the open door. Elsie could hear her muttering their orders to herself so she wouldn't forget them. The girls had decided they wouldn't start eating without her. Moments later, she came out of the doorway, staggering under the weight of a large metal tray containing their glasses. Smiling at the gypsies in the garden, Izzy received glares in return but Elsie could see her natural ebullience was not to be repressed.

'This is a lovely end to a horrible wet day,' Izzy said, attacking her newspaper bundle with enthusiasm.

Elsie sat back, enjoying the last of the sun on her face. The battered fish had been beautifully cooked, as Dorothy had promised it would be. She was washing it down with her half-pint of shandy. Idly she picked at the rest of her chips as she looked over the newspaper they'd been wrapped in. Isolated on the canal, they'd had no access to news from the outside world. She was enjoying sitting there, listening to her new friends chat while she turned the greasy pages of the *Daily Mirror*.

She read of the mass evacuation of London as V-1s were targeted towards the city and sighed: so many people had been killed by these awful bombs. Cartoon Jane was up to her usual misadventures, wearing scanty clothing. Elsie looked at the newspaper's date. It was a couple of days old. The paper shortage meant that news was presented to the public on fewer sheets of much lower quality than before the war. She smoothed the fat-soaked smelly pages and read on. Her hand tightened on the crumpled paper.

## LONG FIRM FRAUD INVESTIGATION

*A Gosport man, Charles Edward Osborne, of Queens Road, who has been helping police with their enquiries into long firm fraud, has been arrested. Hampshire detectives have uncovered what appears to be a full-scale fraudulent commercial enterprise, which involved setting up a bogus company, profiting from selling on goods, then disappearing, leaving suppliers unpaid. The World's Clothing Stores, the Electric Shop and Bunson's Fine Foods, all in the high street, have been targeted, as well as two Lee-on-the-Solent furniture shops. Police have issued a statement asking shopkeepers and companies to be vigilant. A Gosport police spokesman said, 'The austerity of the war years makes this a particularly heinous crime.'*

Unfortunately that was where the article ended. Elsie could hardly believe what she was reading. She pushed the paper towards Izzy. 'You ought to read that.' She put a finger on the article and noted that Tolly and Dorothy were watching them.

'Oh, my God!' Izzy exclaimed, as she pushed away the crumpled paper, only for Dorothy to grab it. It was clear she had connected Charlie's name and Gosport with Izzy, especially as Izzy's face was the colour of chalk.

'You don't know anything about this, do you?' Elsie said.

One look at Izzy's distraught features gave her the answer. 'I'm sorry, of course you don't.' Izzy's eyes filled with tears. Dorothy passed the newspaper to Tolly and pointed to the piece. 'Who is this man?' Dorothy asked Izzy hesitantly.

It was as if a tap had been turned on. Izzy's words flowed like water as she explained her relationship with Charlie and how she'd finally found, with the help of her mother and Elsie, the courage to escape from his clutches.

Elsie saw the dropped jaws and the horrified faces of her new friends. Then the pity, which was the last thing Izzy needed. 'Izzy did a brave thing in running away from him,' she said.

Izzy wiped a hand across her face. The print and grease from the newspaper mixed with her tears to make dirty smudges on her skin. 'I've been on edge all the time in case he should come after me,' she said.

'I never told you about Charlie knocking me about, Dorothy, because I wanted an entirely fresh start. I thought if you knew what a coward I was in not leaving him before, you might not take me on.'

Elsie decided now was the time to tell her that Charlie had been searching for her. 'I didn't want to worry you but he came to my house...'

That was as far as Elsie got. Izzy grasped her arm. 'You didn't...'

'No, I gave you my word and nothing would make me break it.'

Izzy crossed her arms on the table and rested her head on them, her shoulders heaving.

Dorothy said, 'He won't find you here – that's supposing he ever gets away from Gosport and comes looking. From that article,' she laid her hand on the crumpled newspaper, 'it seems un-likely he'll be going anywhere soon. I'm amazed the nasty piece of work managed to fill a warehouse with goods when everything, clothing, food, furniture, is so hard to come by. I wouldn't have censured you because of your background. It's now that matters.' She looked at each of them in turn. 'We've all got secrets and stories in our past that we don't want to reveal. Inland Waterways check to make sure I'm not employing spies or felons but your personal lives belong to you.'

A silence followed, then Izzy said, 'That's fair enough. I didn't know that.

'Charlie has friends who can get anything and a great deal of his stolen gear comes from the American-base stores at Southampton.'

'Well, I certainly wouldn't like to be in his shoes at present,' Dorothy said. 'Don't worry about him coming looking for you. Unless there's insufficient evidence, the newspapers don't usually name a person who isn't as guilty as hell. He could be locked up for a long time.' Elsie, whose arm was around Izzy's shoulders, whispered, 'You've got us now. You're safe here. You do know that, don't you?'

Izzy looked up. 'Yes,' she said. 'I was making believe everything was all right and feeling better, but inside it was eating away at me.' There was silence for a while, then Izzy said, 'Look who's turned up!'

Elsie turned to see a tall man pushing a bath chair across the grass towards a table and benches occupied by boat people. Amazingly Izzy wasn't referring to the good-looking man propelling the elderly gentleman. 'I've got his book! That's Stefan, or Stevo, as he's known,' she said. 'I was

114

reading *The Man in the Iron Mask* to him in the gardens at the Black Cow. The book's on the boat. I should return it to him but I don't think I could bear to go across and chat to him at present after reading about Charlie.'

'Of course not,' broke in Tolly. 'There's no need for you to upset yourself any more. I'll go over and explain you'll return the book. It's safe with you.'

Elsie watched as Tolly jumped up from her seat and was soon striding across the grass. She exchanged glances with the others as the good-looking man with Stevo got to his feet as Tolly approached the table.

'That's Nelson Smith,' said Dorothy, 'known as Sonny. He's the old man's grandson. Undisputed Lothario of the cut.'

Izzy said, 'I've seen him before.'

'Seeing is fine. Look but don't touch. Any girl who expects anything from Sonny Smith gets nothing but heartache for her trouble.'

Elsie watched as Tolly smiled at Sonny, to which he responded, showing perfect white teeth. As he sat down again, Tolly knelt beside the bath chair and began talking to the old man. The resemblance between grandson and grandfather was remarkable: their build and the shape of their faces was similar. Also, Stevo's faded, thinning red hair was reminiscent of his grandson's vibrant curls. But where Sonny's movements were quick, Stevo's were hesitant, probably due to illness or age, thought Elsie. A short conversation followed, with a wave from the old man towards Izzy, then Tolly was bounding back towards the table.

115

'I told him the book would be returned as soon as possible.'

'What did the other one say?' Elsie asked.

'Sonny was very polite and hoped we were having a safe journey.'

'He scares me. He reminds me of Charlie,' said Izzy, with a sniff.

'I thought he was very nice.'

Elsie saw a dreamy look in Tolly's eyes. Dorothy glanced at Elsie and an unspoken thought passed between them. 'Perhaps we've got to watch you where men are concerned, Tolly,' Dorothy said. 'We've an early start tomorrow, everyone. The sooner we arrive at Oxford, the more time we have to ourselves before continuing down the Thames.'

And now Elsie was in bed. She was glad Izzy's secret was out in the open. She, Dorothy and Tolly would give Izzy courage to go forward with her new life. As for herself, Dorothy already knew about her marriage break-up, as did Izzy, and no doubt word would soon get to Tolly.

Tolly wasn't as uncomplicated as Elsie had first thought. She spoke frequently of her work at the Currant Bun back in Titchfield and how she wished, after the war, she could buy the place. Elsie had already thought if Tolly were to lose a little weight she would be eye-catching. Her silky hair, clear skin and happy manner made her a delight to be with. And the girl could cook! Perhaps Tolly's unhappiness, which she couldn't quite hide, stemmed from never having had a proper boyfriend. Oh dear, she thought. She hoped Tolly hadn't set her sights on Sonny Smith: that would surely end in disaster.

She didn't want to think any more about Tolly. Her body ached all over and she was so tired she was almost too weary for sleep. Elsie yawned. Then she remembered Jack and a tingle coursed through her body. She was determined not to feel guilty about being in his arms, even if the others teased her. She hadn't orchestrated it, though it had taken her just a single moment to recognize from the look in his eyes that he wanted her.

Would she ever see him again?

## Chapter Fifteen

Geoffrey stretched his legs in the marital bed and thought how good it felt to have space to move around, alone.

Today Sandra was bringing a few articles from the Crescent Road flat to make the house more homely. He shuddered, thinking of her many cat ornaments.

Already the honeysuckle had disappeared from the conservatory. 'We need to let the light in, darling,' she'd said. He didn't like to antagonize her by saying that it felt baking hot in there now, and the last of the warm summer was yet to come.

Sandra was still resident at the flat though she was eager to join him in Western Way. He was revelling in his freedom from her. To say he missed Elsie was an understatement. He realized now he'd taken for granted how she had looked after him. Clean and ironed shirts had always hung in his wardrobe ready for him to put on. Fresh underwear and socks had been placed neatly in the drawers. When his suits had looked a little jaded she'd taken them to the cleaners.

He'd lost weight. Sandra was ecstatic about that and thought the new clothes she'd bought him from 'her friend' looked better on a slimmer man. He didn't care for the brightly patterned short-sleeved shirts she told him had to be worn hanging outside his trousers.

She'd agreed he should continue wearing his tailored suits to work because that was the standard attire his clients expected of a man in his position. Alas, no matter how hard he brushed them they were beginning to look like cat blankets.

Sandra was growing bigger by the day. He was a little scared of becoming responsible for a son or daughter of his own. Excited, yes.

Hadn't he always wanted children with Elsie? Sandra, however, was not Elsie. She was already talking about a full-time nanny.

How he was going to afford everything was pretty daunting. He had written to Elsie, care of the waterways address she had left him, to tell her as yet there'd been no offer made on the house and that he'd thought it might sell more quickly with someone in residence. He hadn't had a reply.

Of course, his partner at the office and the rest of the staff knew he'd taken Sandra as his common-law wife. He was aware they had lost respect for him. So far it hadn't affected the firm. He hoped to be divorced and remarried quickly and quietly.

Elsie hadn't needed to take on her undesirable job at Priddy's to help the war effort, but she had gone where she was needed, which had brought her a degree of prestige in the town. Naturally this displeased Sandra. Geoffrey was quite proud of how Elsie had done her duty by the country, dealt with the marriage breakdown and settled to working on the narrowboats. He knew it was hard, dirty work.

He glanced at the bedside clock and sighed. It was time to get up. Soon the taxi would arrive spilling out Sandra, her treasures to clutter his house, and her many suitcases. Today, too, was the day on which his nemesis, Fluffy, would move in.

'What d'you want out of this life?' Tolly was manning *Mallard's* controls, Elsie beside her. Dorothy had changed boats, saying she wanted to make sure Izzy was feeling strong enough to cope with a day in Oxford after reading about Charlie. There was no certainty the girls would stay together on their first foray into freedom from the cut. Fields and weeping willows had given way to stone warehouses lining the canal.

'At this moment I want a bath,' said Elsie. 'And, as I've never felt so tired in all my life as I do now, a proper bed wouldn't go amiss. Long term, I'd give anything for a home and children. That's all I've ever wanted. Children are out of the equation so I'll settle for completing this job and seeing what the end of the war brings.'

'Doesn't seem too much to ask, does it?' Tolly replied.

They were looking for a place to tie up both boats overnight. Dorothy had specified the centre of Oxford as being suitable, if there weren't too many work boats already lining the towpath. Failing that, they would have to moor up outside and walk into the city.

'I'd like to own the café,' Tolly said, 'but that takes money.' A dreamy look crossed her face. 'I'd also like just for once to have a man tell me he loves me.'

Elsie felt tears rise. This lovely girl was like Izzy. Neither could see they had qualities that made them wonderful individuals, Izzy because she had been cowed by Charlie, and Tolly because she believed her weight was a barrier to happiness. 'Men aren't the answer to everything,' she said.

'If you don't mind me saying so, that's because you don't seem to have any trouble attracting them,' Tolly replied.

'I'm going to ignore that because I saw the way you acted, talking to that Sonny Smith yesterday.'

Tolly looked horrified. 'Was it that obvious?'

'Well...' Elsie didn't continue. She stared at Tolly. Was it her imagination? She stared harder. Slowly it dawned on her. Tolly's plump face seemed more slender. She was being ridiculous, Elsie thought. It just wasn't possible that in such a short time anyone could lose weight. It certainly wasn't impossible that all the hard work was having a toning effect on their bodies. She herself felt more alive. Yes, she was tired but her muscles didn't argue with her so much when she needed to give that extra turn with the windlass or push harder against a balance beam. And Dorothy had been sending Tolly ahead on foot to the next lock to prepare it for entry. Perhaps the exercise and wholesome food were having a beneficial effect on them all.

'Look up there – think we can squeeze in?'

Heeding Tolly's words Elsie saw a large gap in the line of narrowboats. 'It'll mean tying the butty alongside but there'll be enough room for other boats to pass.'

Tolly waved to Dorothy and Izzy in *Bunting* and signalled she was attempting to slip into the empty space. Dorothy waved back, then gave her a thumbs-up. Manoeuvring the long craft wasn't easy but Tolly managed to line it up perfectly against the towpath. Elsie jumped off and began tying up to rings set in the concrete. It wasn't long before *Bunting* was alongside and Izzy was tying the two narrowboats together.

'Well done,' said Dorothy. 'You lot get more professional by the day. Now, are you all decided on how you'll spend your time here?'

'I'm looking for a phone box to ring up my sister,' answered Tolly. 'Then I'll follow you to the public baths.'

'A bath is going to be my priority as well,' said Elsie. She had already packed her holdall with her toiletries and the cleanest clothes she had.

'Can I tag along with you, Tolly?' Izzy asked.

'Of course you can!'

'I'll expect you all back on the boats by eight in the morning,' said Dorothy. 'Unless, like me, you're planning to sleep aboard anyway.' She smiled at her crew. 'Don't be late back. I've planned our stops to practically the last minute and we need to be in Limehouse on time to pick up our cargo. I suppose you've noticed the strange looks we've had from some of the boaters because we're not carrying a heavy load of some sort?'

Elsie nodded. 'It'll seem strange when we do the pick-up,' she said. 'It'll slow our speed down.'

'If you can call a maximum of four miles an hour speedy.' Izzy laughed.

Elsie was itching to be away. Dorothy had given her directions to the spired city and its various landmarks. She needed to get away from the girls to think. She wasn't used to living in such close proximity to three other women. No doubt each of them felt the same, Elsie thought. Vanity was the least of her worries but she did want to feel clean again and bring the shine back to her hair with a good wash.

'I'll be going, then,' Elsie said. Her first stop would be at the main post office to ask if any letters were waiting for her. She had enough money for her immediate needs and felt distinctly lightheaded at being in Oxford.

'Have a lovely time, everyone,' she called.

Then she was walking down the towpath and eagerly looking for the stone steps that would take her up to the road and whatever adventure was next. Despite the early hour the cobbled street was alive with people going about their business. Elsie took a deep breath. It was good to be on her own. She moved out of the way so a man could pass her at the side of the stone bridge.

The girls, she thought, had become good friends and she enjoyed their company but–

'Hello, Elsie. I promise I haven't followed you.

122

I've a legitimate reason for being in Oxford.' The man paused. 'But I'm not going to deny that I've walked alongside this part of the cut hoping to see you...' His voice tailed off. Elsie stared at the tall man wearing the raincoat and trilby. He adjusted his spectacles. 'I was scared I might not see you again and ... to be honest, I couldn't bear that...'

## Chapter Sixteen

And there it was again. The tingle that started at the base of Elsie's spine and continued through her body, infusing her with heat and light as she looked into Jack Lumley's sea-blue eyes. For a moment she seemed suspended in time but gradually the sounds of traffic and the smell of the canal below came back to her. 'Jack. What are you doing here?' She took in the worry etched on his face.

'My usual hospital appointment with the specialist. I'm aware this is the first stop for you narrowboat women. I couldn't bear the thought that I'd never see you again, Elsie, if you decided to leave the canal here and go home.'

Elsie moved to one side to avoid being jostled by a stout woman pushing a perambulator that was overflowing with children. Jack carried on: 'If you tell me to go, I will. I'll promise not to bother you again.' He tentatively put his hand on her arm. She thought she might look like a scarecrow in her mud-spattered clothing, her hair awry and her face unwashed. How could Jack possibly want her? Elsie was also aware that she didn't want him to go away. No, not at all. 'Look, we can't talk here,' he continued. 'Let's have a cup of tea somewhere, please. I promise I'm not a lunatic or a mad axe-man. But ... but something wonderful happened between us and I know you can feel it too.'

She nodded. She thought her voice might betray her if she opened her mouth to speak so she allowed him to grip her hand and they began to walk across the bridge and into the town. After a while she broke the silence: 'I need to go to the post office, and I must have a bath.' Her words sounded odd, even to her. 'I don't mean I need a bath in the post office...' She tailed off. If she didn't stop saying whatever came into her head Jack would think she was half-witted.

He laughed. 'You mean you need to collect any letters and you need to wash after your stint on the boat?' Elsie nodded.

He was walking quickly and had transferred her holdall to his other hand. She was being propelled along a busy street when he suddenly stopped outside a large building. 'Post office,' he said. 'I'll wait outside.'

As though on automatic pilot Elsie moved along with two other customers towards the counter. After waiting in the short queue she explained what she wanted and was surprised when the woman behind the grille returned with a white envelope and requested Elsie's signature. At the door, Jack waited. When she returned to his side he merely asked, 'Tea?'

Elsie felt his arm link hers. Far from feeling unnatural, it felt right, even though she didn't feel comfortable walking alongside this handsome man in the sorry state she was in. Where could he take her looking as she did?

As though reading her mind Jack said, 'We're going to the Randolph in Beaumont Street. I'll order tea.'

There seemed no need for her to argue with his plans. Elsie tucked the letter into her holdall that he still carried and allowed herself to be led down the busy Cornmarket and past the Martyrs' Memorial to the hotel.

They went into the foyer through the heavy glass doors of the Gothic-looking building, then towards some low tables, set about with comfortable chairs. Immediately they were approached by a waiter, who seemed unfazed by her scruffiness.

'Bring tea, please,' Jack said. He took off his raincoat and hat, laying them on a leather chair. Then he leaned over and put both his hands on her shoulders, scanning Elsie's face with his clear bright eyes, made larger by the dark-rimmed spectacles. Elsie could feel the intensity of his gaze. 'I've only gone and fallen in love with you, Elsie.'

Elsie put her finger over his lips to stem more words. There was a pause while she searched his face, but all she saw were unanswered questions.

Taking her fingers in his hands he kissed them. 'I've never done this before,' he said. 'Spontaneous passion.'

'What if I want it, too?' Elsie sounded surer than she felt.

She leaned forward and kissed him. Tentatively at first, short tender warm kisses, the last one

125

lingering. Her heart was leaping with pure joy. Geoffrey had been her first and only lover. Eventually she sat back on the chair. Jack leaned forward and traced the outline of her lips with his fingers. She shivered with excitement. Was this how it had happened with Geoffrey and Sandra? A sudden awakening of what passion could be like? If so, how could she blame them for following their hearts? Her thoughts disintegrated as the waiter reappeared with a tray that he set on the table in front of them. Jack thanked him and he left with a substantial tip. Suddenly life was back to normal, the magic of his words overtaken by everyday happenings.

Elsie put out her hand to pick up the teapot. Her fingers stilled on the white china handle. Blackened fingernails, a relic of her work on the cut, reminded her again of how she must appear to other people. 'I can't be in here,' she said. 'Look at the state of me.'

'You've every right to be wherever you want. And we can solve that small problem of a bath quite quickly,' Jack assured her. 'Though why you're worrying about what you look like when to me you're the most beautiful woman I've ever met and who's doing a job that many women wouldn't even attempt...'

'I need to wash,' Elsie insisted, furtively looking about her.

'And so you shall. Drink your tea,' he commanded, finishing the job she'd started of pouring tea into the fine china cups. 'I'm in love with you. I've never felt like this about anyone in my whole life and I know you feel the same. I sense you're unhappy and I'm sure I can change that.' Elsie, her thoughts whirling, picked up her cup, which was nothing like the tin mugs on the boats. She thought of how far away from civilization she'd been, yet just steps from busy villages and towns. A thought struck her: she was also far removed from the Elsie who'd left her home in Gosport, wasn't she?

Could she go upstairs to a hotel room with a man who, a week ago, she hadn't known? It wouldn't stop at using his bathroom. How could it?

She raised her eyes and stared across the table at Jack. He pushed his blond hair off his forehead, and it immediately tumbled back. Elsie watched him read emotions on her face that she was unable to conceal.

She had been told Jack had lost his foot when his plane went down. How was she to deal with this knowledge? Her tension was now of a different sort. How would he be feeling? How should she react? Did it matter to her? Of course not. She wasn't perfect, either. She came with the baggage of a husband.

Again, as if reading her thoughts, Jack said, 'There's one thing I have to mention. I had an accident, a plane accident. I was unable to carry on in the RAF...'

Elsie put her fingers across his mouth to stop him. 'I know,' she said. She put her cup back on the saucer. Her eye fell on her wedding ring. Could she really live for today when she was a married woman?

But she wasn't a wife now, was she? Her husband had chosen a different woman and Elsie was redundant. She was a narrowboat woman, who had fallen inexplicably in love with a lock-keeper, who was professing his love for her. There was a war on, and who knew what tomorrow might bring?

Elsie stood up. 'What are we waiting for?' she asked, putting out her hand for him to take.

Together they walked up the carpeted stairs and along a well-furnished corridor. He stopped and opened the door to his room.

Elsie gasped. She'd been incarcerated on the narrowboat for only a short time but she'd grown accustomed to the shabbiness of the surroundings. Now she gave a squeal of surprise at the long velvet curtains outlining the windows, the bed with its opulent quilt, the highly polished furniture, the scent of lavender. Jack laughed.

'The bathroom is there,' he said, waving towards a white door. Elsie pushed it open and immediately felt anticipation rise as she saw the enormous white claw-foot bath. She thought of the primitive washing facilities she'd endured on the narrowboat. She couldn't help the murmur of excitement that rose in her throat as she spotted bath salts, an unopened bar of Lux soap and, hanging from the rail, white fluffy towels that she longed to press her face against. Even the wartime rule of five inches of water wouldn't destroy her pleasure in that scented, hot, luxurious bath.

'Take your time,' Jack said, still smiling. 'I'll be out here if you need anything.'

She came out later swathed in a large white bath sheet. She had towelled her hair almost dry and wrapped a small towel turban-like around her head. She felt an incredible lightness that she knew wasn't only because the grime had gone.

Jack was sitting in an armchair, listening to the wireless. There was a discussion on the attempt on Hitler's life and how the perpetrators had been suspended to hang from meat-hooks on piano wire. The executions had been carried out less than two hours after sentencing in the People's Court.

As Elsie approached, Jack switched off the wireless and stood up. 'You look breathtaking,' he said. His fingers fumbled at the towel until it fell from her head to the floor and her damp hair bounced in a sweet-smelling halo around her face. Jack led her to the bed, which, to Elsie, seemed enormous after the cramped bunk on the narrowboat. With his hands on her shoulders he pushed her down onto the silky softness. She watched as Jack began to remove his clothes. First his shirt, revealing his strong, tanned upper body, his broad shoulders. Then he sat on the edge of the bed and looked at her lying, waiting. 'I lost a foot during a bomb drop. Here at the hospital they like to check up on me. It doesn't bother me now, but I'll understand if you feel you can't cope with the sight of...'

'Shut up,' she said. She moved across the bed, her bath sheet falling away, and put her hands on his shoulders, turning him towards her, kissing his skin and loving the slightly musky, salty taste. Then he was naked, and hungry for her.

They lay together, content yet exhausted. Eventually Elsie murmured, 'So that's what it's all about.'

'You didn't know?'

'I never knew,' she answered, through his kisses.

Elsie wondered at the miracle of it all. She pulled her head away and looked at him. All she saw in his blue eyes was his love for her. Totally unguarded.

Elsie grinned at him. Looping her legs around him she pulled him closer, wondering why such lovemaking had been denied her until now.

They had spent the day discovering each other. A knock at the door woke her. She stretched and pulled the crumpled sheet higher to cover herself.

'Good evening, my little ray of sunshine,' Jack said, wheeling over the trolley he'd accepted from the waiter at the door.

Elsie sat up. 'What have you there?' she asked, now fully awake. She could smell gravy, and her stomach rumbled.

'Dinner. I telephoned down for food.' Jack looked contrite. 'Though if you'd rather we went out or down to the restaurant, it's fine by me.'

'No, I want to stay in this room for ever,' she said, noticing that to answer the door he'd pulled on a long dressing-gown.

'And I want you to tell me more about yourself,' he said, pushing the trolley close to the bed and climbing in beside her. He looked into her eyes. 'If we're to spend the rest of our lives together there must be absolute truth between us. Do you agree?'

'Is that what you want?' Elsie asked. 'Truth and for ever?'

'I don't make a habit of following women. Something happened between us on the lock near my cottage. Call it love at first sight, call it a bolt of lightning, call it whatever you want...' He lifted a silver dome from a dish of pork chops, and the meaty scent wafted tantalizingly towards her.

'Even when there's a war on the Randolph can conjure up wonderful food. One or two?' he asked.

'Can I have two chops?'

'Elsie, you can have whatever is in my power to give you. I love you.'

## Chapter Seventeen

The girls were draped over the stern of *Mallard* eating Tolly's dinner offering of corned-beef hash and discussing their time in Oxford.

'It's such a beautiful place...' said Elsie.

'From what you've been saying, Elsie, it's a wonder you noticed anything except Jack,' laughed Tolly. 'I wish I had a handsome admirer to run after me.'

Elsie knew the girls had witnessed her departure with him. She couldn't help blushing. Izzy jumped in: 'After what she's been through she needs a bit of happiness in her life. But I agree Oxford is beautiful.' Elsie mentally thanked her for ending their incessant teasing.

'Do you know why it hasn't been bombed?'

The girls turned towards Dorothy's voice.

'I read somewhere that Hitler thinks he'll make

Oxford his home when he invades us.' For a moment there was silence, apart from the sounds on the cut around them, as they digested Dorothy's words. 'We'd better hurry up and win this war, then,' said Elsie.

'Did you suspect Jack would be waiting?' Tolly was like a dog with a bone.

'No one was more surprised than me. It was Fate and a hospital appointment that brought us together again, though Jack knew narrowboats usually tie up in that spot because it's easier to get to the public baths from there. He'd got a friend to mind the lock and to look after his little dog. I've always wanted a pet.' For a moment she looked as if she was reliving a wonderful dream. Then she added, 'My husband said dog hair gave him asthma.'

Tolly frowned.

'Jack probably knows we'll be taking Dukes Cut to knock the mileage off our trip to Limehouse,' said Dorothy. 'It's full steam ahead now to pick up our loads. Our next proper stop will be Henley-on-Thames and it's quite a distance, so I don't want any moans about locks or swing bridges.'

'What did you do with your time off?' Elsie asked Dorothy, glad again that the subject of her and Jack had been deflected.

'Paperwork, shopping and enjoying the peace and quiet away from you lot.' Dorothy laughed.

'Until Tolly and I came back to spend the night on the boat,' broke in Izzy.

'Then we all went up the pub.'

'Good, was it?' asked Elsie.

'We played darts until Sonny Smith came in

132

and insisted on joining in.'

Elsie saw Tolly colour.

'He said it could be two against two if he played.' Izzy was scraping her plate. 'And I was amazed at how quickly he could total the scores on the blackboard. I'd been using my fingers...'

'He was only being friendly,' Tolly put in.

Elsie could see she was embarrassed. 'You like him, don't you?'

Izzy said, 'He reminds me of Charlie.'

Elsie frowned at her. 'Did you give that book back to the old man?' she asked, to defuse the argument she could sense was about to start between the two younger women.

'No, he wasn't in the pub,' said Tolly, 'and it was too far for any of us to run back to *Bunting* to get it. Sonny said the book belonged to his grand- mother, Sarah. Apparently she had red hair, just like Izzy's – it runs in their family. He said his granddad was hoping Izzy would find time to read to him again.'

'He's a very charming man, that Sonny,' said Dorothy, raising an eyebrow to show she was teasing them. 'He bought us all a drink.'

'He's too good to be true,' said Izzy. 'Beware of boatmen bearing gifts.'

'Don't be nasty,' Tolly said. 'Does that mean, if you get the chance, you won't read his grandfather any more of *The Man in the Iron Mask?*'

Izzy relented. 'We've already been told not to expect any time off until we reach Henley, so I'll think about it.'

'Perhaps Sonny'll read to him,' Elsie said. She began collecting the plates and cutlery and stood

133

up to take them into the cabin to wash up.

'Did Jack tell you why he was discharged from the RAF?' Dorothy asked Elsie, as she followed her to make tea.

Elsie thought how warm it was inside the cabin. While they'd been sitting out in the night, it had grown colder. 'He told me about his foot but he didn't want to go into details,' she said. 'It certainly didn't put me off him. In fact, I thought how brave he is because unless you knew you'd certainly not suspect he has an artificial foot. He gets about so easily.' She remembered how shy and hesitant he'd become when he was talking about himself. 'I love him all the more for not being perfect,' she added.

'Do you love him, Elsie?'

She noted the seriousness of Dorothy's question. She paused before she said quietly, 'I do. I don't know how it's come about but I want Jack in my life now. I'm an extremely lucky woman.'

'Yes,' Dorothy said. She stared hard at Elsie, then went back to pouring the boiling water into the big enamel teapot, but not before Elsie had seen the glint of tears in her eyes. Elsie put the cleared dishes into the washing-up bowl. She watched as Dorothy finished filling the teapot, then poured the remaining hot water onto the plates so they could soak and be washed later.

Elsie said quietly, 'You know you can talk to me, don't you?' She could hear the murmur of voices outside as Tolly and Izzy chatted. 'I don't want to pry but I've seen you rereading a letter when you think I'm not noticing...'

All at once Dorothy became brisk and business-like. 'What do you mean, letter?' She was gathering mugs together.

Elsie felt the change in the atmosphere. Had she stepped over the mark? Dorothy was her employer and superior. It was then she remembered her own letter. She'd stuffed it into her holdall and there it had stayed. Elsie tried to lighten the mood between her and Dorothy. 'I collected a letter from the post office but then I forgot all about it and it's been at the bottom of my holdall ever since.' She went to the cupboard beneath her bed space and pulled out the bag. 'I must put these away.' She remembered how Jack had laughed at her for washing her dirty clothes in the bath, instead of sending them down for Housekeeping to attend to, as was his suggestion. Self-consciously Elsie had draped all the wrung-out clothing over every available radiator in their room. Now she tipped out her clothes and grabbed the letter.

She heard Dorothy's voice chatting to Tolly and Izzy as she served them tea, strong and sweet with the condensed milk. Dorothy came down the steps and into the cabin. Elsie was reading avidly. Then she sighed and looked across at Dorothy.

'I'd planned on going back to Gosport for a few days, after we'd delivered our goods on the cut,' she said. 'I was looking forward to the time off you'd promised...'

'What's the matter?' Dorothy came and stood next to her.

'Geoffrey's moving Sandra into my home,' she said. She felt Dorothy's arms go around her. 'He says if the place is occupied it'll sell faster.'

Dorothy was nodding. 'What he says is perfectly

logical,' she said, stepping back. 'Does it really matter now you've got Jack?'

Elsie sighed. 'It matters to me because my heart and soul went into that house. He couldn't have afforded to buy it if I hadn't handed over my pay-off after I stopped teaching.' She brushed away a stray tear. 'Still, I should look to the future now, not the past. Jack made me promise to let him collect me from Lower Heyford when our first trip's finished to spend my time with him at the lock-keeper's cottage,' she said. 'At first I refused...' She looked at Dorothy's quizzical face. 'I told him I was popping back to Gosport first, then I intended to stay with him.'

'Forget Gosport, let it be a new beginning for you.'

Elsie stared at her, her mood lightening. 'Yes,' she said. 'It really will be, won't it? Before I turn in for the night I'll have a word with Izzy. It'll be good for the pair of us to catch up on things.'

The days passed in a blur of countryside, villages, lush vegetation, mishaps with steering when mud-banks caught them unawares, and rain that drenched them, slowed them down and chilled them to the bone. Each night, they were happy to crawl into their sleeping-bags and tumble into their bunks, tired out yet ready to face the next day with vigour. Each morning they set off after breakfast a little nearer to Limehouse Basin.

So, too, each morning, Dorothy started the journey with a song. She had a good clear voice that echoed through the sweet-smelling air and encouraged the girls in the butty to join in with her. 'The White Cliffs of Dover' was her favourite but every time she spotted a rabbit in a held she'd break off whatever she was singing to shout, '"Run, rabbit, run."'

Elsie relished her new life. She stole time to write letters to Jack. She was thrilled whenever a letter waited at a postal point for her. She was opening her mind to things she'd never experienced before. She loved the horse-drawn boats with the men who stopped the horses and uncoupled them, allowing them to pass on over the top of a tunnel, then hauled the boats themselves because the tunnels were too narrow to provide passage for horses.

Elsie felt guilty about overtaking these proud watermen, who had inhabited the canals for far longer than they ever would. Usually Dorothy would wave and smile, and sometimes got a wave in return. Henley came and went. Most of the time they travelled within hailing distance of the boat *Aurora* and its butty *Avalon,* owned and worked by Sonny Smith and his grandfather. It was quite usual, Dorothy said, for narrowboats to keep at more or less the same pace on the cut, often mooring at nights within sight of each other as they had at Oxford. Rivalry to enter locks first, so they didn't need to wait for emptying or filling, was rife among some gypsies, and many times Elsie drew back the curtain or stood on the rear of the boat to discover that a neighbouring craft had left before them, making a ridiculously early start, simply to get ahead.

The girls were quickly learning the ways of the boat people. *Mallard* and *Bunting* carried no cargo yet, but *Aurora* and *Avalon* hauled coal. Nevertheless they felt proud when rounding a bend in the cut to discover the two black-painted boats only a short way ahead.

Sonny seemed to have an instinct to discover the best places for mooring up, usually within walking distance of a pub, and Elsie guessed Dorothy was happy to follow in his footsteps so the girls could have a drink and play a few games of darts or crib with the regulars. Elsie, too, was happy with this. It was something to look forward to after a gruelling day. Washing faces, brushing hair, searching for clean dry clothes to put on for 'going out'.

## Chapter Eighteen

Izzy sat back on the hand-embroidered cushion. The old man had closed his eyes and she wondered if he was asleep. Sometimes he shut his eyes as he listened to her read. If she stopped turning the flimsy pages, he'd open one to let her know he was enjoying the sound of her voice and hadn't dropped off.

She loved the cosiness of *Aurora*, though she wondered how two men could possibly keep the boat so spick and span. The wooden walls were hung with pottery plates depicting handpainted scenes of the canal system, and two colourful rag rugs lay over the bare boarding of the floor.

'Well, what happens next in the story?' The rasp

of Stevo's voice brought her back from her reverie. Then he asked, 'Like them rugs, do you?'

'They're lovely. Where did you buy them?' Izzy turned the book over so it lay face down beside her. She loved it when Stevo told her snippets of his life on the cut. When *Mallard* and *Bunting* had moored up near *Aurora* and its butty, Izzy sometimes preferred to sit and read to the old man instead of going out with the others.

'Bought? You can't buy quality like that. My Sarah made those, and that cushion you're sitting on. She was a needlewoman, she was. On *Jonquil* her stuff is all packed away neatly...' The effort of talking brought on a bout of coughing.

Izzy knew better than to fuss around him, which only made him cross. She waited until the red handkerchief came out and he'd mopped his mouth before she asked, 'What's *Jonquil?*'

A smile lit his tired eyes. 'My Sarah's boat. She's moored near Braunston. Sonny looks after her and makes sure she's water-worthy. But she's a tiddly little thing, barely forty foot. No good for work but my Sarah ran her own business from her and lived on her. That's how we met, Sarah and me.'

'Ran a business?' Izzy couldn't help interrupting. His Sarah sounded a wise woman, with a home and business of her own on the cut.

'Sarah made rugs and cushions. She had a sewing machine and it's still on the boat. She'd moor up at busy places and sell her wares.' His eyes closed briefly. 'It took me a good while to persuade her to marry me. Did I tell you you've hair like hers?'

Izzy nodded. 'How come the boat still survives?'

139

'She'd marry me, she said, as long as she could go off on her own sometimes. She was a loner, my Sarah. She loved her books and her painting...'

Again Stevo's eyes closed. Before Izzy had time to speak, he opened them again and said, 'I knew if I wanted that woman I'd have to toe the line.'

'So she was an artist as well?'

'She was self-taught. Had a gift, you see. She painted them plates on the walls here.' He raised a bony hand and pointed towards the pottery dishes. 'It wasn't so much pictures and canvases she painted, no. She'd collect odd-shaped stones and paint birds and animals on them, what she saw on the cut. Popular they was. Many of the women on the canals was too weighed down with children and chores, no time to do anything artistic, so my Sarah's stuff sold well.'

'But you had children?' After all, she thought, Stevo had a grandson, didn't he?

'Only the one.' Stevo was staring at her. A look of regret passed over his face. 'Only the one,' he repeated. 'I thought when Zelda came along my Sarah would get more settled. Wasn't so. She'd take the little one with her, moor up, then after a month or so, come back to me and it would be like being newly married all over again. And she'd sit and read to me...' His voice tailed off. 'Because I loved the bones of her I let her do as she wanted so's she'd be content.' He was speaking as briskly as his breathing would allow.

'When the other blokes tried to take the mickey because I was letting a slip of a thing run rings round me, I'd bop them on the nose to keep them in line. You see, I'd done a bit of bare-knuckle

140

fighting in me youth.'

Again his voice faltered. Izzy had already gathered his life with Sarah hadn't been easy. It was a very masculine business, working the cut. Women usually toed the line. 'You must have loved her a lot,' she said.

'I did. But it broke her when Zelda ran away from us, leaving fatherless Sonny behind.'

It took Izzy a while to understand what the old man meant. 'So Zelda had a baby without being married?' For that to happen on the cut must have caused great distress to Stevo and Sarah. Probably even more shaming than had it happened in Gosport, she thought. And neighbours there could be very cruel with their gossip.

'We never knew who Sonny's father was. But Sonny was the best thing that happened to me. I taught him all I knows.' Stevo smiled.

'Taught him to run after girls?' Izzy laughed, trying to lighten the atmosphere. The clock ticked away while Stevo pondered her words.

'Not me. There was only one girl for me, my Sarah. He's got traces of his father in him, must have. My Sonny knows the difference between right and wrong, and deep down he's a good man. Well, he's looked after me all these years since Sarah died. An' me an' him, we rub along just fine together.'

Izzy looked around the spotless cabin. For one man and an elderly invalid the place was like a little palace.

'You don't like him, do you?' Stevo's question startled her.

Was it so obvious to him? 'It's not about liking

him. I've just left a man who in my eyes is very similar to Sonny, looks and all.' Izzy got up and opened the stove's door and pushed in a log from the stack piled next to it on the floor.

'Is that so? Tell me about the bugger what's hurt you. Because I can tell you've had pain, a little thing like you.' Before she could help herself, the warmth from the fire and Stevo's friendliness helped her unburden herself. He listened carefully without interrupting. Then he said, 'I don't want to upset you but a man like that won't let you go, you know. But you mustn't judge a book by its cover. Sonny's got a heart of gold. I reckon you're like my Sarah, just wants to be on her own to gather her thoughts together.'

'Maybe,' Izzy said.

'She had an unhappy childhood, my Sarah. Until I won her heart, she didn't trust people. I think that's why she liked her own company. I respected that. Sonny thought the world of her. He looks like my Sarah as well, with that lovely hair. Just like yours.'

His voice faltered as they heard footsteps and laughter. Then a chill breeze blew inside the cabin as the door opened. Sonny and Tolly filled the small space. Tolly, Izzy noticed, had a broad grin on her face. They had brought in with them the smells of beer and cigarettes.

'What are you doing here?' Izzy asked Tolly.

'Came with Sonny to walk you back to our boat,' Tolly said. Izzy could tell Tolly had had a few drinks. Her voice was far too loud.

'I'm making hot chocolate,' said Sonny, shrugging himself out of his jacket. 'Want some?'

'Yes, please,' said Tolly and Stevo together.

'No, thank you,' replied Izzy, picking up the book, closing it and setting it back on the arm of her chair. 'We've an early start tomorrow.'

'Haven't we all?' said Sonny, his dark eyes seeking hers.

Again panic took hold of Izzy. She grabbed her shapeless cardigan from the back of the chair, then turned to Stevo. 'I'll see you again soon,' she said. 'Look after the book.' She bent and kissed his weathered cheek, then grabbed hold of Tolly. 'C'mon, you,' she said. 'Time we left.'

Izzy had to squeeze past Sonny, who clearly enjoyed her discomfort.

'Goodnight, girls. Don't I get a kiss?'

Tolly turned to him and puckered her lips. Izzy pushed her roughly towards the wooden steps and out of Sonny's grasp.

With Sonny's laugh ringing in their ears, they left the boat and joined the towpath to walk to *Bunting*.

'So you've had a good evening in the pub, then?' Izzy asked.

'Yes, and I'd have had some more fun if you hadn't dragged me away!'

'I don't mean to spoil your happiness but Sonny's only out for what he can get.'

'You sure you're not just a little bit jealous?'

Izzy decided to let that remark pass. She was well aware Tolly had been drinking and sometimes it was easy for a person's tongue to run away with them.

Tolly, however, didn't want to let things go.

'I think you fancy Sonny,' she said argumentatively. 'I think that's why you spend time with the old man, hoping to get into Sonny's good books.'

Izzy stopped walking and pulled Tolly round so that she was facing her. 'I think you should never reckon to know what I feel. I wouldn't care if I never saw another man as long as I live. I had enough with Charlie. I enjoy being with Stevo, because there's no harm in him.' Those words came out with one breath. 'I thought you were my friend and friends don't say things like that.' Izzy swung away, but she was determined to have the final say. 'But when everything blows up in your face, Tolly, I'll still be there for you.'

Then Izzy swiftly walked away, leaving Tolly to ponder her words. She was in her bunk, pretending to sleep when Tolly finally returned to the boat. She guessed she had been for a walk to think things over. She'd left the lamp turned down low. She heard the other girl clean her teeth and wash, then throw the used water overboard. Last, Tolly extinguished the oil lamp and, as she climbed into bed, Izzy heard her say, 'I'm sorry, Izzy. I know I don't show it but I'm glad I'm sharing with you.'

### Chapter Nineteen

*My darling*
*My belief is that as long as I can pour out my heart to you, I will live. I see what the Germans are doing to us and I think, Why don't you shoot us?*
*I've already been to the tip truck to forage for*

*turnips. No easy task when so many other starving prisoners are doing the same thing. My wound has healed. I am one of the lucky ones.*

*Kramer, the chief, likes to play games by taunting us men with the gift of a turnip. Then, just as an emaciated man has his hands on the precious food, it is given to another prisoner.*

*'We should be getting proper food, Jakub.' Last night Al's voice broke into my thoughts. He doesn't sound the same as he used to – I could barely hear him. 'This is Bergen-Belsen. Don't they know about the Geneva Convention?'*

*He was sitting on the ground in his own mess. I thought my friend would die of typhus, because so many of the disease-ridden bodies are lying dead around us. Perhaps he will die of dysentery. I hope for his sake it might be soon. At least one of us would be put out of his misery. I care a great deal about Alan Jenks.*

*When he dies I'll no longer hear him say, 'I don't know why you bother to write letters. They probably never get to England, burned, more than likely.'*

*The thing is all the time I can hold my precious stub of pencil and beg, steal or borrow some scrap of paper on which to write to you, Dorothy, I feel close to you. You are my reason to live.*

*This morning I had to hold Alan up while we crawled through our special morning shower. In our clothes we filed through a hut and were covered in DDT. Up our sleeves, in our faces and hair and down our trousers. They are worried about the lice. Lice, so the guards believe, spread typhus.*

*After we'd been sprayed we shuffled on, stepping over dead bodies. I can't describe the smell. I know it will stay with me until it's my turn to die.*

145

*Yesterday a woman was screaming at a guard be-cause she had no milk to feed the infant she carried. I watched as she thrust the child into his arms and, crying, shuffled away. I heard later the baby had died a week ago.*
*Jakub*

'What are you getting all dolled up for?'

Tolly looked down at Izzy who was lying on her bunk reading an old copy of *Woman's Weekly*. She let go the waistband of her clean green slacks. 'There's about three inches of material here that was tight on me before.'

'That's why I asked, Tolly. Why are you getting dressed up?'

'I might as well tell you. I'm going to the George to play Aunt Sally.'

'And I suppose Sonny's taking you?'

'You can come if you like.'

'Of course I can – it's a public house so they're hardly likely to chuck me out – but I'm not sitting watching you go all dewy-eyed over that man.' Izzy sniffed and returned to the magazine Tolly knew she had read several times before. She could see Izzy was tired.

Today it had been lock after lock that needed unwinding. It seemed to Tolly they'd never get to their destination, no matter how hard they worked. It was only the thought of spending time in pubs at the end of the day that kept her sane. That, and seeing *Aurora* just ahead of them. 'Any-way, what's Aunt Sally?' Izzy asked.

'It's a game they play up here. Sonny told me all about it. A white skittle is placed on the top of

146

a metal plinth and you have to knock it off with sticks. Sonny's asked me to be in his team. You have to throw underarm and a team consists of eight players–'

'Spare me the details,' Izzy interrupted. 'Are the other two going?'

'I don't know, do I?' Tolly had no idea whether Sonny had invited Elsie and Dorothy. She hoped not. She wanted at some point in the evening to be alone with him. Not that she'd get much chance in the pub because, as always, he'd be the centre of attention, laughing and joking with the men and eyeing up the pretty girls.

'Is Stevo going?'

Tolly was cross. 'Don't keep asking me questions. Why don't you get ready and come out with me when Sonny knocks on the side of the boat? If he's alone, you can go on up the towpath to *Aurora* and play nursemaid to the old man. Can I borrow your curling tongs?'

'They're in my little cupboard.'

'Thank you.' Tolly gritted her teeth in a smile that was more a grimace. She foraged in Izzy's cupboard and, extracting the curling tongs, placed them on top of the stove, allowing only the metal part to heat up.

'Come on in, love. I can tell by that timid knock it's you.'

In the dusk the vibrant paintings of castles and roses set against the black of *Aurora's* walls stood out brightly. *Mallard* and *Bunting* paled in comparison. Izzy traced a flower with her finger before pushing open the cabin door.

'I never used to be so quiet,' said Izzy, lifting the kettle to check it for water, then putting it on the stove.

'Get it all knocked out of you, did you?'

Izzy eyed the old man sitting in his usual place near the fire. Even when it was warm outside she knew he felt the cold. 'So you've come to that conclusion?' Izzy said. She pushed her red curls away from her eyes. She looked around for the book. Stevo had it beside him and passed it to her.

'Told you, you're like my Sarah. Took her a long while before she ever told me about the way she'd been treated as a kid. The awful things that'd been done to her. That's why I never minded when she had a notion to leave me and go to *Jonquil*. I knew she'd come back when she felt she could face the hustle and bustle of the people on the cut. Mind you, I used to get right fed up when she took Sonny with her...'

'You really care about him, don't you?'

'Course I do. He's not just my grandson, he's the son I never had.'

Above the stove there was a wooden contraption to air clothes, two of Sonny's shirts hanging on it. At least, Izzy supposed they belonged to Sonny from the style.

'I'll say one thing for him, he always looks good.'

'Yes, and he's never short of a pretty girl.'

Izzy put a big spoonful of fresh tea leaves into the remains in the pot. She knew boaters never wasted anything, and the stronger the tea the better they liked it. She poured in the now boiling water.

'That's right, let that settle,' said Stevo.

'Our Tolly thinks he's got a fancy for her.'

148

Izzy had barely got the words out before Stevo started laughing. 'More fool her, I say. He's sowing his wild oats and afterwards he'll settle for a girl that's used to living on the cut.'

'I told her so.'

'Then you must tell her again before she gets hurt. You got hurt. That's what's sapped your confidence, girl.'

'When I worked at the munitions factory I was full of meself.'

'An' I bet that was a fine act you put on to cover up the way you really felt.'

His words struck a chord. Had she pretended nothing was wrong and been chirpy and cheeky to disguise how she'd really felt about Charlie knocking her about? If that was so, now that he was no longer around, why had she become so quiet and inclined to live inside her own head?

'You think so?'

'From how my Sarah was, I know so. You don't have to put on an act any more. You can be yourself.'

Izzy busied herself pouring out the tea that resembled tar and lightened it with condensed milk.

'You're a nice girl,' Stevo said. 'If I was fifty years younger...'

'You'd still be in love with your Sarah,' said Izzy. She settled down in the chair with the embroidered cushion and opened the book at the page she'd turned down.

Before she had time to start reading Stevo asked her, 'What you going to do when the war's over? In the pub earlier, so Sonny said, they was saying the Allied soldiers have the Germans on the run.'

'I don't know. Perhaps that means the end's in sight at last. I'll probably sign on for another trip, though. I can't go back to Gosport while Charlie's there. He'd find me in no time.'

'Thought you said the coppers got hold of him?' Izzy looked at Stevo. He appeared tired. His hands on the arms of the chair were bones topped with blue veins.

'The charges don't mean anything,' she said. 'He's got a golden tongue and too many people in high places owe him favours. I need to stay out of his way.' She didn't want to think about Charlie. It depressed her. 'Elsie's fallen for a bloke. She can't do much about that until she's fulfilled her obligation to Dorothy and the job, but I believe she deserves a bit of happiness...'

'I've heard all about that. Nothing much passes me by. Tell me about Dorothy. She's a closed shop, is that one.' He scrabbled for his red handkerchief and blew his nose noisily.

'Dorothy? Well, she never talks about herself. But she's offered to take me home to Southampton with her when we have leave after this trip. Maybe then I'll get to know her a bit better.'

They drank their tea in companionable silence, then Izzy read to Stevo until she saw his head droop and his breathing told her he slept. Then she let herself out of *Aurora* and walked along the towpath towards the dark shape of the butty-boat tied alongside *Mallard*. She was totally alone.

## Chapter Twenty

The empty gasometer reminded Dorothy of a spider's web, delicate, unfed, while its twin bulged fat and full. A train rattled past, smoke belching over dirty grey back-to-back houses. There was a tang in the air, not the smell of cordite that hung over Southampton but a dusty sharpness, like the smell of gas before it was lit. A gigantic crane rose from the landscape, like a ladder reaching towards the heavens. The green countryside had gone, replaced by factories and tall, dark, smoking chimneys.

*Mallard's* hold was like an open mouth, waiting to devour a load, she thought. Men fastened chains around bundles of metal billets, and a smaller crane lifted the load high into the air over the dock and swung it clear of the wharf.

'Keep her steady, Joe.'

'What d'you think I'm doin'?'

'I'm only sayin'.'

These were some of the cries that accompanied the crane driver with his cable and load, while the men guided the rusty billets. *Mallard* sank deeper into the water as the weight of the steel pushed her down.

Dorothy had sent the three girls to buy a meal in the café. It had rained again before they'd reached Limehouse Basin and continued pouring for three days.

Chains unhooked from the billets now swung dangerously close to her as she stood watching the performance. Men were talking animatedly. She stepped neatly aside as a shout warned, 'Watch out.'

By midday the boats were loaded and the girls had returned, making her feel hungry as they talked about liver and onions and apple crumble. She knew she needed a break – a headache had come on. Elsie told her to go for a walk, or at least get away from the boats for a while.

To leave the wharf she had to pass through a crowd of gypsies who were excited about something she couldn't quite see. A woman's voice said, 'Ain't yer got somethin' to put it in?'

'What?' asked Dorothy.

'Gawd bless yer, girl, it's sugar for free. 'Ere!' A brown carrier bag was thrust into her hands and Dorothy allowed herself to be propelled towards the centre of the crowd.

A wooden crate lay broken on the siding below a crane. From it spilled what looked to Dorothy like shiny snow until she realized what must have happened. A malfunction of the crane. The driver was now leaning out of his contraption high in the air and grinning like a maniac. The spillage of sugar was free for anyone who cared to scoop it up. Dorothy thanked the woman profusely and fell to her knees among the scrabbling, sweaty bodies and scooped up handfuls of sweetness, thrusting it into the bag.

'Not often we gets somefink for nuffin', eh?' The woman smiled at her, showing a gold tooth. 'Bloody rationing's killin' us.'

152

With the bag as full as she dared fill it for fear of it bursting before she got back to *Mallard*, Dorothy elbowed her way out of the crush and back along the concrete wharf towards her friends. She staggered under the weight of her bounty, now clutched to her body because she dared not trust the bag's string handles.

Elsie was sitting at the top of the stairs, drinking tea. Immediately she saw Dorothy she put down the mug, jumped onto the wharf and ran towards her. 'What have you got?'

'Sugar,' gasped Dorothy. 'The crane driver dropped the crate. The gypsies were scrabbling about like ants but a woman made a space for me and gave me a bag. Just let me get it in the cabin before it spills everywhere.'

Down in the gloom, Tolly was reading. She eyed the excited pair with their precious cargo, jumped up from her seat and threw down her book. 'I know exactly what to do with some of that,' she said.

At a less busy stretch of Limehouse Water, Dorothy and Elsie walked along the towpath with the two boats' ropes and tied them at the side to begin the tiresome business of covering the loads. The sugar bounty had lifted all their spirits.

Tarpaulin skins had to be stretched and lifted over the cargo. Rain falling into the holds would increase the boats' weight and make for slower travelling. Already time was of the essence. Dorothy noted that the girls, although unused to unrolling the heavy sheets, worked without dissent. Side sheets were held taut and tied down. It wasn't an easy job but nothing on the cut, so far, had been easy. Eventually the boats had been made safe against the inclement weather and were ready for the journey from Limehouse along the Grand Union Canal to Birmingham.

'The London locks are all double-chambered as the traffic's greater,' said Dorothy, 'but don't worry. Lock-keepers are there to assist, which is a blessing as we're used to handling empty boats. When their holds are full of iron they take some manipulating, especially as we'll be fighting against the tidal Thames.'

The girls didn't seem bothered by the logistics but were more interested in Sonny and Stevo's whereabouts.

'*Aurora* and her butty have disappeared,' Elsie shouted.

Dorothy returned, 'Don't worry. He had coal and stuff to unload. I wonder what they've picked up this time and where they're going?'

Her eyes lit on a deeply scored bollard. Countless ropes had gouged deep lines into the metal. She thought of the ropes pulled by horses that had hauled narrowboats along the canals long before engines were installed. Iron posts, worn relics of a bygone age, remained alongside the towpaths. She remembered seeing deep grooves in the brickwork at the sides of bridges, again caused by ropes, souvenirs of days gone by.

Now the load was tied down, Dorothy yelled to Tolly to put the kettle on. She was starving, not having eaten when the others visited the café. The thought of a thick corned-beef sandwich was enticing.

Dorothy was looking forward to travelling once more on the Grand Union Canal. Unique in that it was composed of at least eight separate canals, it linked London with Nottingham, Birmingham and Leicester. Limehouse was a huge dock at a junction of the Thames, busy with craft and crowded with people. Dorothy would be happier when she was in open countryside again.

She decided she wouldn't think about going back to Southampton until they'd dropped off their load at Birmingham. She had asked Izzy to stay with her for a few days and felt apprehensive. But what other option was there? Clearly the girl couldn't return to Gosport. The newspaper had stated the police had Charlie in custody, but Izzy was convinced they would never make the charge stick and he'd be out on bail or exonerated.

It wouldn't be long before he discovered Izzy hadn't gone to her mother's house and clearly intended to have nothing more to do with him. She needed all the help she could get to stay hidden so Charlie wouldn't find her. No, it would be safer for Izzy to come home with her for a well-deserved break. Dorothy sighed. She had secrets of her own that she didn't want discovered, but Izzy's safety came first.

Tolly would be welcomed back into her family at Titchfield, and Elsie was going to Jack. Would they all return for another trip with her? She hoped so. She congratulated herself on having chosen her crew wisely. They were friendly and hard-working. What more could she ask for?

'Cuppa?' Tolly stood before Dorothy with a mug of strong tea in her hands. 'I'll be glad to get out of this place – I've never seen so much rubbish in the canals.'

Dorothy eyed her good-humouredly. 'I thought maybe you'd set your heart on catching up with *Aurora*.'

Tolly's eyes widened. 'You think they're ahead of us?'

'I've no idea.'

'Maybe we'll see them further on.' Tolly's eyes brightened.

'Maybe,' Dorothy admitted. 'We've got a few hours' cruising left before it gets dark. D'you want to carry on? My paperwork's complete. What about the others?'

'We all want to go.' Tolly shoved a bag of biscuits at Dorothy. 'Dip some in your tea.' Dorothy shook her head. 'If you make me a corned-beef sandwich, we'll get out of here and not stop until we find a good place to berth for the night.'

'Aye, aye, Captain,' said Tolly, 'I'll pass on the message.'

The long wail of the air-raid siren cut through the conversation.

'Do we look for a shelter?' Tolly was plainly shaken.

Dorothy realized her girls had been lulled into a false sense of security by the lack of bombing in the countryside. But this was London and Hitler wanted to destroy the city. She made the decision. 'I don't fancy our chances, searching for a shelter here.'

Some of the workers at the basin were scattering, like headless chickens, thought Dorothy. If she'd noticed any signs telling them where the shelters

156

were she'd have urged her girls to run for safety too.

As they huddled together in *Mallard's* cabin it was hard to pretend she wasn't just as scared as Elsie, Tolly and Izzy.

'Can you hear any planes?'

They all listened carefully. 'Perhaps it's a mistake,' Izzy ventured.

'This is London. I wouldn't think they'd set off Moaning Minnie just for the fun of it,' said Dorothy.

The deafening crash that followed set *Mallard* rocking and heaving. Dorothy grabbed Elsie for support.

'What the hell was that?' Tolly asked. Her eyes were big, like saucers.

Everything that wasn't tied down in *Mallard* was moving. Cups slid along shelves, and tins banged against each other in cupboards. Tolly's frightened gaze held Elsie's. And then came the sound of crashing walls, falling masonry. Dorothy expected any moment that something would fall on their boat and rend it apart. Her fingers crossed, she prayed for their safety.

The rocking and shaking seemed to go on for ever. At last the water around them began to settle.

Then came the echo of ambulance bells. More movement outside. This time, running feet, people shouting.

A solid thumping on the wooden cabin top startled Dorothy with its intensity. A familiar voice shouted, 'You lot all right in there?'

The girls looked at each other.

'It's Sonny!' Tolly beamed with delight.

Within moments daylight was entering the cabin as Tolly flung open the door. Sonny stood near the tiller, his white teeth glittering in a broad smile, his red curls bouncing in the breeze. He stuck his fingers into the pocket of his waistcoat, pulled out a watch and looked at it.

'It ain't official,' he said, the watch back in his pocket, 'but general consensus is that that was one of Hitler's new weapons, the V-2 rocket. More deadly than the V-1s an' they don't make no sounds until they land. Somewhere close by has copped it. Poor buggers.'

Izzy broke in: 'Is Stevo all right?'

'Course he is. Take more'n what ol' Adolf can chuck at us to upset him. Our Tommy's with him.' He must have seen the women's confusion at the name, for he added, 'We're giving him a lift back to Birmingham. Makes it easier for me with two loaded boats – he takes the tiller, see?'

Sonny's shadow seemed to fill the cabin as he stood on the steps talking but all Dorothy could think was how kind and neighbourly of him it had been to come over and make sure they were all unscathed. Tolly, grinning like a maniac, looked as if all her birthdays had arrived at once.

Dorothy wondered who Tommy was. The way Sonny had called him 'our' made her think he was a relative.

'A piece of advice,' said Sonny. 'I wouldn't stay here tonight. There's been a dark-haired bloke, a stranger, asking after a red haired girl. The cut people won't let on. They don't like being questioned.' He stared at Izzy. 'I reckon you know who he is.' Dorothy saw Izzy's face drain of colour. For

158

a moment there was silence. Then Sonny added, 'Besides, ol' Adolf could be sending more of them bombs.'

'But I thought we were winning this war?' Izzy said, trying to hide her fear that the man, who could only be Charlie, was looking for her.

'It ain't over until it's over,' Sonny said sombrely. 'Nothing ever is.' He walked away.

The Grand Union had more locks than they'd encountered so far, thought Dorothy, but at least they were out in the countryside again and the late-afternoon sun was shining through the round window onto her makeshift desk in the cabin, where she sat with her eternal paperwork.

Izzy and Elsie had pulled the weighty boats over to a towpath near an orchard. Tolly had disappeared into the trees.

When she returned she was dragging a sack. She had a smile on her face a mile wide.

'C'mon, help me get this aboard.' Eager hands reached out.

'You could get shot for that,' Dorothy admonished her, from the top step on *Mallard,* but she, too, was grinning. The trees were heavy with ripe fruit that scented the air. Dorothy was always happier when she was surrounded by fields and cows, rather than people. Ahead, before they'd moored up she'd spotted *Aurora* disappearing around another bend in the cut.

Now they were on their way again she was content. Her girls were happy, especially Tolly, who'd been let off boat duties as she'd begged to cook the apples.

With her hand on the tiller, Dorothy looked down at herself and smiled. They'd lived through a rocket attack, but when she went home to Southampton she'd better smarten up a bit. She had on a pair of trousers that had long since lost the elastic around the waist so was held up with a large safety pin. The two jumpers she wore kept out the cold breeze and two pairs of socks warmed her feet inside her boots. She'd borrowed a woollen coat from Elsie as her own waterproof was wet inside as well as out. Izzy was at *Bunting's* tiller and Dorothy waved to her. She, too, was dressed for warmth, which was a polite way of saying Izzy looked like a scarecrow. She had been very quiet since she'd heard someone was looking for a red-haired girl.

Suddenly there was a clunk, and a grinding noise came from beneath the boat. Dorothy swore. She guessed immediately what had happened. Something had snagged itself around the propeller. She put the engine into reverse, then swung it quickly to forward. All that happened was that a cloud of foul-smelling smoke floated upwards, then billowed around her. She turned off the engine.

### Chapter Twenty-one

'That's all we need,' said Dorothy, quietly, to Elsie after she'd yelled at Izzy to pull over. Luckily Izzy had been alert enough to steer *Bunting* to the side of the canal instead of ramming into the back of

160

*Mallard*. Tolly poked her head out of the hatch.

'Nothing for you to worry about,' Dorothy shouted. 'I've turned the engine off. Now, I'll have to look in the weed hatch and see if I can free whatever it is that's caught up. Thanks,' she added to Elsie, taking the screwdriver she'd asked her to find. She began unscrewing a flat wooden board on the floor of the boat that the girls sometimes sat on when the weather was good.

When the top of the hatch was uncovered Dorothy swore. 'Come and look.'

'It's some kind of rope,' said Elsie. 'This water's so filthy I can hardly see what's going on down there.'

Dorothy's arm came out of the box covered with silt and weeds. She grimaced at the smell and Elsie followed suit. 'I'm going to need to lean right in but first can you find me something to hack at it with? It feels like it's stuck solid.' Dorothy wiped her arm on a rag, then got up and went to the engine's starter motor. She removed the key and put it on the side shelf. 'I don't want to lose my arm if a sudden motion restarts the propellers,' she said.

'These are all I can find.' Elsie put down an axe, a breadknife and a penknife.

Dorothy stared hard at her finds. 'Is that all?'

Elsie nodded. Izzy climbed onto *Mallard* from *Bunting*. 'Why have we stopped?'

'Stuff caught round the propeller,' said Elsie.

'Go back on *Bunting* and see if you can find something that I might be able to use to free old rope,' Dorothy said urgently. The day was fading now. 'I don't want to be messing around in the

161

murky cut in the dark.'

'Right,' said Izzy. It seemed to Dorothy that it got darker by the minute before Izzy slid back onto *Mallard*. 'You're not going to like it but my offerings aren't much better.' She tipped an assortment of kitchen implements on the floor and a small pair of scissors. Dorothy felt like crying. She let out a huge sigh.

'I really need something like a strong pair of secateurs. The axe is sharp but I might damage the propeller and make things worse.' They'd never be able to free the rope themselves if these were the best tools they had.

'It's no good,' she said. 'You lot'll have to stay here while I go in search of a village or house with a phone so I can let the base know where we are. Tomorrow, some time, they'll get to us and sort out this mess.' She glared at the open hatch. 'I was hoping to make up time we've lost...'

'What's up, ladies?'

'Bloomin' hell! Where d'you spring from?' Dorothy said. A skinny young man with the darkest, curliest head of hair she had ever seen was hanging over *Mallard's* rail.

'I been told to run down the towpath to make sure you was all right.' His cheeky face broke into a wide smile. 'Only you ain't, are you?'

'Who told you to run after us?' Izzy looked terrified.

Elsie put her arm around her friend's shoulders. 'It's nothing to do with Charlie,' she whispered, but Izzy was shaking with fright.

'Sonny said to come back and see what was takin' you so long to reach the lock and the pub.

He's saved you a berth near the Lock Inn.'

Izzy let out a deep breath, clearly relieved.

Dorothy gathered her thoughts. 'Who are you?'

'Me name's Tommy. I'm off to Birmingham to see me sister.' The lad had a broad Cockney accent.

Dorothy suddenly remembered Sonny had mentioned him. 'You're some relative, aren't you?' she asked.

'Sort of,' said Tommy. 'You gonna tell me what's up? I'm losin' valuable drinkin' time chattin' to you lot.'

'We've got some old rope twisted around the propeller and nothing to hack it away with.'

She was talking to an empty space for the young man had climbed aboard and was now on all fours peering down the hatch. 'That's a bugger, ain't it?' He looked up at them with a grin.

'Nicely put. I don't suppose you can help?' Dorothy asked. The boy looked inside the hatch again, more thoughtfully this time. Then he sat back on the deck and asked, 'You got anything to cut it with?'

Dorothy indicated the implements lying around him. 'That's all the sharp things we could find.'

'I'll 'ave to get back to Sonny,' Tommy said, rising and dusting off his brown corduroy trousers. He curled his lip at the breadknife and scissors. 'You shouldn't be on the cut if you don't know how to take care of yourselves!'

With that endearing remark he jumped from the boat and ran back along the towpath.

Dorothy watched him until he was out of sight. 'I wonder if he'll come back with Sonny.'

163

'Well, they'd better get here before the light goes,' Elsie said.

Izzy asked, 'Shall I put the kettle on?'

'Good idea,' Dorothy said, eyeing the hatch with distaste. 'We'll give the lad half an hour and if he's not back by then I'll follow the towpath the way we've come to look for a place with a phone.'

'Oh, don't worry,' called Tolly, her head poking up from *Bunting's* hatch. Elsie could see white stuff on her eyelashes and cheeks. Tolly's eyes were sparkling. 'Sonny won't let us down.'

Dorothy raised her eyes heavenwards.

Before they'd finished their tea the lad came back at a run. He was carrying what looked like a long carpet bag. He heaved it over the side of the boat, shouting, 'Wotcha!'

'I thought Sonny might have come.' Tolly appeared at *Bunting's* hatch. She looked disappointed.

Tommy blinked at her. 'He don't need to be here to see me sort you out.' He narrowed his eyes. 'You the bint allus chasin' him?' Tolly glared at him and ducked inside *Bunting,* but not before Dorothy had seen her face redden.

Tommy pulled off his shirt, exposing his skinny chest. 'You'd better look away, ladies, if you don't want to see a bloke in his drawers.' With a single movement he removed his trousers, then opened up the bag and sorted through it, pulling out what looked like a pair of garden shears. He slithered on his bottom towards the hatch, and put a foot into the murky water.

'What are you doing?' Dorothy cried.

'Don't worry, I knows what I'm about. Jesus,

164

this water's cold.' He stopped in his tracks. 'You 'ave taken the key out, ain't yer? I don't want to get chopped into dog's meat.'

'Yes, I have, but please be careful,' Dorothy begged. Her face showed how distressed she was.

But Tommy could no longer hear her for he had slipped into the icy water with the shears. She could hear a lot of splashing, and every so often Tommy's wet face, curls bedraggled, popped up, gasped for air, swore, then dived down inside the hatch again.

'If you ever told me a person could fit into that small space, I'd never have believed you,' said Elsie. 'I do hope he'll be all right.'

'Well, it looks like he's done this sort of thing before, doesn't it? And it's a good job he's built like a rasher of wind,' said Dorothy. 'I'll be eternally grateful to Sonny and his granddad for looking out for us.'

There was a lot of noise going on below the hatch and every so often water splashed on the decking as Tommy came up, took another deep breath and disappeared again. Only once did he speak sensibly and that was to gasp, 'Bleedin' filthy job, this is!'

Eventually, the shears made an appearance followed by skinny arms and then the rest of Tommy. He climbed out of the hole, dripping, then shook himself, like a dog emerging from a pond. He handed the shears to Dorothy.

'Dry these thoroughly an', if you can spare it, run the blades over with a bit of marge.' He wiped his face with a free hand. 'Sonny's very particular about his tools. Try her now.'

Dorothy said to Elsie, 'Put the key in and see what happens.'

The wet lad, his skin goosepimpled with cold, moved towards the tiller and controls. The boat's propellers whirred into life. Tommy shoved the control to neutral. 'There you go, like new. Okay, best turn it orf. You kin buy me a pint when we get to the Lock Inn.' His teeth were chattering, but he was trying to smile.

Dorothy, who'd gone below to wipe margarine on the shears' blades, shouted up, 'We can't thank you enough. Come down here for something warm in your insides, and I've got a kettle of hot water for you to wash the filth from your hair and body. I don't want you picking up any diseases from that water.'

'Fanks, Dorothy. It is Dorothy, ain't it?' She had just emerged from the cabin holding the greasy shears. She came on deck, bent down and put them in the bag they'd arrived in.

Tolly emerged yet again from *Bunting's* hatch and yelled, 'We're ever so grateful to Sonny for this.'

'No doubt you'll find a way to thank him,' shouted Tommy. 'Most girls do.' Dorothy and Elsie laughed.

Tommy dripped towards the steps leading down into the cabin. He turned and said, 'I'm shutting the door, ladies. I don't want any of you taking a look at me crown jewels.'

## Chapter Twenty-two

When *Mallard*, with Tommy steering, reached the towpath alongside the noisy pub, Tolly said indignantly, 'I thought you said Sonny had saved us a space?' She looked at the boats hugging the moorings. Already she could smell cigarette smoke on the air and hear laughter.

'Well, he can't stay outside and tell people not to moor up, can he? See what he's done? He's pulled the butty in an' tied her behind *Aurora*, so he's taking two spaces, instead of tying the butty in the water next to *Aurora*.'

Tolly could see exactly what he meant but she didn't like anything obvious being explained to her, especially not by Tommy, who somehow seemed to get under her skin. Not in a bad way, though – there was no harm in him. While they'd been travelling the cut, she'd amazed herself by confiding in him her hopes and dreams of one day owning the Currant Bun and making a success of the café.

'Take the tiller while I rearrange our boats so's you can get in the space behind us.'

'I was just about to,' she replied tartly.

He ignored her tone and grinned at her, then jumped out of *Mallard*.

Tolly did as she was told, waving at Elsie, who was steering *Bunting*. Tolly watched Tommy scramble over moored craft. He was a comical person, she thought. Endearing in a funny sort of way. She wondered how old he was. He looked about fifteen but she thought he might be older. Perhaps he was so skinny because he'd grown up without proper food.

*Aurora's* butty was now in mid-stream and Tommy was back on *Aurora* pulling in the ropes to fasten the two boats together, side by side.

Tolly made arm movements to Elsie to show her she was attempting to moor in the space vacated by *Aurora's* butty. Within minutes Elsie had jumped to the towpath and both women had moored *Mallard* and *Bunting* behind *Aurora* and her butty. The pub was a few hundred yards away.

'Yer gettin' good with that boat, ain't yer? And you smells nice.' Tolly preened at Tommy's words. She yelled down into the cabin, 'We're here!'

Dorothy looked up. Tolly saw she'd left her hair in a ponytail instead of its usual bun. 'You look nice,' she said. 'You should wear your hair like that more often.'

Dorothy smiled and began climbing the stairs. 'I'm going to have to thank Sonny and his grand-dad for looking out for us. We'd have lost a lot of time if we'd had to wait for someone from the base to come out and fix the propeller. I can't thank you enough,' she said to Tommy, who was waiting on the towpath.

'Cut people always help folks,' he said. He looked meaningfully at Tolly. 'Even when they can't stand each other.'

Usually the gypsies regarded the Idle Women with suspicion, as Tolly had been told many times. She stuck her tongue out at Tommy and

168

flounced away.

'Come on, Izzy,' yelled Dorothy. After a few moments Izzy came to the steps. She, too, had made an effort. Her cloud of bright hair looked like spun gold.

'I'm not fussed about drinking so if Stevo isn't in the pub I'm going to read to him.' In her hand she held the Alexandre Dumas book.

'He's not on *Aurora* else he'd 'ave shouted at me,' said Tommy. He thought for a moment. 'Well, p'raps not shouted but he'd 'ave banged with his stick to let me know he was aboard. C'mon, you lot, we're wasting valuable drinkin' time.'

Izzy left the novel in the cabin.

'Do you think he's even old enough to drink?' whispered Dorothy to Tolly.

Tommy must have heard her for he came back at her: 'I'm nineteen, not bleedin' nine!'

Tolly knew her mouth had fallen open. The young man glared at them both, then stalked off across the grass and gravel towards the front door of the pub.

'I think we've hurt his feelings,' said Dorothy. All four women were walking towards the noisy bar. Tolly could hear the wireless blaring dance music.

She spotted Stevo nursing a half-pint and sitting in his bath chair, and Izzy made a beeline for him, telling Dorothy she wanted cider if they had any. Tolly followed her.

'Hello, sweetheart,' Stevo said to Izzy. He had a bit of a cough into his handkerchief, then composed himself. 'The news was on just now, and it seems we've got them German blighters on the run for sure. That's the good news, but our boys keep discovering these concentration camps full of dead and dying prisoners of war.'

Before Izzy could reply Tolly cut in: 'Where's Sonny? He doesn't seem to be in here.'

'That's because he's taken Eliza for a walk,' Stevo said.

'What's Eliza? A dog?'

Stevo stared at Tolly, his eyes like ice. 'Eliza's the daughter of the landlord here.' Tolly couldn't hide her disappointment.

The silence that followed was eventually broken by Tommy, who pushed a glass of beer into Tolly's hands. 'Take this. Dorothy sent it over. Now come outside for a minute.' He turned to Stevo. 'The drinks are on Dorothy.' He settled a glass of whisky in Stevo's gnarled hand. 'Sup that up,' he said. 'It'll put hairs on yer chest.'

Tolly followed the lad to the bar where he picked up his own pint, took a big gulp, then strode through the smoke-filled room, letting the blackout curtain fall back in the doorway, so the light didn't seep out. He walked towards a path at the side of the hostelry that led to a garden where there were a few wooden benches and tables. He sat down and motioned for her to sit next to him. 'I don't want to interfere,' he said, 'but it's about Sonny.'

'Well, don't, then!' Tolly stared at him. How could this slip of a lad know what she was feeling?

'You're not the only one to have their heart broken by him. He collects hearts like some blokes collect stamps.'

Tolly snapped. 'What do you mean, he broke

170

my heart? He's never even kissed me.'

The worry on his face dissipated. 'Well, that's all to the good, then.'

'What are you talking about?' Tolly was running her finger round the rim of her glass.

'If he hasn't kissed you, he hasn't laid a finger on you either.'

'No, of course not. What do you take me for?'

A flush of relief lit Tommy's face. He lifted his glass and swallowed. 'I takes you for a girl who knows what she wants when the war's over by opening a successful business, a pretty girl with a lush figure who could have her pick of any blokes. If you've got any sense you'll stop making cow eyes at Sonny. He's a relative of mine but he won't never settle for a girl who's not born to the cut.'

'I'm not pretty,' said Tolly. 'And I'm fat.'

Tommy spluttered into his beer. He wiped his face with the back of his hand. 'I think you should look in a mirror sometime.'

'And I think you need your head examining. Tell Dorothy I've gone back to the boat.' She stormed off, leaving her drink on the table. When she glanced back, he was watching her and shaking his head.

Once more on the boat Tolly refilled the coal bucket and banked up the stove. She thought how lucky they were always to have a supply of wood or coal to use as fuel. Sometimes they 'borrowed' coal from the yards alongside the canal, but mostly the lock-keepers helped them out, and there was always wood for the taking from fallen trees.

Tolly hadn't come back to the boat just because she was upset that Sonny hadn't shown up that evening. She was furious with Tommy. What right did he have to tell her what she could or couldn't do?

She was happiest when she was cooking and the heaven-sent gift of sugar had kept her busy on *Bunting* while the propeller was being fixed. So what if Sonny was out walking with some girl? Wasn't the way to a man's heart through his stomach? She took the clean tea-towels off the delicacies she'd prepared earlier.

*Bunting* didn't possess much in the way of luxury. Certainly not a full-length mirror. There was a small square one on the shelf near the stove and Tolly picked it up.

She scrutinized herself. The weeks of running ahead to prepare the locks and the lack of fattening food had defined her face. She had cheekbones. She knew some of her clothes were baggy and she'd resorted to using safety pins to keep them together but she wasn't prepared for the shock of seeing herself, or most of herself, when she propped the small mirror against the bunk bed and stood back until she had a fair enough image.

She was still curvy but no longer so overweight that she was ashamed to see her reflection. And then it dawned on her. She had stopped puffing so hard when she had to hurry between locks. At home in Titchfield walking anywhere, even in the café, had done her in. She remembered likening it to pulling tree trunks after her whenever she needed to walk. When had she lost that awful feeling of dragging her weight around?

All the recent exercise over the past weeks had toned her. She wouldn't have believed it possible, had Tommy not pointed it out. Of course the lad had never seen her at her heaviest, had he? And he'd said she was ... what was it? Lush?

'That's enough of that,' she told herself, taking the mirror and putting it back in its rightful place. 'Self-praise is no recommendation!'

Tolly approached the stove. She was happy with her afternoon's work. She'd known exactly what she was going to do with the fallen apples she'd gathered from the orchard. It would be a nice surprise for her friends. And for Sonny.

### Chapter Twenty-three

'I don't want to say anything, old chap, but there's egg or something on your tie and...' Eric Tomlin coughed, obviously embarrassed.

Geoffrey stared at him. The young man tipped to join the firm as a junior partner shuffled papers from his corner desk and dared to look up and into Geoffrey's eyes. 'It's just that a comment was made and overheard...'

'What kind of comment? Who by?'

'You know I can't say anything.' Eric coughed discreetly behind his hand. 'We're aware you're going through a change of circumstances...'

'Excuse me, Tomlin, may I remind you you're not yet in a position to speak to me like that...'

Just then the door opened and Milly, the tea lady, arrived with her trolley. The silence that followed could have been cut with one of Milly's cake knives.

She bustled around pouring tea and offering biscuits, which Geoffrey declined as his waistline was expanding, due no doubt to all the fried food he was being fed.

Tomlin held the door open for her to depart, then escaped himself, leaving Geoffrey staring at his cup of weak tea.

He peered down at his dark tie. Yes, it did have a large splodge of something resembling egg yolk. How had he not noticed? Elsie would never have allowed him to leave the house less than immaculately dressed. He sighed. Sandra was more ... bohemian. There was also the matter of the long orange cat hairs covering his trouser legs.

He'd taken a boiled egg, with bread and butter, up to Sandra, who was still asleep, and had left the tray on the bedside table. Elsie would have had a fit if Geoffrey had surprised her with breakfast in bed. Though it wasn't a surprise for Sandra as he did that small chore most mornings. Now her morning sickness had stopped, she ate voraciously. Eating for two, she called it. He wondered if it had made her balloon with her pregnancy. He'd seen pregnant women at practically full term with smaller bumps than hers.

He'd dressed for work in a hurry this morning, having risen early to tidy the living room.

'The baby makes me feel tired,' Sandra had said, when he had asked her about the dead flowers in the blue vase that were giving off a foul smell. 'I can't do everything.'

So he'd had a bit of a tidy-up. But the heart had gone out of his once immaculate home. He'd lost heart too, for there had been several possible buyers to look over the property but as yet no takers, even though he'd dropped the original asking price. Maybe he should take time off and show people around himself.

Alverstoke was a sought-after area, and the price was more than fair. Perhaps Sandra's treatment of possible buyers left a lot to be desired. She could be quite offhand when she wanted. Perhaps they didn't like the 'terrace' she'd created at the front of the house.

He didn't see the point in covering half the garden, destroying flowers that Elsie had planted with such care, to leave a swathe of grey concrete upon which a few deckchairs and tables now sat. Who wanted to sit opposite the road anyway?

But it made sense not to antagonize Sandra – she could be a positive vixen when crossed, especially after she had dropped her bombshell last night: she and the doctor had made a mistake and it was possible the baby would come sooner than anticipated. How wonderful would that be? A son or a daughter of his very own.

He wondered if Elsie had received his letter telling her he had moved back into Western Way. There had been no reply. When he'd telephoned the Rousham Cruisers base, the stupid woman who'd answered had told him condescendingly they were able to forward letters to appropriate places for the crews to pick them up, but Elsie was otherwise engaged. He hated to admit that he missed her.

After he'd drunk his tea, Geoffrey pulled off his tie and put it into his waistcoat pocket, then undid the top button of his shirt, thinking clients wouldn't mind his slight state of undress – it was still warm in late September.

'Get out from under my feet, you silly dog!'

Matey was having great fun pouncing on clods of earth as the spade flicked them over. Jack wiped the sweat from his forehead. Elsie had told him she loved gardening so he was going to surprise her with a plot big enough for her to plant whatever she liked. He wanted to make it easier for her to cultivate by digging it over first. He ignored the pain in his leg as he stared at the small chalet-like shed he'd decorated with left-over paint. Elsie would be able to store her gardening equipment in there. Outside, a small freshly painted bench faced the sun.

The ground at the back of his cottage rolled away to farmland and hills, and Elsie had said how much she liked the peace and quiet of its location. He was excited that she intended to come to him when she'd finished her first round trip.

He couldn't believe now he'd had the courage to wait for the canal boat in Oxford and that he'd actually approached her.

Jack bent down and petted the small white dog, who wouldn't keep still. 'You'd better like your new mistress,' he said. 'She's a wonderful lady.'

At the hotel, he and Elsie had poured out their secrets, hopes and fears. He didn't mind admitting he'd been saddened by the news that she couldn't have children. But it was Elsie he wanted, Elsie he'd fallen in love with. And if he could have her, nothing else mattered.

What if she didn't like the quiet of his lock cottage?

For her he'd move anywhere. Even take up a desk job at the airfield. He'd been offered one but didn't think it a good idea to accept while he was still suffering from nightmares after the crash. It was different now: with Elsie at his side he could do anything. Even move mountains, if she wanted him to.

Matey began barking and running towards the canal. A bell rang loudly.

'You know before I do, don't you, you silly mutt, when someone wants help with the lock?' Jack limped after his dog.


'Out on bail?'

'They'll never make the charges stick, Joey.' Charlie looked the little man up and down.

'Did I hear right your Izzy left you?'

'Nah! She's doing a bit of war work. She'd never leave me.' Charlie felt the small muscle at the side of his mouth twitch. So that was what people thought, was it? That she'd left him? He didn't like Gosport people knowing he couldn't hold on to Izzy. But the bitch had done a runner before he'd got picked up by the police. He wondered if she'd had anything to do with that. Nah, wasn't possible as he never told her what he was up to.

'I'll be fetching her soon, Joey. She says she misses me.'

He thought of the piece of paper in his wallet

177

with her mate Elsie's new address that he'd copied from the original the day he'd broken into their posh house in Western Way. Where the fuck was Izzy? She needed teaching a lesson for making him look a right bloody fool, didn't she? He hadn't found her at Lower Heyford or at Limehouse Basin in London.

But he would find the bitch! He was driving back up to Oxfordshire at the weekend and when he discovered her whereabouts on the canal he'd make her sorry she'd run off.

*My Darling*

*It's been eight days since we've had any food. Water is still available and I'm sure that's keeping me alive. That and the hope I will see you again. Some of the other prisoners aren't so lucky. I tried to take water to a man I'd grown quite close to after losing... I can't even remember my friend's name. His body still lies by the fence. The man was totally dehydrated. I'd managed to find a tin to collect water for him but the rust made it red.*

*I had to pass by the bodies of little children who had been clubbed. Little bodies with their heads dented and caved in. I was told the end of the war was in sight. How could anyone know that? Certainly not these skeletons in blue and white rags. I think if the Germans could do that, kill innocent children, they would never bother to send letters home for us. It's a terrible thing to know you're going to die and no one will know.*

*Jakub*

## Chapter Twenty-four

Tolly could hear the girls laughing as they climbed aboard *Mallard*. One tripped, causing yet more giggles. The scent of spices filled the air in *Bunting* and she guessed any moment now that the others would call over to her.

'Tolly, you wizard thing, come here.' It was Dorothy's voice. Tolly knew that once they'd left the pub, they would return to *Mallard* for a final cup of cocoa. She stood on the stairs and looked out of *Bunting's* hatch.

'Enjoy it,' she called. Then, 'Don't let Izzy eat it all, there's another apple pie here for us.'

'Aren't you coming aboard?' The boats were lashed together, and it would take but a moment for Tolly to step over the ropes onto *Mallard*. But she had other plans.

'Has the pub turned out now? Did Stevo get home safe?' Tolly wasn't particularly worried about Stevo, but she wondered if Sonny was back.

'Of course,' said Dorothy, poking her head out of *Mallard's* hatch. 'Guess what? Izzy's been given a bag of stuff that belonged to someone called Sarah.'

'Sonny's grandmother.' Tolly had remembered who Sarah was.

Dorothy smiled at her. 'Sure you don't want to come in with us for a while?' Tolly shook her head.

Dorothy said, 'Thanks again for the apple pie. I can't wait to dig in.' And then she was gone, leaving Tolly to stare along the dark waterway. For a moment she listened to the night sounds.

The sound of a glass shattering inside the pub broke her thoughts. Smiling to herself she went down the stairs to reappear, moments later, with a covered, fragrant dish.

Carefully, Tolly stepped over the ropes and slid past the now closed hatch and *Mallard's* door, then onto the towpath. All she was aware of was the sound of her shoes on the gravel.

It was a boat-length to reach *Aurora,* and when Tolly climbed aboard she could hear voices coming from the cabin. The door was closed because of the blackout so she knocked, carefully holding the pie in her arms.

When the door opened she slipped inside while Tommy slid back the blackout curtain. Tolly looked about her. Stevo sat in his usual seat near the fire and Tommy gave her a warm smile. 'This is a nice surprise,' he said. 'What you got under that tea-towel?'

'Sonny not here?' Tolly had no need to look about her in such a small space for it was obvious that only Stevo and Tommy were on board.

'He's out with his girl.' The words fell from Stevo's mouth. He was staring at Tolly. 'By gum, that smells good.'

Tolly's hands were shaking as she passed the dish to Tommy. 'We had a bit of luck with getting hold of some extra sugar so I made some pies. Thought you'd all like to share this.'

Tommy took the warm dish from her. 'That's

really kind of you.'

Tolly stared at him. It seemed to her that his eyes could see right inside her. He knew she'd made the pie especially for Sonny, who had committed the sin of not being there to receive it. Worse still, the old man had let slip Sonny was still out with the girl from the pub.

Tommy whipped off the tea-towel and gave a long, low whistle. 'Would you look at that, Stevo! Bin a long time since anyone's cared about our innards.' The browned top was thick with sugar.

'You gonna sit and have a cuppa with us, love?' Stevo asked.

Tolly knew she could no more drink tea than fly to the moon. 'I won't, if you don't mind. Dorothy's been talking about getting a move on towards Blisworth Tunnel with a really early start.' Well, it was a half-truth, Tolly thought. Dorothy had mentioned the tunnel.

Stevo nodded knowingly. 'Well, we'll all need our wits about us going through that haunted place,' he said.

'Stevo, you stop that! No need to scare the poor girl.' Tommy put the pie carefully on a shelf. 'Want me to walk back with you?'

Tolly had now regained her poise and pushed away her disappointment at not seeing Sonny. 'It's only next door,' she said.

Stevo chipped in: 'Has Izzy looked in the bag I sent over?'

'If she has, she's said nothing yet to me of what she's found.' Tolly turned to walk up the steps. 'I'll say goodnight.'

Out in the night air she took a deep breath and

began the short walk back to *Mallard* and *Bunting*. Only she didn't stop at the moored boats. She was telling herself Sonny had every right to go out with whoever he chose. Even so, it had been a blow to her that he hadn't come back to *Aurora* with the other two. She took another deep breath, then let the air out slowly.

A short walk along the towpath would clear her head.

There was no reason that Sonny should think of her in a romantic way, she tried to tell herself.

Yes, a walk would make her feel better.

After all, if Izzy was back in *Bunting* now, there was no way Tolly could stand listening to her happy chatter. She had to admit she felt hurt.

Why? Surely Tolly had made apple pies for everyone. No, the truth was Tolly had baked a pie especially for Sonny. The other pies had been an afterthought: she had made them to use up the apples and sugar, and she knew the girls would appreciate them. She wanted Sonny to look her in the eyes and say thank you and know she'd made it just for him.

Why didn't Sonny want her? He must know how she felt about him. She looked just as pretty as some of the girls she knew he'd been with. She'd lost weight and looked better for it – hadn't Tommy told her so?

She'd thought she could make him notice her by cooking for him. But it had all backfired, hadn't it?

Tolly stepped around a puddle left from the last rain. She didn't want to walk too far along the towpath in the dark. Through the gloom, the shape of the lock loomed ahead. Turning back, she heard a rustle in the undergrowth. Then a giggle. A man's voice, coaxing, gentle. Tolly recognized that voice. It was Sonny's.

She moved quickly, not bothering that the tears in her eyes were obscuring her vision, and ran back along the gravelled path towards the moored boats.

## Chapter Twenty-five

'No!' Dorothy exclaimed. 'This is the right way to do it.' She pulled the hooked tool through the canvas, dragging the piece of cut flowered material with it, Izzy watching her carefully.

'I can do that!' Izzy yelled, once the tool and material were back in her hands. Dorothy watched for a few seconds. Then she leaned across and slipped another log into *Mallard's* stove. The scent of pine was filling the cabin.

'Didn't take you long to get the hang of that, did it? You're fairly ripping along the lines now. Good for you.' Dorothy smiled at Izzy. Her red hair curled around her face and her determination showed as she methodically pulled piece after piece of cut cloth through the holes in the sacking, making the rug grow.

'Wasn't it kind of Stevo to give this to me? Sarah started it,' she said, then went on, without waiting for Dorothy to reply, 'I really like doing it. It's kind of soothing as well as being productive.'

'Yes, well, you can't sit in here all day making a rag rug. There's locks outside that need opening and work to do on board and bridges that need lifting...'

'Yeah, yeah,' chanted Izzy. Rug-making had taken her mind off the very real possibility that Charlie was looking for her. Dorothy blessed Stevo.

'Anyway, I need to ask whether you've decided to join me in a second trip?'

'We haven't finished this one yet!'

'I need to know because at the office they'll be sifting through new enquiries from other women. If I've a full quota they won't need me to take on newcomers and we can stay together.'

'In that case, count me in.' She looked at Dorothy. 'In fact, I don't know when I've ever felt so happy, even if it is hard work.'

Dorothy said a silent prayer of relief but to Izzy she said, 'Thank you.'

She'd already asked Tolly, who'd agreed to stay on. Her only worry was Elsie who, from the time she woke until the time she went to bed, spoke about Jack and what she was going to do at the cottage when her tour of work finished.

Izzy seemed to read her thoughts, for she said, 'Elsie is so lucky to have found someone who obviously adores her, isn't she?'

Dorothy thought of the letter she kept beneath her pillow. She lived in fear of one of the girls finding it but she needed it with her because it was all she had left of Jakub. She answered Izzy's question with a smile. 'Elsie deserves to be loved.'

Since Dorothy had invited Izzy to stay with her

184

in Southampton at her mother's house she should probably tell the younger girl about herself, but it was easier to put things off. The weeks they'd all worked together on the cut had made the women firm friends. It was only Dorothy who couldn't share her feelings so easily and openly.

How would her three friends feel if they knew what she'd done? If they knew the lie she was living? She wished she'd never offered Izzy a few days' break at her home, but she couldn't allow her to go back to Gosport where it was more than possible her ex-boyfriend Charlie might find her and hurt her again.

She thought of little Alfie. Into everything, he was. Slow to walk and talk but that, she thought, was a blessing in disguise at present. She wondered if she'd be able to find something suitable as a present for him. There were hardly any toys in the shops now. Near the tunnel ahead there was a shop that sold all sorts of domestic and canal paraphernalia. She'd seen toy cars in there, wooden ones made by a local wood carver. Perhaps they might have something suitable for a small boy.

She wondered, too, if she dared ask Tolly to make a cake for Alfie. Tolly was never happier than when she was baking and they had plenty of sugar still from the spillage at Limehouse, even though they'd given some to Stevo.

Dorothy sighed. If she asked Tolly to make a cake, she would have to lie when she said who it was for. It was best she said nothing.

'I'm sorry but I really need to lie down for a while.' The disembodied voice floated down into the cabin.

Izzy blew out her cheeks and put her rug-making to one side. 'I'd better go and relieve Elsie at the tiller. She was very pale this morning.'

When Izzy had taken over, Elsie was most apologetic. 'I'm sorry, Dorothy, but I feel really rough.'

Dorothy put down the paperwork she was trying to sort through and pulled out the bunk bed. Elsie looked like a ghost. 'I hope what you've got isn't catching,' she said. 'Get in your sleeping-bag and try to rest. Do you want a cup of tea?' She looked at Elsie worriedly.

'Oh, no, that's the last thing I need.' Elsie practically collapsed on her bunk. 'I just feel so peculiar. I mean, I loved that apple pie Tolly made but in the morning I brought it all up. You don't think there was something wrong with it, do you?'

'I wasn't ill, and neither was Izzy. And when I had a word with the old man he was full of praise for Tolly's baking. So was Tommy. I reckon you're having a bilious attack. Will you be all right if I leave you on your own and take over the steering of *Bunting*? I think Tolly could do with a break.'

Dorothy looked at Elsie whose eyes were closed. She didn't reply so Dorothy went up top, closing the door to keep the heat in the cabin.

'Slow down,' she said to Izzy. 'Let *Bunting* nudge up against us at the rear and I'll be able to change places with Tolly. She can come and annoy you. I'd rather be on my own. I'm fed up with her moaning about Sonny. Trouble is, it's all in her head. To the best of my knowledge Sonny's never made a move on her so she's got no reason to think she could be his next fancy woman.'

Izzy stepped aside so Dorothy could handle the

tiller. 'She kept me awake,' she said, 'with her snivelling because he was in the bushes with some young woman from the Lock Inn.'

Dorothy relented. 'Tolly hasn't had much experience with men.'

'Meaning you've had plenty yourself?'

Dorothy knew Izzy didn't mean to hurt her with words that were hastily said. She turned away, looking across at the fields and trees without really seeing them. Tears rose to her eyes and she blinked them away.

She was going to have to let Izzy into her secret. Would Izzy still have respect for her when she knew the truth?

At her initial meeting with both Izzy and Elsie, Dorothy had known the two women could keep secrets. Mentally she crossed her fingers. Her job could be at stake here. 'Actually, I do know about men and losing the man you love...'

Izzy was staring at her wide-eyed, but before either of them could say another word, the sound of Elsie being sick interrupted them. Dorothy sighed. 'Look after the boat. I'll see to Elsie.'

The smell of vomit assailed her as she went down into the cabin. Elsie was sitting up in her bunk, mortified.

'I'm so sorry. I didn't mean to...' The words mixed with her tears.

Dorothy fetched a bowl and shoved it at her. 'Aim for that next time,' she said tartly. She poured water onto an old piece of cloth and began mopping up the stinking mess on the floor. Elsie was crying hard now. She tried to get up.

'Stay there!' warned Dorothy. She'd thrown the

187

dirty cloth overboard and dunked the floor mop into the canal. She sprinkled San Izal disinfectant liberally and began scrubbing the floorboards. When she was satisfied everything was sanitary, she rinsed the mop in the cut, then hoisted it onto the outside roof of the cabin, its usual resting place, to dry out.

'Is she all right?' Izzy said.

'Well, I'm certain what she's suffering from won't kill her,' Dorothy said, ducking back into the cabin, this time leaving the door open.

'The heat from the stove will soon dry everything out,' she said to Elsie. 'Tell me when you first began to feel sick.' Her voice was soothing now.

'Yesterday morning,' answered Elsie, 'but it went away and then I felt fine. It came back this morning.'

Dorothy sat down on the edge of Elsie's bunk. She picked up one of Elsie's hands and held it tightly. She looked into her eyes and said, 'I may be mistaken but it rather sounds as if you may be pregnant.'

Elsie said, 'I can't be. I only went to bed with Jack that once in Oxford. Geoffrey and I have tried all our married life for a baby. We always thought it was my fault I couldn't conceive...' Elsie stopped babbling. A look of wonderment crossed her face.

Dorothy said, 'But it wasn't Geoffrey you were sleeping with in a hotel in Oxford, was it?'

## Chapter Twenty-six

'Haven't you finished reading that blessed book to the old man, yet?'

'*The Man in the Iron Mask* is a good story, but Stevo usually falls asleep after a few pages. He loses concentration easily.'

'Perhaps it's your boring voice.'

Izzy threw a spoon at Tolly.

'Ouch!' she yelled.

'C'mon, children, play nicely,' Dorothy remonstrated. 'Whatever would Elsie think if she knew you two were squabbling like kids?'

'She'd think it was normal,' said Tolly. 'After all, we're waiting around doing very little so Jack can take her into Lower Heyford to see that doctor she liked...' Tolly tailed off while she tried to remember. 'Dr Wells, yes, that's his name.'

'I've never seen a man so happy that he might become a dad,' said Izzy. 'Though Elsie can't quite believe it's true.'

Well wrapped up against a chill wind, the girls were sitting at the rear of *Mallard*, glad that the rain had stopped and a weak sun had broken through.

'Of course not, after ten years of trying for a baby and nothing happening. You'd not think it was possible either. When Elsie started being sick that was only part of it. Her breasts hurt and she said she felt tired all the time.' Dorothy paused.

'Those symptoms are a giveaway. I'm so happy for her...' She sounded as though she was remembering something. Then she snapped back into leader mode: 'We won't go through Blisworth Tunnel until Elsie's back. It's easier this side of the tunnel for Jack to find us.'

'We're all keeping our fingers crossed that she's pregnant, but won't this hanging about mess up your calculations for how long this round trip should take?' Izzy asked Dorothy.

'As long as the loads get to Birmingham, we do have some leeway.' Dorothy sighed. 'Of course it means that Jack will want to take care of her and straight away move her into the lock cottage.'

'She won't do that,' Izzy broke in.

'Is there something you're not telling me?' Dorothy knew Elsie was especially close to Izzy and of course the two would share secrets because they'd known each other long before they became narrowboat women.

'She won't mind me telling you,' Izzy answered. Dorothy and Tolly stared at her expectantly. 'Of course Jack will want her to move in with him but it mightn't be for a while. As you know, her husband is selling their house and a flat in Alverstoke that he bought for the woman he's now living with, who has moved into Elsie's house with him.'

There were murmurs of disgust from Dorothy and Tolly.

'Elsie thinks her husband might drag things out if he finds out about Jack and especially about the baby.' Izzy frowned. 'She told me she would sign on with you, Dorothy, for another trip.'

Dorothy was smiling and couldn't stop herself

saying, 'Oh, damned good show!'

'Well, Elsie reckons having a baby is a natural function, and during the first half of her pregnancy there's no reason why she shouldn't work.'

'I hope she asks the doctor and gets the go-ahead on that,' put in Tolly.

'I'm sure she will,' Izzy said. 'It's one of the questions on her list.

'You see, if she moves in with Jack immediately she's worried her husband won't keep his promise to give her half the money from the sale of the house. She said Jack wouldn't care about the money, he'd take her with the clothes on her back, but she thinks she deserves to get what she's owed. Geoffrey was at fault for making his girlfriend pregnant.'

'Then he should pay her!' shouted Tolly.

'All Elsie wants is time to sort out her life with Jack and to have what Geoffrey promised. She really loved him and her home. Of course, that's in the past now,' she added. 'What she's worried about is whether the doctor will say it's fine for her to stay on with us for a while.'

'Yes, but if Dr Wells says–'

Izzy interrupted: 'Elsie and I chatted about her work on the narrowboats, how excited she is about the baby and how her love for Jack is very different from her feelings, in the past, for Geoffrey. Geoffrey cares about Geoffrey, Jack loves Elsie, and it's about time she had some happiness. Ultimately you two will be told of her decisions, but I know she won't mind me sharing all this with you.'

'I'm pleased you have,' said Dorothy. 'I'm more than happy to have you all for a second trip. We have to unload this cargo and pick up another, coal this time from Birmingham to Banbury, then get back to Lower Heyford.'

Before anyone had time to say what they thought, a boat's horn sounded.

Dorothy looked back the way they'd already travelled and was surprised to see *Aurora* and her butty-boat sailing along the cut.

'I thought they were ahead of us,' said Izzy. Again the horn sounded.

'I don't think he's hailing us for the fun of it – I think something's wrong,' said Dorothy.

'We'll soon find out. He'll be here in a moment,' Tolly said.

When the boats drew level, Sonny was at *Aurora's* tiller, his face like granite. Tommy allowed the butty to drift against *Aurora* and jumped aboard *Mallard*. He looked tired and drawn.

'The old man took a turn for the worse last night.'

Izzy said quickly, 'Have you called a doctor out to him?'

Tommy looked at her glumly. 'No point in calling out doctors when we all know the end is near.'

'What do you mean?' asked Dorothy.

'He's been livin' on borrowed time for ages. But he coughed up a heap of blood in the night. We need to get to Braunston – he's got family there and memories.'

'Is he conscious?' Dorothy again.

'Yes.' Tommy nodded.

'He should be in a hospital,' Tolly said sharply.

'Us boat gypsies don't have no time for

hospitals. We takes care of our own.'

'So who's with him now?' Izzy was frantic.

'He's asleep.'

Izzy looked to Dorothy for confirmation. She nodded. 'Tolly can steer *Bunting*, I'll take this boat and you two can steer your own craft. Izzy, get on *Aurora* and see what you can do to help.'

Izzy threw Dorothy a grateful look, then asked, 'Will Elsie find us?'

'For God's sake, woman, if a grown man and woman can't spot four narrowboats going slowly along a canal there must be something very wrong with their eyesight. Take what you need from here and get on *Aurora*.'

'Thanks, missus,' Tommy managed. 'Me and Sonny was hoping you'd let Izzy come aboard. The old man likes her and he needs someone with him while we carries on to Braunston.'

Dorothy looked over to Sonny whose face was impassive. He hadn't said a word. But he raised a hand in greeting.

'Don't take no notice of him. He worships that old man and can't find a way to put his feelings into words.'

Dorothy sniffed. 'I know a lot of people like that,' she said softly. 'Let's get going, girls.'

After bathing Stevo's face and forehead, Izzy read to him while he lay in his bunk on board *Aurora*. It didn't matter that he slept and might not hear her voice.

The old man's heavy breathing filled the small living space. Izzy made tea and took mugs to Tommy and Sonny. Sonny had upped the speed of the boat to press on quickly to Braunston.

A few short weeks ago Izzy had never dreamed she'd be clambering over boats while they moved along the canal. Or that she'd be breaking her heart because she knew she was about to lose someone she had grown very fond of. Izzy directed her words at Sonny: 'You want to go to him? Tommy and I can manage the boats.' He looked at her gratefully.

Sonny stayed in the cabin with his grandfather for a long while. He came up the steps as the sky was darkening. 'I don't think we'll make Braunston tonight,' he said. 'We can't travel with the lights on because of the blackout. It's his brother, Sol, he wants to see. They had a meeting at the Lock Inn. Sol had come up by car.'

Izzy remembered she'd been introduced to an old man with salt-and-pepper hair in the pub. She also remembered that had been the night Tolly had become upset because Sonny had gone off with the girl. She kept that to herself. 'Should I go and sit with him again?'

Sonny's eyes softened. 'Did he tell you my grandmother Sarah used to read to him?'

'Many times,' said Izzy. She put her hand to her mouth. 'Oh, I meant to tell him I'd mastered rug-making with Dorothy's help. Stevo gave me some stuff that used to belong to Sarah.'

Sonny smiled at her. 'You remind him of her,' he said. He looked into the gunmetal sky. 'I'm tying up in a bit,' he added.

'I'm sure Dorothy will want to stop for the night, as well,' said Izzy. 'Before you tie up I'll sit a while longer with Stevo.' She didn't wait for a reply but went back down into the cabin and the tiny stool near the bunk.

She picked up the old man's hand, the skin like parchment. 'You're the only man I've ever been able to talk to and not be afraid of,' she whispered.

The terrible long-drawn-out breaths continued. She couldn't bear it, the waiting until another breath started, but hated even more the thought that another wouldn't come.

His mouth had fallen open. She used her other hand to brush back the thin hair from his forehead. Once, she surmised, he had been every bit as good-looking as Sonny. The life he'd lived had left its mark. Sarah had been a lucky woman to be loved by this man, Izzy thought.

Each time a breath was wrung from him she thought it might be his last. Izzy laid her head on his cold hand.

'I'll take over now.'

She hadn't noticed or heard Sonny enter the cabin. He put his hand on her shoulder. Izzy had been so deep in thought she'd not felt *Aurora* rock as the two men had tied the boats together and moored for the night.

Without a word, Izzy got up and Sonny took her place. It was time to return to her own boat.

As she stepped onto the towpath Tommy called goodnight but she didn't reply.

None of the girls felt like cooking a meal so that evening they had cocoa and chunks of bread and jam.

It was three in the morning when Dorothy woke Izzy from a fitful sleep. She had bunked in with her, taking Elsie's sleeping-bag. The gentle knock on the cabin door had woken her. Tommy, his face grey, his eyes red, told them, 'He's gone.'

Izzy said, 'I'll go and see Sonny.' She began pulling a jumper over her pyjamas.

Tommy stilled her. 'He don't want no one, not even me. He'll sit with Stevo till morning. Sonny's in a bad way. Best we leave him. It's what we do.'

Tears poured down Izzy's face.

### Chapter Twenty-seven

Elsie returned to a subdued crew. Jack and she were ecstatic because the doctor had confirmed her pregnancy. She had persuaded Jack that she would stay with Dorothy for at least another trip or until she had had favourable news from Geoffrey on the sale of her beloved house.

'When we reach Stoke Bruerne we can pick up any post that's been forwarded for us,' said Dorothy.

Tolly's sister Reggie wrote often with news of what went on in Titchfield. Dorothy received only missives from the Grand Union Canal Company. Izzy sometimes had letters from her mother, but Charlie's name was never mentioned.

Sonny visited *Mallard* and *Bunting* as soon as it was light. He had brought with him *The Man in the Iron Mask*. 'First I need to thank you, Dorothy, for your kindness,' he said. 'I've washed and laid out my grandfather and soon he'll be laid to rest with Sarah. Stevo would want Izzy to have this. I hope you'll allow Izzy to stop awhile in Braunston. Boatmen's marriages and funerals are held there. You'll be sailing through anyway, and my grandfather has left her something besides this book. Stevo's brother will meet us there to hand it over. Ten in the morning, the Green Man. I can't ask you to stay for the funeral as by the time we've notified relatives and arranged everything you'll have overshot your deadline for the company.' He paused. 'Anyway, it wouldn't be fitting. We're not your kind of people.'

The gypsies did things their own way.

Dorothy looked into his finely chiselled face, his red curls hovering on his forehead, brown eyes red-rimmed, and she knew that the death of his grandfather had hit him hard. 'I'm sure Izzy will agree. I'll talk to her later.' She didn't want to wake Izzy for she'd cried herself to sleep in Elsie's sleeping-bag.

He nodded towards the book. 'It meant a lot to my granddad that she sat with him.'

Dorothy said, 'I often wondered why you didn't read to him. Or that he didn't finish it himself.'

He stared at her. 'Stevo never learned to read. Nor did I.'

Dorothy allowed his confession to wash over her. 'But I've watched you in pubs chalking figures and numbers on the scoreboards.'

He shook his head, 'Doesn't mean a thing. I got a quick brain, and you don't need to know how to read to add up scores.'

'But place names, notices along the cut?'

'Bless you, us gypsies have been brought up on the water and we know it like the back of our

197

hands. No need to read stuff that don't bother us.'

'You've never enjoyed a novel, then?'

He shook his head and his glistening curls bounced. 'Why would I need to read about made-up stuff? Real life is so much better.'

'But Stevo appreciated Izzy reading to him?'

He smiled, showing his strong white teeth. 'She reminded him of Sarah. My grandma could read and write, and she often shared whatever she was reading.'

Dorothy had the feeling that their conversation was at an end. After all there was nothing more for her to say, and Sonny was moving from one foot to the other, obviously wanting to leave. 'Will you ask Izzy?' he said.

Dorothy nodded. 'Of course I will, and she'll be there.'


Tunnels and locks came and went, flights of locks that climbed hills and tunnels so long it was eerie going through them even with the lights on.

The four boats sailed within shouting distance of each other.

Sometimes, when they stopped, Tommy boarded *Mallard* and told them tales of the ghosts of navvies killed when the tunnels were being excavated. He talked of the men who lay on their backs on top of the narrowboats and walked the craft through the tunnels to save the boaters from treading through the canal muck when there was no room alongside for the horses to pull the craft. Legging, he called it.

Dorothy noticed the girls were more than tired. The round of hard work and daily boating chores were taking their toll. That, and Stevo's death.

Braunston was a canal village. Boat builders, woodworkers, canopy makers, hull blackers, rope and fender merchants, all types of trade were plied there and it was a hub of activity.

*Aurora* and her butty went in ahead of *Mallard* and *Bunting*. Tommy had told Dorothy that Sonny would need a death certificate and there would be lots of paperwork to attend to so that Stevo could be laid to rest after a good send-off.

'I wasn't born on the cut. I had schooling,' he said. 'I'll help sort everything.'

Dorothy and the girls watched the two boats containing their sad cargo move into a disused arm.

'Look at the crowd of people waiting to meet them,' said Tolly. 'The news must have got about somehow.'

It had begun to rain again.

After mooring just outside the village and eating a pot of stew, not one of the girls felt like going out but Izzy had a scrub down in soapy water in the cabin. At least tomorrow she would be clean. Her clothes weren't up to much: most had shrunk or become misshapen since she'd been living on the canals but she sorted out the best of them, intending to look as decent as possible to meet Stevo's brother.

Izzy tossed and turned all night in her own bunk on *Bunting*. What could Stevo's brother want with her? Tolly had been extremely quiet. She'd attended to her chores aboard the boat but there seemed to be an unspoken barrier between her and Izzy.

Izzy, well aware of Tolly's unrequited passion for Sonny, wondered if jealousy was at the bottom of it. It had been Izzy Sonny had asked to come aboard to sit with Stevo.

Eventually morning came, and after breakfast, Dorothy and Izzy walked back along the towpath to Braunston, to the cobbled square and the Green Man. During the night the rain had stopped and now a weak sun pushed through the clouds. Everything smelt fresh and new.

A pony and trap stood outside the pub with no driver. The piebald had a nosebag and was munching happily. Izzy patted it but Dorothy gave it a wide berth.

'You'd better look inside the pub. At least you can remember what Sol looks like, which is more than I can,' Dorothy said.

'Ah, on time I see. I like that.' A small man, whom Izzy recognized as Sol, thanks to his resemblance to Stevo, was emerging from the wide wooden doors of the pub. He went to the trap and unclipped a step at the side. 'Easier for you both to climb up,' he said, smiling. He ushered them into the open interior where Dorothy and Izzy sat opposite one another on padded wooden seating.

'I'm sorry about your brother,' Izzy said. Sol had climbed up into the driving seat after unhooking the pony's nosebag and setting it aside.

'It was to be expected,' said the man. 'Call me Sol. May I call you Izzy?' She nodded. 'And you must be Dorothy. Are you both comfortable enough?'

He didn't wait for a reply but shook the reins

and the pony began clip-clopping over the cobbles.

Izzy stole a look at Dorothy, who smiled back at her.

The pony pulled the trap through the busy village, then alongside the canal. 'I couldn't ask you to meet me at our destination,' Sol said. 'It's difficult to find unless you're from these parts. Sarah liked the peace and quiet, you see.'

'I don't understand,' began Izzy.

'You don't have to, girly. Stevo told me it was the very home for you.'

At the word 'home', Izzy stared hard at Dorothy, who, she could see, was just as puzzled. She looked through the trees at the ribbon of canal that sparkled, now the sun was trying to cheer it up. Late autumn fruits grew on the bushes in the lane, which was barely more than a track. Trees met overhead and the little trap was bouncing along beneath a canopy of branches.

Sol stopped the pony, with a click of his tongue, in a clearing. After climbing down he came around and reset the step so they could alight onto the grass. He helped them both down. He was dressed in the traditional boatman's garb of corduroy trousers, open-necked shirt and braces.

'Off you go.' He pointed through the trees at an overgrown path and Izzy stared at him. 'It's best you see her first.' He chuckled. 'Stevo would have liked to watch your face the first time you set eyes on her.' Izzy set off, full of curiosity, with Sol and Dorothy following.

The grassy path led down to the cut. Alongside the towpath and backing into trees was a small fenced garden. Part of it was overgrown but it was easy to see someone had had a go at cutting the grass. A water tap was set in concrete. A washing line was hanging lengthways.

A narrowboat was tied to mooring stakes buried in the towpath. It was quite short, barely forty foot long. Izzy could see it wasn't like an ordinary narrowboat. The canvas cover had been done away with and a wooden roof made the boat totally enclosed, except for the back where the tiller rose, like a long-necked swan. The shiny black paint-work was covered with bright traditional paintings of castles and roses. Izzy drew in her breath. The boat's name, *Jonquil*, was adorned with tiny roses.

'What a pretty little thing!' Izzy cried.

'See that brass chimney? Put your hand just inside the top and you'll find the key.' Sol ambled over to stand beside the women.

Izzy scrambled along the side rail and climbed onto the roof. She waved the key in the air. 'Got it!' she cried.

'Whose boat is this?' Dorothy asked.

'It was Sarah's. But Stevo has left it to Izzy.'

'What?' Dorothy was shaken. 'Surely he can't do that.'

'Don't see why not. He's been looking after its upkeep all these years. She's been out of the water and she's had her bottom recaulked. Lovely and dry inside, she is.'

Izzy was sliding down to the door.

She inserted the key in the lock. The door had a tiny stained-glass window. Then she was inside the boat, and looking around her in amazement. It was nothing like the freight craft she and the others were living on. She stood gazing at the stove in the corner of what was obviously the main living area. There was a comfortable sofa and a shelf full of books, and as she walked over the colourful rag rugs strewn about the varnished boards she saw a separate area, which was given over to a small stone sink and a tap. Shelves and cupboards formed this space into a sort of kitchen. Everything was clean and tidy – in fact, it looked as if the owner had just popped out for a moment. She could smell dried flowers. Looking about, she saw dishes of pot-pourri placed on shelves.

As she went past the sink she kicked against a small, raised, oval rubber protuberance set into the floor. She stepped on it and there was a sort of sucking noise. Izzy turned on the tap and water fell into the sink. It took Izzy a few moments to realize that the rubber oval 'flushed' the sink and emptied it. There must be a re-fillable water tank somewhere hidden from view, she thought. Excitement rose in her. Sarah had obviously decided she would not use buckets!

Pushing open another narrow door, she walked into a bedroom. Not with hidden bunks but a real wooden bed! It wasn't made up but a folded pile of blankets was topped by a patchwork quilt. There was even a mirror screwed to the wall. And a chest of drawers.

Izzy heard voices and turned to see Sol and Dorothy in the living area.

'This is so lovely, Sol, a proper home.'

Sol began to laugh. 'It's yours now, love.'

Izzy was sure she'd misheard him, but Sol was

203

still talking. 'The little Lister engine has been looked after an' all. Stevo wanted you to have this boat. He said you was so much like Sarah you'd appreciate it. You can go where you wants, whenever you wants. He never did get round to clearing out her work stuff. There's still rugs and bits and bobs she'd make to hawk from place to place lying around in here. He thought maybe you'd make some use of them, too.'

Izzy was dumbfounded. 'I can't possibly...'

'Oh, yes, you can. It was what he wanted.'

'But doesn't Sonny have any say in the matter?'

'Ain't Sonny's boat. It was Sarah's. Besides, Sonny's now got *Aurora*, her butty, and four other boats and crews as well. He's only too pleased to have this one off his hands so he won't have to spend out on it to keep it up to scratch.'

Izzy moved quickly towards Sol and enfolded him in her arms. 'You don't know what this means to me,' she said. He smelt of pipe tobacco and peppermints.

'Don't make no mind what I thinks,' he said. 'Stevo knew you better than you knows yourself.'

Dorothy had tears in her eyes but Izzy was crying so much with happiness she couldn't hear the rest of his words.

## Chapter Twenty-eight

Geoffrey approached the back of the house in Western Way. A puncture on the way to work had meant he'd had to contact the garage, who'd promised to collect his car from Foster Gardens, change the wheel, repair the tyre and return it in the morning.

'Can't it be done any sooner?' he'd asked.

'No,' had been the mechanic's flat reply. He had then quoted Geoffrey what seemed to him an exorbitant price for the repair and collection of his vehicle. Geoffrey had slammed down the office telephone and, not feeling in the mood for clients, had consequently caught a bus home earlier than usual, getting off at Alverstoke and walking the rest of the way. He'd left his car keys for the mechanic and forgotten to remove his house keys from the keyring.

A chill autumn wind bit into his cheeks as he strode along, kicking angrily at the brown and yellow leaves now lying on the pavement.

He intended to write a letter, care of the address Elsie had given him, telling her he now had money to send to her as her share of the Western Way home. Not that he had managed to find a buyer for it yet, but he had been lucky enough to sell the flat in The Crescent. The money for that dwelling would equal Elsie's share in the marital home. He thought she would appreciate a handwritten letter, rather than a typed missive from his secretary.

The bicycle looked new. It was propped against the wall near the front door and, as he inched around it, he wondered who it belonged to.

Something told him not to barge into the house. He wanted to know if the bike's owner was inside. Most of his friends owned cars. They would have no need to call on him during the day, knowing the hours he worked.

He shut his eyes to the desecration of the garden. Sandra had had so many plans to change the layout and had engaged various people to cut down bushes and cement over flower plots. Alas, her plans hadn't matured to fruition.

Not that he'd protested: he wanted Sandra to be happy, and content with the house for as long as they lived there. He'd also thought any garden renovation would add profit to the place. Now he realized what a shambles it had become in the short months Elsie had been gone.

He was glad he had the money in his account to pay off his wife. He would hate her to come back to Gosport and see her beloved garden in this state.

Last night there had been an air raid on Portsmouth and unhappily Gosport had suffered. Piles of locally made red bricks had lined the streets this morning. The smell of cordite hung in the air. Keast's, a shop not far from his office, was now rubble. It looked as if a bomb had also descended on his garden.

He heard Sandra laugh as his hand twisted the new handle on the unlocked back door. He stepped inside. The laugh had come from the living room. He could now hear faint music from the wireless. In the sink the breakfast dishes were piled up and the tap dripped over encrusted fat.

Quietly he moved towards the open living-room door and peeped inside.

Sandra half lay, half sat on the brocade sofa. She was still in her nightwear. A satin dressing-gown, the same creamy colour as her nightdress, was hiked up above her plump hips showing the roundness of her pregnancy and the hand of the dark-haired man who was fondling her private parts.

Geoffrey wanted to rush into the room and hit out at the unknown man, but he couldn't move as Sandra murmured contentedly, then squeezed her legs together, trapping the hand while she leaned into the man and kissed his well-shaped mouth.

Geoffrey, his heart beating so fast and loudly that he thought the pair would hear it, felt sickened. Last night when he had suggested to Sandra in bed that they had sex she had complained that she felt unwell. She didn't seem to be unwell now.

He stepped back and retraced his steps into the garden. He knew he wouldn't be seen as his garden led down to Stanley Park and wasn't overlooked. He unlocked the small gate that led into the park and allowed the autumn colours to swallow him.

He walked blindly, without caring where his steps led him. He made no sound as the tears rolled down his cheeks. All he could think of was that he had stupidly squandered everything he had ever wanted and worked for.

'You're not cross that Dorothy came with me instead of you?'

Izzy looked into Elsie's face to make sure she really wasn't upset and was relieved when Elsie gave her a hug. The white tea-towel waved in the air like a flag. They were washing up after corned-beef hash and peas.

'If I'd come I'd have wanted you to take me for a trip down the cut in your boat. Imagine how cross Dorothy would have been about that. We're behind time as it is, so she says.'

'I don't know that I'd dare up moorings and just take off...'

'But that's exactly why Stevo left *Jonquil* to you, so you'd do just that! It's what Sarah did. Besides, after being on *Mallard* and *Bunting*, there's not much you don't know about narrowboats, is there?'

'I suppose not,' Izzy said wistfully. 'If you're going to live with Jack in his cottage, will I be able to come over and see you three?' She meant Jack, Elsie and the baby, but Elsie quickly said, 'Four.'

Izzy knew she looked confused.

'Matey, the dog. He's a proper little character. You should get a dog. It would be company for you when you venture off in *Jonquil*. Do you know how excited I am about the baby? I've got you to thank for my happiness. If you hadn't torn out that advertisement for this job from the newspaper, I'd never have met Jack.'

Elsie put down a dried saucepan. Again she hugged Izzy. 'You must feel happy, knowing horrible Charlie can never find you?'

'That's true,' Izzy said. 'You won't think I'm silly if I tell you what I've been thinking about doing after I finish the second trip with Dorothy?'

'Of course not. Why ever would I think that of you?'

'I found lots of unfinished work on *Jonquil*. There's all kinds of stuff – tapestry, ready cut material, sacking for the backs of rugs, pins and needles, embroidery silks and iron-on patterns. It's all put away in cupboards and drawers. It seems Stevo had had the boat cleared of her personal effects but left her work materials. I liked having a go at finishing the rug Stevo gave me and I'd have finished it by now if I'd had the time. When he told me that Sarah used to go from village to village on the cut selling her wares, I wondered if I might have a go at that myself.' She paused and before Elsie could answer said, 'I dunno about getting a dog. It might be nice to have a cat, though.'

'That's a brilliant idea. All of it's a brilliant idea! Is that why you said you might see more of me when I live with Jack?'

Izzy blushed. 'You probably think I'm being silly. I can understand why you love Jack and want a family, but it's not for me. I want to explore, see a bit of England's countryside, and if I can earn my living at the same time, all well and good.'

'I'm sure you'll make a success of whatever you do.' Elsie hung the wet tea-towels to dry over the wooden clothes horse propped near the stove. 'I only wish I could talk a bit of sense into Tolly. She's asked me if I'd walk back with her to Braunston tonight. Don't look like that, I know it's

209

a fair distance.'

'That girl!' Izzy sighed. 'She's like a dog with a bone when she gets an idea in her head. I suppose she wants to run after Sonny?'

'She wants to go to the do they're having to celebrate Stevo's life in the Green Man.'

'But we're not invited! We're not gypsies!'

'I tried to tell her that but she thinks everything's changed now that Sonny has control of all those boats. She's heard he might marry ... and I'm scared she'll do something silly, like, like...' Elsie fizzled out.

'Offer herself up on a plate?'

'Exactly!'

There was silence in the cabin.

'She must know the water gypsies only wed their own,' said Elsie, eventually.

'If you try telling her that she won't listen. Apparently if they marry outside the clan it can bring all sorts of trouble. Are you going to walk back to Braunston with her?'

'Am I heck!' said Elsie. 'I'm pregnant, not stupid!'

'Does Dorothy know about this?'

Elsie shook her head. 'No, but if she did, she'd worry.' She smiled. 'But I have thought of a way we might be able to stop Tolly getting hurt.'

'How?'

'It involves Tommy.'

'Tommy?'

'Yes. Haven't you noticed the way they're always bickering? Him and Tolly?'

'What's that got to do with it?'

'I've seen the way he stares at her. In all the best

romantic novels the hero and heroine are always the last to know they're in love because of all their arguing.'

'I think that baby's sent you doolally,' said Izzy.

'If you say so, but at least help me keep Tolly safe? Which she won't be after she's thrown herself at Sonny and he's drunk himself silly with grief and doesn't care who he sleeps with. If you can get off the boat and go back to Braunston before she arrives there, this plan could work.'

Izzy stared at her. 'It had better be a damn good plan, then.'

## Chapter Twenty-nine

'I don't know why I let Elsie talk me into this,' grumbled Izzy. She was running along the towpath. Dorothy seldom moored up until the last vestiges of light had gone from the day, and kept strictly to blackout regulations. Izzy nearly stumbled in the darkness but managed to right herself. She swore as she rubbed at her twisted knee.

She'd left Elsie to explain her disappearance to Dorothy and guessed Tolly would take a while dolling herself up to look good for Sonny. Tolly had begged Elsie to let her borrow the print skirt she'd brought with her that had lain unworn in her holdall. It fitted her as if it had been made for her.

Eating simply but well, the hard work and fresh

air had transformed Tolly. No longer plump and awkward, her hair was glossy, her cheeks pink.

Izzy hated the dark. She could almost see well enough to keep to the towpath and had brought a small torch but hoped to conserve its failing battery. Her biggest fear was that she'd be unable to find Tommy in Braunston.

She'd seen how he looked at Tolly. Elsie was right: if there was one person who could help them stop the girl making a complete fool of herself it was him.

Again Izzy stumbled. She had to stop to catch her breath. She wasn't sure if she was actually still going in the right direction but decided that the towpath, though overgrown in places, should eventually take her back to the village.

Her mind drifted to *Jonquil*, her boat. She felt a surge of excitement. She need never go back to Gosport at all now, except to visit her mother. On *Jonquil* she would be safe, thanks to Stevo.

Dorothy had asked her if she would prefer to spend their well-deserved break living on her own craft, but Izzy was grieving for Stevo and had already said, if Dorothy didn't mind, she'd sooner be with her than on her own, wallowing in sadness.

Was Dorothy trying to discourage her from visiting Southampton?

She had the feeling Dorothy regretted inviting her to her home.

No, that wasn't possible, she thought. It had been Dorothy's idea.

Izzy had a stitch from running and she was sweaty with the exertion. Again she stopped to catch her breath. The clean sweet night air was tainted with woodsmoke. She couldn't be far from Braunston, surely.

She breathed a sigh of relief that, even if Tolly was now on the towpath, she was behind her, giving Izzy more precious time to find Tommy. But where to look?

The towpath merged into the square.

The Green Man was busy, music flowing from its darkened windows and door. She wished she'd brought a scarf to cover her bright hair. Izzy waited impatiently for someone to come out of the large main door. She didn't think she would be welcome if she walked straight in. She knew she wouldn't have long to wait as people were going in and out all the time.

A man now stood in the doorway, his hand ready to push open the door. Izzy, not wanting anyone to recognize her, swiftly crept inside after him and positioned herself in a darkened corner, her eyes searching through the cigarette smoke for Tommy.

Satisfied he wasn't there, she left and walked back towards the cut and began looking for *Aurora*. She discovered the boat had been moved from the deserted arm and moored nearby. *Aurora* and *Avalon* were in darkness. She listened carefully at a window but was satisfied no one was on board. She wondered where they had taken Stevo's body.

It was then she heard fiddle music coming from a large nearby barn. When she reached the wooden building she had to stand on tiptoe to look though the only window that showed a tiny

213

chink of the light that illuminated the inside. The blackout curtain hadn't been pulled across properly.

She saw Tommy lifting wooden benches from the back of the hall and setting them out in rows facing a stage. This was probably where the service or get-together would be held, she reasoned. She could see no sign of Sonny. But how to get Tommy's attention?

The barn was filled with men setting up tables and arranging vases of flowers. On the stage, four musicians were tinkling out tunes with fiddles and tambourines. Practising for the next day's spectacle to honour Stevo, thought Izzy.

Luck was on her side as Tommy came close to the window. She tapped sharply on the glass. Tommy's brow furrowed and he looked about him. Izzy tapped again. He came towards the window, then pulled back the curtain and peered out. The moment he saw it was her, he dropped the blackout curtain back into place. Would he come out to see what she wanted or ignore her? After all, she wasn't supposed to be there. No, she thought. Tommy would wonder why she was outside.

Izzy stood waiting in the shadows. It wasn't long before Tommy was at her side. She stepped forward to greet him but he pushed her gently back into the darkness. 'This is a gypsy do. You shouldn't be here.'

'I know that. Why d'you think I'm hiding? Though what anyone would do to me, I can't imagine,' Izzy said.

'It's a mark of respect that only Stevo's people

214

see him off. What d'you want?' His first words had been brusque but now his manner had softened.

'It's Tolly. She's got a bee in her bonnet that if she comes here tonight she can persuade Sonny she's the one for him.'

She knew she should be more precise but surely Tommy would know what she meant.

'It will spoil Stevo's do...' His voice petered out as he grasped her meaning.

'I want you to convince her to come back to the boats,' Izzy said.

He looked cross. 'And how am I supposed to do that?'

'Tell her you care about her.'

He made a choking sound. 'Why, I've never...'

'No! That's the trouble! You've never said anything, only mooned after her with those big brown eyes of yours. What with Elsie finding Jack, and that damned criminal Charlie on my tail, I'm positive she thinks she's still the fat girl no one wants.'

'But she's beautiful! She wouldn't? Would she?' His mouth was now hanging open at the possibility.

'Yes, she would. She thinks she needs to prove she can entice a man. And not just any man. Sonny.'

'You mean she'd sleep with him?' His eyes opened wide.

Izzy snapped, 'If she offers herself, he'll take her, won't he?'

'Last time I saw him, he was drunk in the pub. But that wouldn't stop him. Most blokes when they've had a few can hardly raise a glass but Sonny? He'd bed any woman to add another notch to his belt.'

'Tolly seems to equate making love with real love. You've got to stop her before she ruins herself.'

'What's given her this daft idea?'

'She heard him and some girl in the bushes the other night when we stopped at the Lock Inn, back along the cut. Why d'you think she made him that apple pie? She's desperate for his attention.'

Tommy was gazing deeply into her eyes. Izzy could see he was disturbed by what she'd said. 'And you think she'll take notice of me?'

'Yes, because you really care about her.'

'Does it show that much?'

Izzy put her arms around his thin body. 'Only to people like me who've not seen a lot of real love. Please help her before she does something she'll regret.'

'So, instead of biding my time, you're asking me to show her my feelings and get my hopes shattered?'

'If you really care about Tolly, you'll stop her making a fool of herself. She hasn't had the experience to see that she could be really hurt by Sonny, left high and dry.'

'But it doesn't matter if I get hurt?'

'If you really care about her, you'll risk that.'

There were more furrows in his forehead. 'I'll have to let them know I'm going off for a while.' He jerked a thumb towards the window. 'They'll understand, probably think I need a bit of time on me own,' he said. Then he sighed. 'You go

216

back to the boat. Get off the towpath if you see or hear her coming. She mustn't know you've been talking to me.'

'You'll do it, then?'

'Of course,' he said.

## Chapter Thirty

'She's coming!' Tommy practically pushed Izzy through an open gate, then strode towards the tiny wavering light that was coming ever closer along the towpath. He began jogging towards the dull glow, which was barely bright enough to show Tolly the way.

'Whatever are you doing here?' Tolly cried. 'You scared me half out of my wits!'

'I've walked up from the village specially to see you,' Tommy began. That at least was not a lie.

'How did you know where we'd moor for the night?' She stood defiantly in front of him.

He could smell a light perfume and his heart ached because he knew she'd not put it on for him. 'C'mon, Tolly. I know these cuts and their likely overnight mooring places.'

'I can't stop and talk, Tommy. I'm on my way back to Braunston.'

He deliberately stood in front of her, barring her way. If it made her angry then so be it. 'Why? To see Sonny?' He could feel his resolve weakening.

'Of course.'

Suddenly he felt deflated. Whatever had possessed him to think he stood a chance with this beautiful woman, whose head had been turned by Sonny?

'So, you're going to cause a rumpus tonight of all nights? You're going to butt in where you're not wanted, show up Sonny and spoil the gypsies' send-off for Stevo? How could you even think of doing that, Tolly?'

'Maybe he'll be glad I came to see him. I only want to comfort him.'

Tommy knew what she meant – didn't he feel the same for her? But what chance did a scrawny bloke like him have against Sonny with his glistening curls, his brawny body and his way of dressing that was the envy of every man on the cut?

Sonny was who he was, the legitimate heir to almost all Stevo had possessed. And what was Tommy? Who was Tommy?

'You'll be a laughing stock.'

The moon had pushed her way out from behind the clouds. He saw the sudden fear in Tolly's eyes. And he knew her like he knew himself.

'How can you say that?'

'Because I know him. I know Sonny's ways.'

If he stood any chance of making her change her mind, it was now or never.

'Look, let's sit here and talk for a few minutes.' He struggled out of his jacket and laid it on the grass. 'Sit,' he commanded. Tommy heard a crack, a twig breaking, perhaps.

'What's that? Is someone else around?' Tolly exclaimed, whirling around to look.

Tommy shook his head, dropped down, then pulled her onto his coat beside him. 'Who's going to be out here? It's just an animal.'

If Izzy had made the noise, he hoped she was on her way back to the boats now.

He felt Tolly shiver. He noticed she was wearing a skirt. He'd never before seen her dressed in anything other than the usual attire of scruffy trousers and thick jumpers to keep out the chills. Pain again bit into his heart that she'd smartened up for Sonny, not him.

'I've got a story to tell you,' he said. He felt her bristle with impatience as she sat close.

'Get on with it,' she said.

'All right,' he said. 'My mam and da died of influenza in 1930. A neighbour took me in. I was living in Birmingham then, but although Marie was kind to me, her husband drank and when he came home, well into his cups, he'd knock us about. Cos I was the cuckoo in the nest I got the brunt of it. We never had much to eat.'

'So you weren't born to the canals?'

He shook his head. 'No, but I might as well have been. One day Eric broke my arm after hitting me about the head with a lump of wood. I ran down to the cut, scared out of my wits he'd do something worse. There was a couple of black boats waiting to go into the lock and I hid on one. We was way out in the countryside before I was discovered asleep in a cupboard. My arm was swollen up something terrible and the pain had knocked me out, you see.

'Stevo put my arm in a splint and made me eat.' Tommy pushed back his long, curly fringe and showed Tolly a scar. 'I was only a little 'un but when I told Stevo how I came to be hiding on his

219

boat he let me stay. I knew Marie cared but what could she do? She had her own children to worry about.

'Sonny and I became good pals. He was older than me and showed me how to look after a narrowboat. I thought Sarah was the loveliest woman I'd ever seen.' He paused. 'Even then she used to go off on her own, but she always came back.'

He glanced at Tolly – she was listening avidly.

'I was never as good-looking or strong as Sonny but Stevo treated me like I belonged, like I was another grandson. When I was twelve I stopped off in Birmingham to see if I could find Marie. I always felt guilty about never letting on to her that I was all right.

'When I found the family they were in a right state. The eldest girl, Marlene, was on the game.' He saw Tolly frown. 'Selling herself for money.' He saw Tolly nod and felt her hand creep into his. It gave him the courage to carry on.

'The husband had been hanged for killing Marie in a drunken temper one night. Marlene said she'd look after the two little 'uns sooner than them go into the workhouse. She got a job in a factory but because she was only a young 'un herself, it didn't pay much. She went out at night near the docks to make more money. She didn't tell anyone she was pregnant but it had begun to show. Although I was skinny I was strong, still am.' He flexed his muscles. 'I only knew the boats, so I got work humping stuff, shovelling coal at the wharf. Of course, no one believed I was strong enough until I showed them I was. Marlene lost the baby. She was like a sister to me. I stayed because they, and Stevo, were all the family I'd ever known.

'She met a bloke who took her on with the two little 'uns and they went to live just outside Birmingham. They're still together and she's got a little boy of her own now. She's who I was going to see when I cadged a trip on *Aurora*.'

'"Was" going to see?'

'It was a shock for me to find out Stevo was so ill. Somehow I thought he'd always be there, you know? I been back and forth working the cut with Stevo an' Sonny for a long time. Now I've discovered he's left me something.'

'A boat?' He had her full attention now. She shivered so he pulled her closer.

'No. Sonny gets all the business. He'll look after it. Stevo knew that.'

Tolly looked crestfallen. 'Dorothy told me Sonny can't read. I could teach him.'

'Bless you, he wouldn't thank you for suggesting that! Sonny's the sharpest thing on two legs on the cut. What does he need with letters?'

'Well, I know you can read. I've seen you reading.'

'Yeah, well, I'm one of the lucky ones. But I got a proposition for you, Tolly.'

She stared at him. His heart was turning somersaults. Here it was, the time to ask her.

'I know you got your heart set on a café back in Titchfield. I got a fair amount that Stevo's left me. See, it isn't only Izzy who's come into some good fortune.'

'But what's that got to do with me?'

He took a deep breath. 'I'll buy the café and

221

you run it.'

He could almost see the cogs turning in her brain as she gasped. She knew, without him saying another word, that the price she had to pay was to go back to *Mallard* and *Bunting* and forget about Sonny.

He closed his eyes. He'd said his bit. He hadn't told her he loved her, but how could she fail to see he cared? He wanted her answer, but he didn't want her to refuse or feel rushed.

Izzy was astute enough to realize he cared for Tolly, had asked for his help. But she could never have envisaged he would come up with this offer to save Tolly from herself.

After a long while, when all he could hear was animals in the undergrowth and water lapping on the cut, he ventured, 'Well, what do you say? I know you think Sonny will give you excitement. I won't. I can't. You are a fantastic cook and I believe you can make a success of the Currant Bun. But I'll stay in the background or help, as you wish, and maybe, just maybe, some day you'll have feelings for me, because I really care about you.'

'You'd do this for me?' In the moonlight he saw her eyes were moist with unshed tears.

'Stevo knew I never had money before, except the pittances I worked for. I don't want money for myself, but I do love you, and if I can help to make your dream come true, well...' He was shaking. He'd finally told her of his love.

Tolly leaned her head on his shoulder. 'I've never had any man care about me that much to want to do something so wonderful,' she said. 'But you can't just hand over money without wanting something in return?'

So, she was considering his offer. 'I'll stay in the background, a sort of sleeping partner, I think it's called.'

'Oh, no!' she cried. 'That wouldn't be right, no, not at all. If you really are serious about this, Tommy, I could throw my arms around your neck and kiss you to death.'

He didn't tell her that was exactly what he'd love her to do but he listened as she carried on: 'Come back to *Bunting* with me. Let me show you the plans I have for the café. The war isn't going to last for ever, is it? Soon I'll be going home to Titchfield for a few days – why don't you come with me? You could see the café, meet my dad and my sister.'

He felt happier than he'd ever been. Yes, he'd take her back to *Bunting*, make sure she boarded the boat, but he didn't fancy getting shouted at for waking the other girls. Dorothy could be a Tartar when she was roused. Besides, if they weren't going to a pub they often went to bed as soon as it got dark. He'd soon catch up with Tolly after Stevo had been laid to rest. They could talk and plan then to their hearts' content.

Tolly was practically hanging off his neck. He twisted around and tenderly, his heart thumping wildly, allowed his lips to graze her forehead. Then he whispered, 'C'mon, Tolly, my love, let's get you back to the boat.'

# Chapter Thirty-one

Elsie was reading when she heard the low hum of voices outside. The candle flickered.

Dorothy was still asleep. The top of her head showed above her sleeping-bag, her long hair snaking down on the blankets. She looked younger when her hair wasn't pulled back in that tight bun, Elsie thought.

The voices quietened and she heard footsteps on the stones of the towpath. There were no loud noises, no crying. She gave a sigh of relief. At the soft but heavy tread of rubber-soled shoes on wood, *Mallard* swayed as someone tripped across the deck to the craft tied next to it. She guessed Tolly was returning to *Bunting*. She hadn't heard Izzy come back but had there been trouble she would surely have known about it by now. Izzy moved quietly, like a cat. She blew out the candle, satisfied that now she would be able to sleep.

Elsie put her book on the floor. As she moved a crackle of paper reminded her of the two letters she'd been reading earlier. She'd collected them from the post office at Braunston and marvelled that Jack seemed to guess exactly where and when the boats would arrive so she could pick up her letters from him.

She smiled in the dark. She'd never received love letters from Geoffrey. But, then, she'd never believed in love at first sight until it had happened to her. Jack's declarations meant so much to her. She put her hands across her abdomen. Sometimes she felt so happy it seemed incredible.

The other letter had been sent on from Lower Heyford.

Geoffrey wanted to arrange a meeting, time and place entirely up to her. He said he didn't expect her to come home: he would travel to wherever she wanted.

Her first thought had been to write back and tell him she had no intention of meeting him. But what if he had a buyer for the house? The money she was owed needed to be addressed. Plus, she no longer wanted to keep her and Jack's relationship a secret. A meeting seemed a small price to pay to have everything out in the open. Elsie yawned. Time to sleep. Dorothy had muttered something about wanting to arrive in Warwick tomorrow. Contentedly, she closed her eyes.

'Wake up!'

Izzy, freezing cold despite her run along the towpath, was only pretending to sleep. She'd thrown herself into her sleeping-bag fully clothed, and now, still shivering, she made a show of telling Tolly off for disturbing her. Tolly mustn't know she'd had a hand in whatever had happened tonight.

'Go away, let me sleep.' Izzy opened one eye to see what Tolly was doing.

Even if everything had turned out for the best, Tolly would be mortified if she thought Izzy had interfered in her life.

Tolly was putting on her pyjamas by the light of

the stove. Then she plonked herself on the edge of Izzy's bunk. 'Wake up! Something wonderful's happened!'

'What?' Izzy pushed back her sleeping-bag and glared at her.

'You've got your jumper on?' Tolly stared at her.

Izzy searched for an excuse. 'I'm cold!'

Tolly nodded. Izzy could see she was so excited she wouldn't need to ask any more questions.

'Tommy's going to buy the Currant Bun. I shall run it!'

Izzy couldn't help herself: a strangled cry came from her throat. Never in her wildest dreams had she imagined Tommy would go that far to hold on to the girl he cared about. She knew he had a silver tongue and she'd hoped he could persuade Tolly not to go into Braunston and make a spectacle of herself. But this was something she'd never envisaged. Tommy must really love the girl.

'Tell me everything,' she begged. She had to know how this had come about.

Eventually, when Tolly had explained about the money Stevo had left to Tommy, Izzy asked, 'But how can you take money from one man when earlier today you were out of your mind with wanting Sonny?'

Tolly smiled. 'The café means more to me than any man. I think I wanted Sonny to notice me because no man has ever looked at me with longing in his eyes. I mean, have you seen the way Jack looks at Elsie? Like he could eat her up! Sonny's a gorgeous man and I thought if I threw myself at him...' She paused. 'Well, baking him an apple pie didn't win me any favours, did it? At least if he

226

chucked me over afterwards, like he does most of the women, I'd know what it's like to be made love to by a man.'

Izzy looked confused. 'But why?' She was well aware of the answer but she wanted Tolly to put it into words.

'I was willing to give myself to Sonny. But it's what's inside a person that counts. It's more than mooning after someone with good looks. Tommy's kindness showed me he obviously cares more about me than he does about himself.'

She looked at Izzy with moist eyes. 'I'm going to take Tommy home with me to meet my family. He's lost Stevo, who really cared about him. My dad and Regina will love him.'

'Will you care about him?' Izzy asked. 'Could you eventually see yourself loving him?'

'How can I not?' Tolly replied. 'He's saved me from myself.'

*Dorothy Darling*

*It will be over soon. The inmates can't take it in. Probably don't see any future after what has already happened in the past. Please God I live to see this liberation. The numbers of inmates are dwindling daily. Typhus causes more deaths than starvation. Kramer our camp commandant does not care what happens to us. No one here receives letters. Most are too weak to bother to write. I am certain correspondence is read, then burned. Life is so cheap, what price letters? There are enormous open graves here at Belsen and the German guards today were ordered to straighten out rotting bodies. Those who have not died of malnutrition or sickness had been dosed with phenol. Two minutes*

227

*and one injection of carbolic acid adds another body to the pile. They like to lay the corpses in rows because it's easier to bulldoze the dirt over them. I found this label from a tin and I cried. It's from my home country. Polish beetroot. The paper is quite dry, surprisingly. I'm wondering how come it's not been eaten. I am using it to write on, my darling. Always I think of you. It gives me strength.*

*Jakub*


*Dear Geoffrey*

*We will be climbing the Hatton Flight locks on our way to Birmingham and should reach them this Friday at some time. As you state you would like us to meet as soon as possible, I can be at the Hatton Fields public house on Birmingham Road some time in the evening. I trust you'll understand why it's impossible for me to give you a definite hour.*

*Elsie*


## Chapter Thirty-two

'Do you want me to come with you?'

'After the day we've had?' Elsie stopped scrubbing her arms with carbolic soap and looked at Dorothy, whose face showed lines of fatigue and anxiety. 'You must be shattered.'

'I'm worried about you meeting Geoffrey.' Dorothy was washing the plates and pots in a bucket of soapy water. They'd eaten Bovril fritters and the bottom of the frying pan had caught and

228

blackened. She was cross because no matter how hard she scrubbed the marks wouldn't come off.

'I telephoned Jack from that phone-box way back along the cut. He wanted to come with me. I told him that would certainly put the cat among the pigeons. My current man meeting my husband?' Elsie laughed, then let out a groan and rubbed her hand across the base of her spine.

Dorothy gave her a look.

'It's just normal aches and pains. Who'd have thought we'd climb twenty-one locks? No wonder Hatton Flight is sometimes called the Stairway to Heaven! I hurt all over. Stairway to Hell more like. Two miles of locks!'

'Wait until we hit Birmingham. It's nothing but locks. Are you sure you're capable of working so hard, what with the baby?'

Elsie began cleaning her teeth. When she'd finished, she spat in the dirty water and said, 'Do you think the gypsy women worry about things like that? The doctor assured me—'

'All right,' said Dorothy, interrupting her.

There was hardly room to move in the small cabin space with both women busying themselves. Elsie knew she'd have to hurry if she wanted to get to the pub before it closed. If it was even open. Spirits and beer were in short supply due to war shortages; sometimes pubs closed early or often didn't open but left a sign on the door: 'No Beer'.

Dorothy had suggesting mooring *Mallard* and *Bunting* on a quiet strip of water above the locks, which would make it easier for Elsie to walk back along the towpath and take the lane towards the Hatton Fields, a popular public house.

'I haven't even heard whether he'll be there.'

'Didn't you telephone?' Dorothy looked puzzled.

Elsie shook her head. 'Not when I phoned Jack. My mind was consumed with the Hatton Flight. In fact I should have washed my hair but there hasn't been time for anything, let alone finding another telephone box.' Elsie was now pulling a brush through her fair hair and wincing as it hit tangles. She looked at herself in the small square of mirror. 'Do you think I look all right?'

'Your skin's the colour of a russet apple, your hair's shining and you're wearing a skirt. What more could a husband who did the dirty on you want?'

Elsie threw the hairbrush at her. Then she eased her feet into a pair of slip-on shoes and did a little twirl in the small space.

Dorothy was right. Elsie looked and felt healthier than she ever had before they'd met. Tanned and fit, she was also happier than she'd ever been. She hoped when she returned from her meeting with Geoffrey she'd still feel the same.

'Sure you don't want some moral support?'

Elsie hugged Dorothy. 'You're a good friend,' she said, 'but I'd better do this on my own.' She broke away and pointed towards the stairs. 'You can see the pub if you stand out by the tiller, and I don't intend to stay any longer than I have to.'

Dorothy picked up a greying tea-towel and began drying dishes. It was a signal for Elsie to leave.

She picked her way along the towpath, past the lock, then hurried towards the sound of noise and music. Such a lot had happened and she knew she'd changed so much since she'd left Gosport.

Elsie took a deep breath, opened the pub door and went inside, tucking the blackout curtain in place behind her. The cigarette fumes and smell of stale beer enveloped her as she made her way through the crowd. How would she and Geoffrey feel when they met each other? Although she'd hated him when he'd virtually dismissed her from his life, she knew now that that had been his greatest gift to her.

'Small lemonade,' she said to the girl, in a tight sweater with piled-up blonde hair, behind the bar. Elsie took a sip of the tepid liquid, then looked about her. The place was busy, the wireless playing, and Elsie recognized several gypsy boaters.

She almost dismissed the scruffy man sitting in the corner wearing a plaid suit. His trilby hat and dark raincoat lay upon a chair. He was staring around the bar, and when his eyes fell on her, he frowned. He blinked, almost as if he hadn't recognized her. Then he smiled.

How could anyone age so much in such a short time? wondered Elsie, as she made her way towards him, a smile plastered on her face. His usually immaculate hair was greasy, and much longer than she remembered. Had his face always been so heavy-jowled?

She put her glass on the table, then pulled off her gabardine raincoat. It was grubby, torn and covered with grass stains. She tried to roll it up before she made room for it on the same chair as Geoffrey's hat and coat.

Geoffrey rose formally to his feet. For a moment

Elsie thought her husband was going to shake her hand, but he pointed to an empty chair next to the table. 'I managed to save you a seat,' he said.

She saw he had put on weight, despite the fullness of his over-large suit. The long jacket was ill-fitting. The baggy trousers tapered to his ankles. She could smell the Brylcreem plastered on his hair.

'My, aren't you the pinnacle of fashion,' she said, and immediately chastised herself for her sarcasm. Geoffrey appeared not to have noticed. Elsie felt very dull in her old but cleanish clothes. She was aware that Geoffrey's eyes hadn't left her. A quick look around the room told her that a few boatwomen were sitting with their men. They wore colourful skirts and gold jewellery.

She saw Geoffrey look away, then brush at some long red hairs on his jacket. 'Sandra changed her hair colour?' The words came out of her lips unbidden.

Geoffrey gave her a mournful smile. 'Her cat. It gets everywhere.'

He smiled then began foraging in his inside pocket and pulled out his wallet. He extracted a folded envelope and gave it to her.

As Elsie bent forward to take it she could smell his cologne. It briefly passed through her mind that working on the cut she seldom noticed men's cologne. Mostly it was sweat, cigarettes and diesel fumes. Sometimes snuff.

Now Geoffrey was speaking: 'Before I even tell you how well you look and how glad I am to see you, I need to hand over this cheque.'

'Have you sold our house?' The words escaped

232

along with a feeling of sudden loss.

'Not yet, but the cheque's for the equivalent of what you'd receive if, when, the sale goes through. I thought you might need the money.'

'Need? It's what I'm owed, Geoffrey.'

He looked at her intently as she opened the envelope and stared at the cheque.

Elsie nodded. She was satisfied with the amount, and Geoffrey never did anything that he wasn't a hundred per cent sure of.

'You've been very accommodating to me.' He sought her eyes. 'Which is in part why I needed to see you.' He leaned across the table and picked up the hand that wasn't holding the cheque. 'Elsie, you can come home again, soon, to live.'

It took a while for his words to sink into her brain. He was actually telling her she could come back to Gosport!

'To you? And Western Way? Is that what you mean?' Her words crackled in her throat.

He nodded. Elsie's brain was whirling. Never in her wildest dreams had she expected him to say that. Only he wasn't asking her, was he? He was telling her she could return home.

'If I don't come back right now, does that mean you'll cancel the cheque?'

He squeezed her hand, then held on to it. 'Of course not. You'll need time to think over my offer. When we bought the house in Western Way you put in a great deal of the money you'd earned from teaching. I'm merely returning to you what belongs to you. It's quite possible I might not need to sell the house after all.'

'Oh!' was all Elsie could find to say. She bent

towards her coat and tucked the envelope into her pocket. Through the fluffy cloud that had suddenly become her brain, she remembered Sandra. 'What about Sandra? It can't be long before she's due to give birth.'

'Don't you worry about Sandra. Some interesting information has come to light.'

Elsie saw a shadow pass across his eyes. Immediately she guessed something bad had happened. The big romance was at a standstill, perhaps. She removed her hand from his.

'I'm going to file for custody of my baby. Sandra isn't fit to be a wife, let alone a mother. You on the other hand have always wanted children. I've decided we can make a go of our marriage and cement it with my child.'

Elsie stared at him. He really believed what he was saying! His arrogance was beyond measure. Then she realized he had always been like that, able to put himself and his own wishes before anyone else's. He was assuming she would drop everything and do his bidding, just as she always had.

Oh, she had no doubt he would find some way to remove Sandra's child from her. After all, he was good at his job. But what a hateful action for him to take. A child needed its mother, its rightful mother. She thought of her own baby, snug and safe within her. How dare he contemplate depriving another woman of her child? Elsie had never wanted another woman's child, she'd wanted her own. They had never discussed adoption.

She thought of all the years they had been disappointed with no sign of a baby. But she was now pregnant, which meant that their lack of success was nothing to do with her. She'd been so caught up in her own happiness and good fortune that she hadn't stopped to think what this meant for Geoffrey and Sandra's baby. Now, though... Surely it couldn't be his.

Elsie knew then she had to tell him. She no longer loved him but she could not allow Sandra to make an absolute fool of him. She picked up her warm lemonade, took a long draught and put down the glass. 'I'm never coming back to Gosport, Geoffrey. I've met someone and I'm pregnant.'

There, she had told him.

Geoffrey's face crumpled like a screwed-up envelope as the information reached his brain. 'Are you sure?' His face was grey, like used putty.

'I've seen a doctor.'

'But ... but...' he blustered. 'We tried for years.'

'I know. But I've fallen in love...'

'You can't be pregnant!'

'Geoffrey, listen to yourself. Don't raise your voice. It's a fact.'

There was silence while he simply stared at her. 'But ... but...' he repeated. 'That means the fault lies with me!' His forehead creased with the effort of trying to reconcile himself to the awful truth. 'It's highly unlikely the baby Sandra is expecting is mine!'

'Well, yes, Geoffrey, I'm afraid so.'

# Chapter Thirty-three

With his elbows on the table Geoffrey's head was in his hands. His shoulders heaved. Elsie knew he was crying, but he wouldn't thank her for acknowledging it. He'd been dealt a terrible blow. She wanted to reach out to him because she felt sorry Sandra had taken him in, hook, line and sinker. Geoffrey, so sure of his own virility, had been blind to the possibility that the cause of their failure might lie with him.

'You all right, mate?'

Elsie was startled by the voice she knew so well. She looked away from Geoffrey's crumpled figure and up into Jack's familiar eyes above her. He shook his head at Elsie and she knew he didn't want her to let on to Geoffrey that she knew him. The only possible reason for that would be because Jack realized Geoffrey couldn't take the news that he was Elsie's lover. Certainly not at this crucial moment. No, Geoffrey was clearly in no state to absorb further shocks. Knowing Jack as she did, she doubted it would be long before Geoffrey knew the truth. Jack didn't like secrets.

Geoffrey raised his head and stared at Jack. 'Who the hell are you?'

'I've been watching you, and it's clear you're upset. D'you want to get out of this crowded place for some fresh air?'

Faces were turned towards Geoffrey and Elsie.

Even the darts players had halted their game and were staring.

'It's not air I need but peace and quiet. I've booked a room here. I'll go upstairs.' Geoffrey rose shakily to his feet. Elsie saw all the cat hairs on his trousers and her heart went out to him. This wasn't her fastidious Geoffrey, this was a broken man. And why shouldn't he be in pieces? It's one thing to understand that your wife and yourself can't conceive a child, another to discover that you're infertile and that another woman is lying to you about her pregnancy.

'I'll come with you,' Elsie said, rising.

She watched as Jack put out an arm to help him up. Geoffrey fumbled in his pocket for his room key. 'I've had a bit of a shock, old man,' he said hesitantly.

'I can see that, and I don't suppose you want to share it with everyone in here.'

The wireless was playing 'Pistol Packin' Mama'. Elsie thought in the future, when she heard that song, she'd always shudder.

Eyes were upon them. Elsie looked at Jack and saw the genuine concern on his face. He turned to Elsie and took a note from his trouser pocket. 'He needs brandy. I think we all do. Can you do the honours?'

Elsie returned to the bar and was immediately served. 'He all right?' asked the blonde. Elsie nodded and, clutching the three glasses, followed Jack and Geoffrey out into the hallway where wide stairs led up to the bedrooms.

Jack took the key from Geoffrey, then opened a door along the short corridor. Elsie thought he looked tired, and his leg seemed to be bothering him. Inside the basic, clean room, Geoffrey sank onto a chair.

'Drink this,' said Elsie. She offered him a glass and he swallowed the brandy in one gulp. He put the glass on the bedside table and looked at Jack. Elsie set down the other two.

'Thanks for your support,' he said. 'I'll be all right now. You can go.'

Jack shook his head. 'No, I don't think so. There's a few things need to be clarified about Elsie and myself.'

At Jack's words, Geoffrey's brain seemed to spring back to life. 'Wait a minute,' he said. 'You,' he stared at Jack, 'and her?' He looked at Elsie. She nodded.

'I couldn't let her come and meet you on her own, could I? Not that Elsie knew I'd be here.'

Elsie felt suddenly grateful that their secret was out. Geoffrey put his hand to his head, as though everything was too much for him.

'I didn't mean to hurt you,' began Elsie. 'Back in Gosport you made it clear that you wanted me out of the way...' She trailed off. She was glad now that Jack had unexpectedly turned up and she hadn't had to face Geoffrey on her own. Elsie knelt down on the carpet near her husband. 'I expect a similar thing happened between you and Sandra,' she said. 'Falling in love. Quite out of the blue I fell for Jack. We couldn't help it.'

Geoffrey put a hand on her shoulder. He stared into her eyes. 'I've treated you appallingly,' he said, in a very small voice.

She wanted to tell him that everything had

turned out fine. But it hadn't, not for him.

He let out a huge sigh. 'It's all my own fault. I've been well and truly hoodwinked,' he said. Then, with some force, he said, 'The bitch!'

Jack moved in close to Elsie. 'You're not going to get violent, are you?'

His body had tensed. Elsie saw his hands were clenched into fists.

Geoffrey said, 'I didn't mean Elsie. I meant the woman I lost my head over, ended my marriage for.'

'Sandra?' Jack offered.

'I see you've talked about us.'

'I'd like to think we didn't leave any skeletons in the cupboard, Elsie and I.' Jack sighed. 'My name's Jack, by the way, Jack Lumley.'

Geoffrey said, 'I think I'd like to be on my own, now.'

'Will you be all right?' Elsie's voice held a plaintive note. But she could see Geoffrey had regained his composure.

'As all right as any man whose dream of becoming a father has just been shot down in flames.' He looked at Jack. 'And talking to my wife's paramour who has impregnated her isn't exactly going to make me feel better, is it?'

Jack said, 'If you're sure you're going to be all right, we'll leave you.' He turned to Elsie. 'Or do you intend to stay for a while?' Elsie was now standing.

'Go,' said Geoffrey. He eyed the two untouched drinks on the dressing-table. 'But you can leave those,' he said.

Elsie and Jack made a move towards the door.

Jack paused. 'I never meant any of this to happen but I'll look after Elsie.'

Geoffrey said, 'Good luck to you both.' Elsie thought she saw again the glimmer of tears in Geoffrey's eyes. He turned away. Then he glanced back at her and whispered, '*I* should have looked after you.'

Jack opened the door and the two of them filed into the corridor.

'I won't go without saying goodbye,' Geoffrey called to Elsie. He came and stood in the doorway. 'I'll catch you up on the canal.'

Elsie stood on tiptoe and kissed his cheek. She felt as though a load had been lifted from her shoulders. Knowing Geoffrey as she did, she guessed he'd have a sore head in the morning. He'd probably order more brandy from the bar. Then he'd be planning how best to get rid of Sandra.

Down in the smoky bar, ignoring the curious looks from the drinkers, Jack asked, 'You're not angry with me for coming here, are you?'

Elsie shook her head. 'There was no need,' she said.

'Oh, yes, there was,' Jack murmured. She wanted to snuggle into him but it didn't seem right with all those eyes upon them. She thought instead of the blow that Geoffrey had taken, and how his dream of a son or daughter had been shattered. She didn't love him any more but she was still saddened by how everything had turned out for him.

'My car's outside,' Jack said. 'Come home with me. I'll make sure you're back at the boat early in the morning.'

She thought of the welcoming house, his cosy bedroom, lying in his arms. It was very tempting. Elsie shook her head. 'If I come to the lock cottage I'll never want to leave it. Dorothy will be worrying. I must get back to her.' She remembered the cheque in her coat pocket. She took it out, stared at the envelope, then said, 'I'll not be coming to you with nothing. This is my share of the house money.'

He frowned. 'We don't need Geoffrey's money. Return it. I can provide.'

'It's not Geoffrey's,' Elsie said. 'It's mine.' She patted her stomach. 'And I'm sure we'll find an excellent use for it.'

Jack shook his head. His fair hair fell across his eyes and he used a hand to brush it away. 'I think I've bitten off more than I can chew with you,' he said, gathering her close. 'You're a hell of a woman, Elsie. Did I ever tell you I love you?'

## Chapter Thirty-four

On their way at last after a scrambled-egg breakfast – somehow Tolly always made the powder taste like real eggs – and a prolonged catch-up on all of last night's happenings, Elsie was now walking along the towpath, careful not to slip in the mud, and watching the shimmering water of the cut. It had rained during the night but now a light yellow sun had ventured out.

It had been Elsie's turn to clear the weed hatch, not a job to look forward to at the best of times. Her fingertips still felt frozen as she held tightly to the lock key given to her by Jack. Thank God all she'd had to do this morning was to make sure the propellers were clear of rubbish by leaning down into the hatch and feeling about in the murky water. She marvelled at Tommy, who had crawled into the cut's icy depths to clear the rope that had been entwined around the propellers. Tommy and the café were now all Tolly talked about from the moment she woke to the time she fell asleep.

Geoffrey walked beside her.

He'd surprised her by appearing at the moored boats while they were eating and asking Dorothy if she minded him taking up some of Elsie's time.

'Shrewley Tunnel's on the agenda for today. It's more than four hundred yards long, and once we enter the tunnel we can't stop, but if you,' she'd nodded at Elsie, 'want to walk up towards the next lock together, you can talk in relative privacy.' Dorothy had taken pity on the downcast man.

Elsie's mind kept turning over all that had happened last night. She hoped Geoffrey knew how he was going to sort out his life. She had loved him once. She felt no animosity towards him. He had done her a good turn, if anything. If she hadn't become an Idle Woman she'd never have found Jack. Whenever she thought of Jack and her baby, a trickle of warmth ran through her body.

It had taken all of her willpower to return to the boat last night when she had really wanted to go home to the cottage, shut the door and stay for ever, safe with Jack and Matey. She wondered now if she had done the right thing in saying she would sign on for a second trip with Dorothy.

'I'm sorry about the way things turned out between us,' Geoffrey said. 'It's been a double blow to my ego finding out you don't want to come back to Gosport.' He suddenly smiled at her. 'Actually, I can see what a pompous prig I've been, expecting you to jump at my bidding. I know now I could have been a better husband to you.'

'I think we've both learned a lot from what's happened,' she said, gazing at him. She thought he looked out of place in his silly suit, which did nothing for him, except make him look ridiculous. She wasn't going to tell him that, though, was she? Perhaps now he knew the truth about Sandra he'd go back to thinking for himself. His dark suits suited both him and his profession. Geoffrey's repeated apologies weren't moving things forward. She was about to change the subject when he said, 'I daresay you'd like to marry Jack.'

Elsie's eyes opened wide. 'You'd allow a divorce?' It was a dirty word.

'I owe you after all the unhappiness I've put you through.'

'You'd allow me to start proceedings? You wouldn't contest?' She looked up into his face. He nodded and smiled. Her grin almost split her face in two. Had Geoffrey suddenly reverted to the caring man he'd been when they'd first met?

She was so happy it was easy to walk along in companionable silence. Fields spread into the distance around them. The harvest had been cut and the colours ranged from dull yellow to brown. The water rippled in a light breeze, no sign of another boat coming along the cut. Ahead a brick bridge rose above the water. A road ran over it. Along its banks blackberry brambles, the fruit ripe, glinted and beckoned. She looked across towards *Bunting*, half expecting Tolly, at the tiller, to start making noises about gathering fruits. There was, after all, still a little of the sugar left. A car was parked in a layby along the narrow road.

Elsie's heart lurched. A dark-haired man was leaning nonchalantly on the open door of the Chrysler. With horror, she recognized him.

'Oh, my God!' Elsie turned and stared at *Bunting*. Tolly waved to her. It had been her turn to cook breakfast but Izzy had volunteered to wash up. She was hidden in the cabin.

'What's up?' Geoffrey asked.

'That man leaning on his car, it's Charlie!' Elsie could see her words meant little to Geoffrey. 'Charlie was Izzy's boyfriend. He knocked her about. She ran away from Gosport to escape him. The last we heard he was detained by the police. She'll be horrified to find he's followed and found her.'

'Just a moment, I know him. I was in court the day he was charged. He's out on bail. He's not supposed to move away from Gosport.' Geoffrey squinted for a better look.

Elsie saw Charlie slam the door of his car. Then he half walked, half slid down the bank towards the area of the towpath near the base of the road bridge. Elsie was sure that immediately *Mallard*

244

nosed her way through, Charlie would jump aboard looking for Izzy.

'I wasn't personally involved in the case, which hasn't ended yet, but I certainly know all about it. He's a nasty piece of work. Look at that!'

Charlie was now standing on the deck of *Mallard*. Dorothy didn't look very happy about it and was remonstrating with him.

Elsie pulled on Geoffrey's arm. 'We'd better get on board.'

Elsie and Geoffrey piled on next to Dorothy from the same spot where Charlie had boarded. There certainly wasn't room enough for them all on the rear of *Mallard*.

'Who the hell d'you think you are? This is private property!' Dorothy hissed.

'Look here, man.' Geoffrey's voice was overshadowed by Charlie's more strident tones.

'Hold your horses. I'm looking for Izzy.'

'You can't just jump on my boat,' insisted Dorothy. Elsie saw she couldn't do much to persuade Charlie to get off because she was holding onto the tiller. Elsie was hoping Dorothy wouldn't tell him that Izzy was on the other boat trailing behind.

'There's barely room for me to steer,' Dorothy shouted.

'I can soon sort out that little problem,' Charlie said. 'You think about telling me where my Izzy is while I sit up here out of the way.' He jumped up and perched on the cabin's roof, his legs dangling down in the stairway. He had an amused expression on his face as he smoothed the material of his dark suit. As always, thought Elsie, he was im-

245

maculately dressed. 'I'm well out of the way up here,' he said. 'Izzy's got to be around some- where.' He bent forward and looked down inside the cabin, then sat upright again, facing Geoffrey, Elsie and Dorothy. Now all three of them had to gaze up at him sitting high above them.

'Where have you hidden her, then? There's no room in there, even for a little 'un like Izzy.' Charlie smiled, showing his strong teeth, and his eyes swept past them to the boat trailing behind. 'Of course.' He slapped his head as if he'd made a mistake. 'I'm on the wrong boat. She'll be on that one.'

Elsie interrupted. 'How did you find us?'

The bridge was behind them now and the tunnel ahead loomed closer. The scenery had reverted to fields and lush foliage with the crispness in the air that autumn brings.

'Wasn't hard, darling. Not when you left a letter to your hubby there.' Charlie nodded towards Geoffrey. 'On your table it was.'

'You broke into my house?' said Geoffrey, his face like thunder.

Dorothy was watching the cut ahead and began fumbling at the controls.

'Come on, I didn't touch anything. I knew Izzy would tell your missus where she was going and I was right. Elsie left you a note, didn't she? Didn't take me long to win over the girl in Rousham's Cruisers to tell me whereabouts.'

'She's not here,' Elsie cried.

'We're coming up fast to a tunnel,' Dorothy shouted, 'You'll need to get down. It's difficult for me to slow.'

'Yeah, and I suppose you expect me to get off this boat and go away like a good boy?'

'You need to move.' Dorothy was white-faced. 'I can't stop in time.'

'Trust me to pick the wrong boat,' Charlie said. 'Izzy needs to know who the strong one is in this set-up.'

Charlie got no further for the almighty crack that was the back of his head on the blue-grey bricks of Shrewley Tunnel echoed in the sudden darkness as the boat sailed into the opening and he was flung forward.

'Oh, my God!' Dorothy was trying to slow the boat and hurled the engine into reverse. But too late: Charlie had been knocked from his high seat down into the footwell.

'Reverse!' shouted Elsie, to Tolly in the butty. Her face was a mask of horror at what had happened. Izzy had appeared on the stairs with a tea-towel in her hand, clearly mystified at the commotion.

'What's going on?' Elsie saw the words form on Izzy's lips. Geoffrey had fallen to his knees and was examining Charlie. Already blood was creeping through Charlie's dark curls and staining the back of his shirt collar.

Elsie watched, surprised, as Geoffrey seemed to know exactly what he was doing. But for some reason he was searching Charlie's suit pockets.

Dorothy had managed to reverse the boat towards the landing stage near the entrance to the tunnel. The butty had bumped into the back of *Mallard*. Tolly, quick-witted as usual, had handed over the tiller to Izzy, jumped to the towpath, holding a rope, and was pulling *Bunting* towards the side of the canal.

'We can't do anything for him here,' said Geoffrey. 'He's breathing. Keep him warm. Don't move him. Try to keep that young woman away! I'm going for his car.'

Elsie knew 'that young woman' meant Izzy.

'What do you mean, his car?' asked Dorothy. She had regained full control of *Mallard* and was tucking the boat in at the front of *Bunting*. Geoffrey climbed over the side onto the towpath and threw another rope towards Tolly. He began jogging back the way the boats had travelled.

'Why go for Charlie's car? Why not find a phone box and call an ambulance?' Dorothy asked.

Elsie was attempting to cover Charlie with a blanket, but Dorothy winced at the amount of blood that had poured from the back of Charlie's head and was now pooling red and dark on the wooden planking. She took off her coat and wedged it beneath his neck hoping to stem the bleeding. His hair was wet and matted. 'Oh, my God, it's all my fault!' Dorothy cried.

'You tried to warn him. He wouldn't listen,' said Elsie. 'And it's probably quicker to take him to a hospital than it is to find a phone box to ask for an ambulance to come. Trust Geoffrey, he's had first-aid training.'

'Maybe an ambulance wouldn't be able to reach us here on the towpath.'

'You're probably right.'

Dorothy looked towards Tolly. 'I'd better help her,' she said.

Izzy was standing at the back of *Bunting*, her

face like chalk.

'Help us tie up,' shouted Dorothy. Izzy seemed to gather herself together and threw out the other mooring rope. Dorothy jumped to the towpath, picked up the rope before it drifted back into the water and began to haul in the butty behind *Mallard*.

'What happened? What happened?' Izzy asked over and over again.

Dorothy ignored her. 'How far away is Charlie's car?'

'Can't be that far away,' replied Elsie. Dorothy was tying a rope around a fencepost. Izzy had jumped from *Bunting*, landed on the towpath and was climbing onto *Mallard* when she saw Charlie lying motionless on the deck.

'Jesus! That's Charlie! What's happened? Is that blood? Is he still breathing?'

'I think so,' Elsie said trying to hold Izzy back from touching him. The enormity of what had happened made Elsie's gorge rise. She grabbed the side rail and was sick into the cut.

Dorothy shouted, 'Pull yourself together.' The sharpness of her tone jolted Elsie, and she wiped her mouth with the back of her hand.

Both boats were stationary now, tied to the fence and to thick hedge branches.

Elsie held Izzy. Tears were running down her friend's face. 'Is he going to be all right?' she whimpered.

Elsie could feel Izzy shivering with shock. 'Leave him be. He needs air. Geoffrey's good in emergencies.'

Izzy's small body was cold.

The boats had been tied, and they were well out of the way of any passing craft. Dorothy was looking worried. Tolly was unusually quiet. In Elsie's arms Izzy was still shivering. Elsie suddenly realized she was cold, too. 'Tolly, put the kettle on!' she yelled.

### Chapter Thirty-five

Geoffrey returned to find Charlie unconscious but wrapped in several blankets to keep him warm. The minutes had seemed like hours to the girls waiting for him.

'I've parked his car on the road above the tunnel,' Geoffrey said. He took Charlie's pulse, then pushed back the matted curls. 'The blood's stopped flowing,' he announced. 'Warwick and Coventry copped V-2s last night. A farmer walking along the road told me. Clearing-up operations are in progress. Thank God we don't need to hang around waiting for hospital transport.'

'If the blood's stopped does that mean Charlie could live?' Izzy asked. Her face was stained with dirt and tears. Geoffrey guessed that, however badly Charlie had treated Izzy in the past, there had been a time when they'd loved each other. She had a right to remember that.

'It's why I've collected his Chrysler,' he said. 'I know you shouldn't really move accident victims, but with those big raids to attend to it could be hours before an ambulance gets here.'

'Do you know where the nearest hospital is?' Dorothy asked. Her face was chalk white.

'I've a pretty good idea and I've got a tongue in my head!' Geoffrey scooped the big man up in his arms, staggering under Charlie's weight as he manoeuvred him off the boat. He was breathless as he mumbled to Dorothy, 'Can you follow me? I've got to climb that rise to the road and he's no lightweight.'

Without replying, Dorothy did as he had asked, walking in his shadow. Only once did he stumble and knock against her. But he was able to use her as ballast and not lose his grip on Charlie. The blood smelt of metal, strong and pungent. Geoffrey heard Dorothy's sigh of relief when they reached the road.

All the women followed him to the car, sad and dejected.

'Warwick Hospital can't be far. Elsie, do you want to come with us?'

Izzy gave a sob when she saw that the blood from Charlie's head had transferred itself to Geoffrey's jacket. 'I think it should be me,' she said, looking at Dorothy, who nodded her assent.

'Get into the back of the car and fold that blanket on your lap, then.'

Izzy did as she was told while Geoffrey, as carefully as he could but with great difficulty, laid Charlie across the back seats so that his head rested on the folded blanket.

'I'll get in touch with the police, Dorothy, and report the accident. There's no need for you to hang about here. You've got a job to do for the war effort.' He climbed into the driver's seat and the car burst into life. He wound down the window. 'Don't clear up the blood, and don't tread in it. The police may want to look at the boat if Charlie doesn't survive.'

Geoffrey drove slowly into the centre of the lane. Soon the car was a small dot and eventually disappeared.

*Mallard* and *Bunting* were moored above Knowle Locks when Geoffrey caught up with them again.

Elsie could see Izzy had been crying.

'He's gone,' was all Izzy said, and flew into Elsie's arms. Dorothy disentangled Izzy from Elsie and took her down into the warmth of *Mallard's* cabin.

Geoffrey didn't step onto the boat but made a sign that he wanted to talk to Elsie.

She left the boat to join him. He was grim-faced. 'He died at the hospital. When you finally reach Birmingham you may get a police visit, you may not. So leave the blood. The hospital concur it was an accident and we did the best we could to save him. But they will do an autopsy.

'What I need from you, Elsie, is a few details of why you think Charlie came to find Izzy. Talk to her when she's settled down and make a note of how her life with Charlie was. I need to know as much as I can in case they do decide it was more than an accident. This is just a safety measure. I've also contacted the Grand Union Canal Company in my capacity as a solicitor. The assertion that this was just a horrible accident will bear more weight coming from me than Dorothy, who might be put in a compromising situation when it comes out that Izzy was trying to hide from Charlie.'

Elsie walked to the car with him. While he'd been talking she'd realized how far apart, back in Gosport, as a married couple, they'd become. She should have felt she could confide in Geoffrey when Izzy was constantly in fear of Charlie. How sad it was that it had taken Charlie's death to regain the art of communication between them.

'I'm talking to you, and the others of course, in a purely professional capacity now because I was present when the accident occurred. I'm sure nothing more will come of this.'

'You did all you could to help Charlie,' Elsie said. 'That was good of you. And the one bright thing to come from this is that Izzy won't need to keep looking over her shoulder now.'

Geoffrey touched Elsie's cheek. 'I'm driving back to the pub at Hatton Flight. I told the police I'd leave Charlie's car there. Then I'm returning to Gosport. You know where I am if you need anything, professional or otherwise.' He smiled at her. 'I'm glad you're going to be happy, Elsie. Jack's a lucky man.'

Elsie wanted to ask how he would deal with Sandra but whatever Geoffrey did now was none of her business.

Dinner that night was a one-saucepan stew, courtesy of Izzy, who said she needed to keep busy. Nevertheless it was a sombre affair, with only a cup of cocoa for pudding. All the girls wanted to do after finishing their chores was sleep.

Dorothy was reading by the light of the stove

but was unable to pay attention to the words on the page, for they seemed to run into one another. She'd volunteered the visit to Southampton because she knew Izzy was scared of going back to Gosport. She wondered if now Izzy would see a trip on her own boat as cathartic, but if the girl wasn't ready to be alone she wouldn't go back on her promise. Her fear that her own secret would come to light must take second place.

'Are you awake?' she called softly to Elsie.

Elsie grunted back at her. 'I'm making tea. Want a cup?'

Dorothy sat up in her bunk. The book toppled to the floor. 'Love one. You are signing on for another trip, aren't you?'

Elsie ladled water from the bucket into the kettle. 'I've been meaning to talk to you about that. Today's made me see that life's too short to plan very far ahead. Back in Gosport I worried about getting blown up during an air raid. This war work is worthwhile but I so want to be with Jack. Today showed me that death can happen any time.'

'I understand,' Dorothy said. 'All of us needed to get away, do something different...'

'You needed to escape? From what?'

Dorothy didn't doubt that Elsie wouldn't gossip to Izzy and Tolly but fear stopped her confiding. 'Just life at home in Southampton,' she said. 'I've got to know many of the gypsies and most are good folk. Even the hard work and long hours don't bother me any more. But I still want something more...' She swallowed a tear. 'I envy you, Elsie. You have happiness before you now.'

'I'm thankful for that ... the baby and Jack,' Elsie said. 'Mind you, Tolly is pretty happy too. She's going to get her café.'

'Yes, and I wouldn't mind betting one day she'll look at Tommy and see what a good man he is.'

'It's funny how things work out. I expect in *Bunting* Tolly and Izzy are talking things over as well.' Elsie was quiet for a moment. Dorothy could hear the kettle bubbling on the stove. She knew it wouldn't be long before Izzy gained the courage to strike out on her own, making a life for herself now she had a floating home to work from.

'If you don't do another trip, you have my blessing,' Dorothy said. 'But I hope you change your mind. There are only about thirty of us women working the canals at present.'

Elsie was pouring boiling water into the teapot. 'Really? I'd have thought there'd be more.'

'It's too hard. The work is dirty, heavy. I've stuck it because it's necessary for me to be away from home...'

She realized what she'd said and waited for Elsie to ask her what she meant. But Elsie was putting mugs on the makeshift table and either hadn't heard or was too polite to ask.

'I must admit that you three girls have become more than employees to me,' Dorothy went on. 'I look upon you all as firm friends.' She bent down, picked her book up from the floor and tucked it beneath her pillow. She was comforted by the crackle of the letter there.

Elsie handed her a mug of sweet tea. 'I won't be needing my car that's parked at the basin. There's petrol enough in it. Why don't you use it

255

to travel south?'

'That's kind of you,' Dorothy said. 'If you're really sure?' She wasn't ready yet to divulge her secret to Elsie but, oh, how she wished she was.

## Chapter Thirty-six

It was raining when *Mallard* and *Bunting* arrived at Tyseley yard in Birmingham. Rubbish floated in the cut and Dorothy did her best to skirt around old bedsteads poking out of the dirty, smelly water. Dank buildings and tall walls lined the canalside and filthy smoke belched from factory chimneys. 'This rain is going to make it harder to clean the boats,' she said.

At the goods yard, materials of all sorts were being loaded onto trains and lorries. Cranes perched, like strange birds grabbing food for their young, as narrowboat holds were emptied or filled. Dorothy went to the Grand Union Canal Company office, filled in the never-ending paperwork and received her next instructions.

With the boats tied up and Dorothy back in their midst, the girls went into a café while waiting their turn for *Mallard* and *Bunting* to be unloaded, then reloaded.

Condensation ran down the windows and gathered on the grubby net curtains. The air smelt of grease. Omelette and chips seemed the safest bet, even though Dorothy knew the omelette had never seen a real egg, just as the marked tablecloth had never seen a wash. 'We're taking scrap metal on board here,' she said, around a mouthful of soggy chips. 'We deposit it at Banbury and then we're home for a while.'

Smiles spread across their faces.

'I know all about Banbury,' Tolly said. 'Banbury cakes come from there, fruit filling inside pastry...'

'And don't forget Lady Godiva riding through the market town in the nuddy!' Elsie said.

'Lady Godiva took off her clothes in Coventry,' Dorothy said, 'though likely a local girl rode in the May Day procession showing a bit more than she should.' She was glad her charges had cheered up.

'And then from Banbury it's straight back to Lower Heyford?' Elsie asked.

'Yes,' said Dorothy. She looked at Elsie, whose face was now one big smile. No doubt she was looking forward to seeing Jack. Outside dusk was gathering. She wondered when the elderly waitress would think about drawing the blackout curtains. She looked at the grey-haired woman with cut-outs in her slippers for her bunions to poke through and asked, 'Shall I draw the curtains?'

After wiping her nose with a grimy handkerchief, the woman said, 'Blackout's been lifted. Didn't you know? Not fully, but we're getting there.'

Tolly let out a belly laugh. 'It's finally coming to an end,' she said. 'This damn war will soon be over!'

Dorothy laughed too. 'Wonderful,' she said. 'We didn't know!'

'Well, there ain't no wirelesses on the cut, is

there?' The old woman shuffled off, wafting body odour.

'Wonder how she knew we're from the cut,' Tolly mused.

'We look like ragamuffins, that's how,' said Elsie.

'Is the canal company going to reprimand us for taking longer than we should have?' Izzy asked, putting down her cutlery.

'When I phoned from Tyseley depot and picked up the post nothing was said. I was expecting them at least to ask for details about the accident.' It was easier to refer to 'the accident' than 'Charlie's death'.

'And did they?' asked Elsie.

Dorothy shook her head. 'My superior mentioned Geoffrey's name so I knew he'd told them what had happened but they didn't quiz me. Knowing a solicitor can be a blessing. I'd wondered if I might lose my job.'

'It wasn't anything to do with you, though, was it? And Charlie was trespassing on our boat!' Tolly was indignant.

Dorothy saw the glisten of tears in Izzy's eyes. 'Stop talking about it. Some of us don't need to remember...' She paused, then foraged in her handbag. 'Anyway, I picked up the post.'

Tolly said, 'Anything for me?'

Dorothy handed her a letter.

She stared at the envelope. 'It's from Tommy,' she said. 'He told me he'd write.'

Then Dorothy passed one to Elsie. 'No need for you to wonder who that's from – it's got kisses on the back.'

Elsie snatched it and said, laughing, 'Why shouldn't my Jack put kisses on his letters?'

'Sorry,' Dorothy said to Izzy. 'Nothing for you or me!'

Back at Tyseley, after walking around the shops, which seemed virtually empty of stock, and marvelling at the lights shining onto pavements and spilling into the sky, Dorothy discovered the holds on both boats had been filled with scrap metal. She identified parts of planes, old saucepans, bits of iron railings. 'One good thing, we didn't need to clean the holds for that,' she said. 'Saved us more back-breaking work. But we'd better get them covered before the rain adds even more weight.'

She looked at both boats lying low in the water. 'I'll get the office to sign us out and we'll find somewhere to moor up for the night. Best we top up here with diesel and water, though,' she said.

Sooner or later Dorothy knew they would have to pass back through the tunnel where Charlie's accident occurred. Thank God they wouldn't reach it tonight, she thought. It was so nice to have the girls happy, and she hated the thought of them becoming depressed again.

As soon as the tarpaulins covered the holds, the rain ceased and the sharp cold air smelt of smoke.

Dorothy wasn't sure if it was because on a return journey the countryside looked different or if each woman was trying to spare the others' feelings but the tunnel came and went. Nothing was said.

At Banbury the scrap was unloaded. Dorothy

was aware of the girls' low morale but it was to be expected. All of them were tired and the memories didn't help.

With the holds empty they soaked mops and scrubbed down the boats in readiness for their return to Lower Heyford.

'Don't worry about yourselves,' Dorothy said. 'When we reach the basin of Rousham Cruisers you can use my little house to have baths and clean yourselves up.' She still hoped that Izzy would prefer to stay on the cut in her own boat. Elsie had told her Jack would be more than willing to give Izzy a lift to Braunston, where *Jonquil* was waiting for her. But Izzy declined.

'I think I'd prefer to be around people for a while instead of on my own. Going to Southampton with you, Dorothy, is just what I need. I'll cope better.'

With Dorothy in charge of *Mallard* and Izzy steering *Bunting*, the two boats entered the basin at Lower Heyford.

Amazingly, Tommy was already at Rousham Yard, looking completely different. He wore a suit and was waiting in the office, talking to Maisie, the office girl, when Dorothy pushed open the door. He looked disappointed that Tolly wasn't with her. He'd brought with him a huge bunch of flowers. Dorothy wondered where he'd got them. Digging for Victory had put paid to flower cultivation.

'The girls are at my house bathing and making themselves beautiful,' she said. 'You can either go across now or wait for me.' She told him she had paperwork to deal with. Maisie put the kettle on and Tommy left them to it.

260

Dorothy had already spotted Jack's car and heard the excited barking of a dog. She so hoped Elsie would think again about doing another trip with her. An arrow of sadness pierced her heart that no one was waiting for her.

Maisie handed her a letter from Head Office and Dorothy opened it with trepidation.

She'd been exonerated of blame for Charlie's death. She wondered what had happened to Charlie's body. Geoffrey had told her it would be sent back to Gosport. Casualties of war were buried with dignity even if no relatives came forward, he'd assured her. She assumed that would also be the fate of accident victims. Dorothy decided she would make it her business to find out, in case Izzy asked her.

The letter gave the date and time that she should start the next trip. There was also a footnote warning of cuts by the company. The sparse information was as she'd expected. With the war coming to an end, men would return from fighting. Women who had taken on their jobs would be required to step down, the work needed for the men. Also the railways could go back to hauling materials when the fear of bombing diminished. Idle Women would disappear.

After completing her paperwork and chatting with Maisie, Dorothy went to look at Elsie's car. Elsie had given her the key and, after removing the tarpaulin, she made sure the tyres were sound and started the engine, which, amazingly, fired first time.

Then she went over to *Mallard* and *Bunting* to give the boats a final check for cleanliness. She needn't have worried – both craft were spotless. She smiled, remembering her crew's horror at the Keating's Powder. The girls had already packed up their belongings, which lay safely in grubby hold-alls and bags on the concrete path, awaiting collection.

Such a lot had happened on this trip. She'd made friends. Even the awful rain hadn't managed to dampen their spirits too much. Neither had the heavy locks and stiff lift bridges, nor the dark, damp tunnels filled with the ghosts of the men who'd perished while building the cut all those years ago.

First to leave was Elsie. Jack looked happy to have her and her belongings in his care and the little white dog danced over the car's seats. Dorothy steeled herself not to shed a tear when she hugged her through the open window.

Tolly was next, hurling instructions at Tommy, who'd hired a taxi for the occasion. He looked delighted as he stowed Tolly's bags in the boot.

Dorothy hugged each of them and hoped they would return.

Soon she and Izzy were alone in the small, comfortable cottage.

Izzy said, 'It's funny without Elsie and Tolly, isn't it?'

'We'll meet up again, and quite soon,' Dorothy said, though she, too, felt dispirited.

Izzy looked relieved. 'When I come back,' she said, 'I shall visit the Black Cow and meet up with my friends there. I promised I would.'

Dorothy smiled at her. 'Friends are everything,' she said. 'Now, as we're not leaving until tomorrow morning, who is cooking tonight, me or you?'

Izzy volunteered to make a hasty meal and they got ready for an early start. Tomorrow she and Izzy would be on their way to Southampton. Dorothy wasn't looking forward to it.

## Chapter Thirty-seven

Izzy wasn't sure what to expect on reaching Southampton and the place where Dorothy lived. Southampton, not far from Gosport and a big dockland city in its own right, had also experienced severe bomb damage. Dorothy's home was in a terraced house near the docks. Huge cranes loomed over freighters and the smell of oil hung in the air.

'I hope you weren't expecting something more grand. My mum sacrificed a lot for me. Now it's my turn to keep her.' The backstreet house had a small front garden surrounded by privet hedges.

Although Dorothy had the key ready in her hand, the door opened and a woman who was obviously her mother flew into her arms, then hugged Izzy. A smell of baking followed her from the hallway.

'Come in,' she cried. 'I expect you two could do with a cup of tea. How nice to meet you – Izzy, is it?'

Dorothy's mother told Izzy her name was May. Small and dark, she had on a wrap-around pinny over a skirt and jumper.

'I've put you two together in the back bedroom. If it's not suitable one of you could sleep on the sofa, here.'

She pointed out an uncomfortable-looking piece of furniture near the fire. Against one wall a Morrison shelter was kitted out with blankets and pillows. A large dresser held plates and knick-knacks. Everything shone with polish.

'Don't fuss, Mum,' warned Dorothy. She was looking about her expectantly.

'We've been living in such cramped conditions, I'm sure everything will be fine,' assured Izzy.

May smiled, then put a finger to her lips, motioning them both to be quiet. 'Alfie's asleep,' she said, as though that explained everything. She hugged Dorothy again and disappeared into the scullery.

'Alfie?' Izzy looked at Dorothy.

'My little brother,' Dorothy said. 'He's a toddler, a right handful. I'll go out and bring in the bags. You make yourself comfortable.'

Izzy nodded. They'd had to park the car away from the house as piles of bricks left over from the last bombing still cluttered the road. Was it her imagination or had Dorothy been glad to get out of the room? She hadn't mentioned a brother. But, then, she thought, Dorothy never spoke about her home. She wondered how old May was. If Dorothy was in her early thirties it must have been quite a surprise for May to discover she was pregnant again after so long. Perhaps Alfie was one of those 'change' babies, she thought. Often when a woman was coming to the end of her childbearing years, starting the change of life, they sometimes fell for a late baby.

Perhaps Dorothy's father was in the services. Could that be why Dorothy didn't talk about him? Loose Lips Sink Ships, and all that. Of course, he might even have died. Didn't Dorothy say she provided for her mother?

Izzy shook herself. Thinking about people dying reminded her of Charlie. She tried to push him from her thoughts. Instead of wondering about Dorothy's life and her family tree she should be grateful she didn't have to go back to Gosport where every street would remind her of Charlie.

She should be planning for her new life. She thought about the rug-making equipment she had brought with her, intending to sit indoors and work on it while Dorothy spent time with her mother.

Eventually Izzy would venture out in her boat on the waterways, selling the things she'd made. She really wasn't looking forward to another trip for the canal company. But she'd promised Dorothy and couldn't very well let her down, could she?

A little later, sipping tea and eating cake May had made, the three women chatted about the past trip on the canals. Izzy thought how comfortable she felt in their company. She decided that before they went back to the basin at Lower Heyford she would take a trip home to Gosport. It would be nice to see her own mother now she had nothing to fear.

A child's cry interrupted Izzy's thoughts. Both May and Dorothy rose to their feet.

'I'll get Alfie,' May said. Dorothy's face was in-scrutable as her mother told her to sit down again.

It wasn't long before May clattered downstairs with a blond, blue-eyed toddler in her arms. Izzy saw tears in Dorothy's eyes as she put out her arms to take him from her mother.

Izzy was surprised when May snapped, 'Don't get him all excited. You know he won't sleep tonight if you do.'

The little boy's podgy arms went towards Dorothy and he was saying, 'Do-do, Do-do.' He had a broad smile on his sleep-creased face. Izzy remembered Dorothy buying a wooden toy car at a shop in Braunston.

At the child's words a smile lit Dorothy's eyes, and she enfolded him in her arms, holding him close.

'He's wet,' said May. 'Hasn't quite got the hang of using a potty. I'll take him out to the scullery and wash him.'

Izzy thought the little boy was going to cry. His bottom lip trembled as Dorothy relinquished him. And Dorothy was loath to let him go, thought Izzy. Quickly May distracted him by shaking a coloured rattle, then taking him from Dorothy.

As May and Alfie disappeared into the scullery, Izzy couldn't help asking, 'Where's his dad?'

'Away,' was the only answer she got. Izzy nodded. It was as she had thought. So many men were fighting abroad. So many women had been left at home to bring up children alone.

'I help as much as I can,' Dorothy said.

Izzy decided she would do whatever she could to make things easier for May, Dorothy and her baby brother. She didn't suppose May got much of a break from the little boy. She would offer to mind him while May and her daughter went into the town and looked around the shops or had a meal in a café. They'd find it easier to talk together without the distractions of a little boy. She could always take Alfie to the park she'd spotted in the centre of the city. The more she thought about it, the better the idea seemed.

'I'm taking my stuff upstairs. Coming?' Dorothy asked. May had closed the scullery door.

The back bedroom was comfortable. A double bed stood in the centre of the room with its brass bedstead against the wall. There was a washstand with a jug and bowl on top of it. Dorothy opened its door to show her a chamber pot inside. Once upon a time Izzy would have died to think she might use that in a shared room, but after the bucket on the boat she was ready for anything. A wardrobe stood in the corner and a dressing-table with a mirror caught the light from the window. It was all very clean, smelt of lavender polish, and homely.

'Which side d'you prefer to sleep?'

'The window side,' Izzy said.

'Fine by me,' Dorothy replied. She began removing dirty clothes from her holdall. 'I must get the copper going for hot water to wash this lot,' she said. She took out her brush and comb and a little bag of make-up and set them on the dressing-table.

Izzy saw her put a piece of paper beneath her pillow. She was surprised to see the blush on Dorothy's face.

'I always tuck it under my pillow.'

'Oh?'

'It's the last communication I had from the man I love.' She seemed troubled but then she removed the piece of paper and passed it towards Izzy. It had been handled so many times the paper felt like a piece of thin cloth.

*Darling Dorothy*
*Please excuse this writing but I'm in a lorry only a few miles from Dover. A dispatch rider caught up with us on our way back to Camberley. We have orders not to return to camp. I can only think we are on our way to France or Belgium. I will write again as soon as I can. I'll ask someone to put this in the post for me. At least you'll have some idea where I've gone if you don't hear from me soon.*
*Love Jakub*
*PS You mean all the world to me.*

'Oh, Dorothy, you haven't heard from him since?' She was looking at the date on the letter.

Dorothy shook her head. 'I miss him so much. We were going to marry. I have no idea if he's dead or not but that letter is very dear to me. At least I know he loved me.' She sighed, wiped her eyes with the back of her hand, then sniffed and said, 'I'm sorry. You've had enough problems of your own. You don't need to hear about mine.'

Just then May called up the stairs, 'I'm going to take Alfie to see the children playing in the park. Do you want to come?'

Almost in unison Dorothy and Izzy called back, 'Yes.' They laughed. Dorothy said, 'I'll get Mum to fill the copper with water and tomorrow we can wash out all our dirty clothes and get them on the line in the garden.' A smile still lit her face. 'It'll be lovely watching Alfie playing on the grass in the park,' she said. 'I don't know about you but I'm starving. Mum's made a stew for our evening meal.' She gave Izzy a hug. 'We should take advantage of not having to open heavy locks and lift iron bridges.'

'You two coming or not?' May's voice came from downstairs.

'Coming,' they chorused.

## Chapter Thirty-eight

Izzy felt she was truly on holiday with so little manual work to do. She swept the house, peeled potatoes for meals and generally made herself useful. Not having to rise early, then lounging in an armchair, listening to the wireless, made her feel very lazy.

She'd hoped last night in bed that Dorothy might continue with her story about Jakub but all she'd received was silence, until Alfie had woken, crying. This morning she had a headache.

'The Allies are surrounding Aachen in Germany,' said Izzy, when Dorothy and May returned home from shopping in Kingsland Market. 'I heard it on the wireless.'

'All the stallholders are talking about it,' Dorothy said. 'Does it mean Germany will surrender?'

'Hitler will never give in,' said May, then to Alfie, who had let out a high-pitched yell in his

269

pushchair, 'Oh, do give over, Alfie.'

'He's been grizzling all morning,' said Dorothy. 'We couldn't look at anything in the market because as soon as we stopped he cried. I think he's got more teeth coming through.'

Dorothy bent down and unclipped the little boy from his harness, pulling him into her arms. Izzy could see how much she cared for the little chap.

'Damn,' said May. 'I didn't buy potatoes. That's because he started crying when we reached the butcher's stall and he saw the dead rabbits hanging up.'

Izzy said, 'Why not leave him with me and the pair of you go back and pick up the things you forgot?'

Kingsland Market was two minutes up the road near the bridge.

'Really?' said May. She looked delighted.

'Are you sure?' asked Dorothy. 'Perhaps I should stay here as well.'

'You're coming with me,' snapped May. It was almost, Izzy thought, as though May resented Dorothy spending any time with Alfie. She told herself she was being silly.

'I wouldn't offer if I didn't mean it,' said Izzy. 'Go now, before I change my mind. I can see to Alfie. I do know how to look after a little one, you know.'

'I'm not waiting to be asked twice,' said May. She had started undoing her coat but now she refastened the buttons. 'We won't be long,' she added.

Izzy moved the pushchair into the living room,

then took Alfie from Dorothy. 'Go on, go out with your mum for five minutes, I can cope.'

Dorothy dropped a big kiss on Alfie's forehead. 'Go to Auntie Izzy.' The little boy grinned.

'Oh, will you put another log on the fire? It's so nice that Alfie's stopped whining for a moment,' May said. 'You've definitely got the magic touch with kiddies.'

'Go on – quickly before I change my mind,' persisted Izzy. 'Shoo!'

Lack of sleep had contributed to Izzy's headache. Dorothy had also woken and a couple of times slipped from the bed to listen to May at the bedroom door as she attended to the child.

A few moments later Izzy was alone with Alfie.

Alfie was tangling his sticky fingers in her hair as the front door closed. 'Let's find you something to play with, shall we?' she said.

She had seen how Alfie would play for a long while rattling pots and pans so she deposited him on the floor while she removed the fireguard and livened the fire with a couple of bits of coal and a log. Alfie had already struggled to his feet and walked unsteadily around the furniture, following her. She went into the scullery to rinse her hands and find something for Alfie to play with. Izzy took down saucepans, lids, and took out wooden spoons from the drawer for him to use as drumsticks, then looked down at the floor expecting to see his little face grinning up at her.

A familiar sound, that of the shovel in the fireplace scraping the hearth in the living room, assailed her ears.

She was just in time to snatch the shovel away

from him before Alfie poked it into the fire. Izzy had forgotten to replace the fireguard.

Grabbing the wriggling child, she fell into an armchair and began to wrestle off his outer garments. Alfie took exception to her removing his coat and started to scream. Izzy persevered with his coat, and shoes that had to be unbuttoned. Not an easy feat when the little boy was wriggling like an eel. The one item of clothing Alfie wouldn't allow her to remove was his blue hat with fluffy bobbles.

'Right, little man, you can keep it on,' she said, giving into the child squirming in her lap. Happy now, he slipped from her knees and, while she quickly put the fireguard back in place, toddled away, knocking into items of furniture as he disappeared into the scullery.

Remembering the pots and pans that he loved were on the floor she breathed a sigh of relief. Izzy began turning his coat right side out, in readiness to leave on the newel post in the hall where it usually hung. Her sigh of relief had dissipated when she listened and heard silence.

It took mere seconds for her to fly into the scullery, grab the child by the legs and forcibly remove him from where he lay beneath the galvanized wash copper. To manage that, she had to lie on the floor to turn off the gas tap. Alfie had been studying the flames burning beneath the water-filled copper that had been lit to boil for her and Dorothy to wash their dirty clothes.

Alfie thought it was a game and chuckled as she swung him up into her arms, and safety.

'It's obvious I can't leave you on the floor down

here,' Izzy said. A string of dribble fell from his plump lips. 'There are too many bad distractions for you. We'll go upstairs. You could wear a person out in no time.'

Izzy remembered May had muttered something about Alfie being overtired and needing a nap.

In May's bedroom Izzy placed Alfie in the white-painted, high-sided cot.

He stood gripping the bars and staring at her, tears on his cheeks. One word came from him: 'Noooo!' He shook his head and the bobbles on his hat danced frantically.

The noise cut through her head like a saw. Izzy gazed around the room, which looked over the street, hoping for inspiration. It contained a double bed with a cotton bedspread, on which May's nightgown was folded, the cot, a small white chest of drawers, a bigger brown chest of drawers and a wardrobe with the door ajar.

Izzy thought, Be firm. She turned away from him. Before she reached the door, the screams forced her to turn back.

Alfie's face was blotchy with tears. Her heart shattered into little pieces. He was only a baby, wasn't he? Her resolve weakened, she strode back to the cot, lifted him out and carried him through to the back bedroom. Izzy climbed onto the bed she'd shared with Dorothy and eyeball-to-eyeball started a staring contest with Alfie. He giggled and so did Izzy – he looked so lovable in his blue knitted romper suit and blue hat. Izzy pulled out his jumper and blew on his fat belly and he laughed. She did it again, feeling lighter and happier now she seemed to have the upper hand with him. The more she blew on his skin, the more he laughed, kicking his legs high in the air, his arms flailing and tangling in her hair.

''Gain,' he said, and yawned.

''Gain,' he demanded, so the game continued. He smelt of little boy, milk and talcum powder. The game went on and on, until Izzy was thoroughly sick of it. But his laughter was infinitely better than his tears. And then came the blessed moment when he didn't say, ''Gain,' and Izzy saw his eyes flicker and close. He was asleep.

She lay with the child in her arms, remembering that the gate was fixed so he couldn't topple down the steep stairs. 'You're so lovely,' she whispered, watching his body rise and fall with his breathing.

She'd already assured herself that, apart from rugs and shoes, there was nothing on the bedroom floor with which he could hurt himself. Ever so softly, so she wouldn't wake him, Izzy kissed his downy cheek.

Then she, too, closed her eyes.

It was the air-raid siren that woke Izzy – and the sound of the front door banging open. She looked across the bed for Alfie. He was gone!

'Izzy!'

Dorothy's call cut through the noise of the siren. Izzy fell off the bed and was rewarded with Alfie's cry of delight. 'Do-do!'

Where was he? Nothing looked out of place in the bedroom. Nevertheless Izzy looked beneath the bed.

'Izzy!'

'Coming!' she called, stumbling towards May's

274

bedroom. She breathed a sigh of relief. Alfie sat on the floor near the open wardrobe door stuffing paper into his mouth. He turned and smiled at her. A piece of chewed paper fell to the lino.

Around him lay the remains of letters he'd obviously discovered in a shoebox at the bottom of the wardrobe. All were crumpled, some were wet with spittle. A quick look around told her this was the only part of the bedroom he'd desecrated.

Without bothering to look properly at what he was eating, Izzy stuck her finger into his mouth and pulled out the slimy paper. She slammed the door shut, snatched a letter held in his wet hand and continued scooping up the paper until the floor was clear.

With Alfie under one arm and a handful of soggy paper in the other, she marched into the back bedroom and shoved the offending material beneath the bedspread.

Alfie began to wail.

The smell coming from him was eyewatering. Potty? She'd forgotten May was attempting to train him.

'I – we're up here,' she yelled.

By now Moaning Minnie had ceased her caterwauling and, holding the child firmly, Izzy carefully unclipped the gate at the top of the stairs and began to descend.

She heard the whine of the V-2. Dorothy was unclipping the bottom stair gate. The noise of the unmanned rocket ceased.

Izzy stood with her back against the wall of the stairway and waited, holding her breath. And prayed, her face against Alfie's head.

Izzy heard, 'Oh, my God,' from May somewhere near the front door.

Alfie was silent. The loud bang that followed set him screaming and pieces of distemper fell from the ceiling, the house reverberating with the aftershock.

From the hallway came a shriek.

'Alfie!' May appeared at the bottom of the stairs and Izzy practically fell down the last of the steps thrusting him into May's outstretched arms.

'Too late for a shelter. Get into the Morrison,' Dorothy commanded.

In the living room, the cage-like refuge welcomed them. Another whine and the following silence had Izzy's heart pounding like a drum. The dreadful explosion, when it finally arrived, sounded close. The docks? she wondered. Working on the peaceful canals, which Hitler didn't seem bothered about, she had forgotten how mind-numbing a raid could be.

Izzy could almost feel the fear coming off Dorothy and May.

Alfie wriggled on May's lap as she said, 'Has Alfie behaved himself?'

Izzy breathed shallowly. Somehow Alfie's blue bonnet had swept back and now lay around his neck. The pom-poms were wet and chewed. 'He's been a perfect angel.'

# Chapter Thirty-nine

Dorothy gazed out of the bedroom window at the washing dancing on the line. It wasn't often a breeze caught their blouses and jumpers: on the narrowboats wet washing was hung around the stove to dry. It should have been easier to fix a line outside the boat but the stiff breezes that came from nowhere resulted in clothes disappearing, even when pegged.

She breathed a sigh of relief. Wearing the same clothes day after day seemed quite natural on the cut – everyone lived in a similar way. After all, you couldn't change after every little shower.

The V-2s had passed and done their damage elsewhere, and the little house was still standing, unscathed. Her mother had taken Alfie to the park and Izzy was downstairs wiping out the copper and mopping the scullery floor where water had splashed when they'd rinsed the clothes in the big stone sink.

She sat down on the bed and heard paper rustle. Pulling back the bedspread, she saw twisted, torn and chewed envelopes and screwed-up type-written pages ... addressed to her. She picked up a lump of what at first glance appeared to be masticated bread. Surely this was Alfie's work. Using a fingernail to dissect it, she saw what was undoubtedly pencil marking, almost indecipherable.

One half of a page was readable. It was from

Regimental Headquarters dated December 1942 and said,

*I regret to inform you, as named next of kin of Jakub Kowalski, that your fiancé is reported missing by the War Office. He may have been captured and could now be a prisoner of war. You may be assured they will make every effort to locate his position.*

*There was a heavy bombardment of the port by the Germans...*

Here the typewritten sheet was torn away.

*Battalion attacked. I hope you will not give up hope of his eventual retu*

And there it ended.

Dorothy began reading the scraps again. She looked once more at the date. Surely that couldn't be right. How had she not known about this letter when the last communication she had received from Jakub was in May 1942?

She was sure her heart's thudding would be heard all over the house.

There was part of a wrapper from a tin, round red fruit-like objects on the paper. She couldn't see what they were, and the printing was in Polish, that much she could tell. On the glue-covered reverse she found writing so small she would need to find the magnifying-glass to read what she could.

Her heart gave a huge lurch. It was from Jakub. She knew his fine copperplate script. Surely this couldn't have come through the post. Wouldn't it have to have been enclosed in an envelope? Why hadn't she set eyes on it before?

From downstairs she could hear Izzy singing along with the wireless. Her voice was lusty and carried well, though out of tune.

How had these fragments of letters come to be strewn beneath the bedspread?

Dorothy picked up another partly chewed missive. This time it was a printed postcard.

*Dear Dorothy*

*I have just arrived in Hanover, this Field Service Postcard says in German, I am a POW. I am well and in Germany.*

*Jakub*

She let it slip from her fingers. Hanover? But she had had no idea where he was. She picked up a crumpled letter. The beginning and end of the page were missing but she could see once again it was Jakub's handwriting. There were too many holes in the paper for her to be able to read more than

*Last letter from you in April. I am in hospital my arm a small wound. Keep in touch with Regimental Headquarters London.*

Dorothy spread out the pages and envelopes. Her muddied brain was still trying to make sense of the fact that these letters had been delivered after she'd thought she'd had the last letter from her beloved Jakub.

Why had she not known of their existence? Dorothy couldn't help herself. She read the information in those scraps of paper again and let out a single scream that had Izzy rushing upstairs and bursting into the room.

'Dorothy, whatever's the matter?'

Immediately Izzy saw what Dorothy had in her hands, she put her arms around her. The sounds were terrible, like those of an animal in pain. Amazingly, Dorothy didn't shake her away.

'It's possible Jakub's alive,' Dorothy said, when the comfort of Izzy's arms had soothed her enough to talk without sobbing. 'All this time I thought he was gone, dead, and now it might not be so.' She looked into Izzy's eyes. 'Do you know where these pieces of paper have come from?'

Izzy looked guilty, then said hesitantly, 'I fell asleep this morning with Alfie and he got into your mum's wardrobe. You came back and then there was the V-2. I only had time to hide these – I was more worried about Alfie.' She gave a strangled sob. 'I meant to come and sort them out, but with the raid and then the washing, I forgot.'

Dorothy said, 'Do you know what this means?'

Izzy shook her head. 'I never examined the pieces, never had time with you yelling up the stairs at me and Moanin' Minnie doing her bit.' Izzy was breathless. 'I took the bits off Alfie and didn't dare put them back in the wardrobe for fear May would discover I hadn't been looking after her little one properly.'

'Alfie is *my* child!'

The silence was almost deafening. 'Alfie belongs to me,' repeated Dorothy.

Izzy, obviously shocked, stared at her. Then she picked up one of Dorothy's hands, and whispered,

'Tell me.'

Dorothy took a deep breath. 'Mum and I were living in Portsmouth. One night I went to Kimbell's dance hall with a friend. I met Jakub with some of his Polish mates. They had a weekend army pass. He walked me home. We met up again and it wasn't long before I fell in love with him. My dad had been killed in action – he was in the navy and my mum was going around the bend with grief. She was pregnant from Dad's last home leave. It was a shock – she'd thought she was over all that business – but her little boy was born dead.'

Izzy pulled her hand away from Dorothy's to stroke back strands of hair that had escaped the scraped-back bun. 'Oh, how awful,' she said.

'Awful's not the word,' said Dorothy. 'I was worried for her sanity.'

'What happened?'

'Jakub was going to be sent to Camberley. I'm not making excuses for myself or my behaviour but one night we went too far. By the time I knew I was expecting, I'd received this letter.' She patted the pillow that covered it. 'He never knew he was going to be a father when he went away.' She stared hard at Izzy.

'So there was I, pregnant and unmarried. All the neighbours would be pointing their fingers at me. I'd be ostracized. Lose my job, I was working at Lyons' then, in the tea shop. Mum came up with a way out of our problems.'

## Chapter Forty

Dorothy saw that Izzy was confused. 'It sounded like the best way out of our difficulties. I had the baby, and we moved to Southampton. It wasn't hard to rent this place – the owners had gone into the country to escape the bombing, you see.' She stared at Izzy. 'From the moment we arrived, Mum pretended Alfie was hers. She lavished all the care and attention on him that she couldn't give to her own baby. I got a job on the narrow-boats.' Dorothy gulped. 'To tell the truth I couldn't bear to be around and watch my son being loved so much while I had to take a back seat and pretend he was my brother.'

'Did Jakub find out about the baby?'

'I'd written to him. I had what I thought was his final letter before he went abroad. There was no reply to any of my letters. I believed him to be dead.'

She looked at the horror on Izzy's face. 'Maybe you have no idea what it's like to be an unmarried mother. People can be vicious.'

'C'mon, Dorothy. I come from Gosport. Life's no easier there.'

'Are you pointing the finger at me?'

'Not at all. I don't know where you got the courage to do such a brave thing.'

Dorothy breathed a sigh of relief. 'I couldn't bear it if you judged me,' she said.

'I wondered at you looking at Alfie with such love in your eyes. But I could see sadness as well.' Izzy paused. 'May goes to great lengths to stop you getting too involved with him, doesn't she?'

Dorothy shrugged. 'She gave me a new start without all the tongue-wagging. I cried a lot, thinking Alfie would be called a bastard. Mum's idea seemed the ideal answer, and it was helping her get over the shock of first losing Dad, then her own child. Alfie's not forward for his age, especially with walking and talking, but when he began calling her Mum, and me Do-do, oh, how that hurt. But there's no other way. I have to put up with it. I work to keep the home going.'

Izzy was staring at her. 'I see what you mean. But your Jakub might very well be alive in that prison camp.'

The enormity of the situation wasn't lost on Dorothy.

'It also means my mother has been keeping letters from me.'

Again, silence descended. Only their breathing could be heard in the small back bedroom.

'First, you've a right to look in her wardrobe and see if there's anything else she's hiding from you.' Izzy's voice was clear. 'Normally I'd say you should not look at her private stuff, but this is different, isn't it?' She pulled Dorothy up from the bed.

Dorothy said, 'Even if there's nothing else of mine there, I'm going straight over to the park and having this out with her.'

Izzy held her back. 'Don't be foolish. What's the point of that? You really shouldn't argue in front of Alfie. Things are bound to get heated, and why let complete strangers know your business?'

'But I need answers.' Dorothy was adamant.

'And here's me thinking the job on the cut taught you patience. Why don't you wait until the little one's in bed? I'll come up here out of the way and you can speak to your mum in private.'

'I can't wait that long,' Dorothy said.

'Of course you can. If anything, the longer you wait, the more you'll cool down. Besides, like I've already said, she's your mum and anyone can see how much she loves you and Alfie.'

Dorothy stared at Izzy. The young woman was right. 'Come with me,' she said, leaving the back bedroom.

In the bottom of May's wardrobe the shoebox sat askew on top of other boxes. Dorothy removed it and foraged inside, discovering birth certificates, marriage lines, the usual paraphernalia her mother would keep safe. The rent book was up to date, and there was also a blue post office savings book. She flicked open the pages and looked at the large amount credited. 'Look at this,' Dorothy said.

'I'm ahead of you. See who she's saving the money for!'

May had been putting money away for Dorothy every week since she'd begun work on the narrow-boats.

Dorothy saw her own name on the book, which meant she alone could withdraw the money. She gasped. 'Why would she do this?'

'Perhaps because she's your mum and she loves you? I don't know how many times I have to say that before it sinks into your head.'

'I feel guilty now,' said Dorothy.

'Maybe you should.' Izzy was putting everything back into the box. 'Just remember to listen to her side of things.'

'She should have given me my letters.' Dorothy was insistent.

Izzy ignored her. 'It looks like the box had fallen down,' she said. 'I'm sure the door wasn't locked so it was easy for Alfie to get at it while I slept.' Dorothy heard the guilt in her voice.

'While you slept,' she repeated. 'But there aren't any more letters here for me.'

'No,' said Izzy. 'And I think she meant you to have those, some time, or she'd have destroyed them.'

'Well, they're torn up now.'

'Not by May,' Izzy said. 'And she didn't exactly hide them where they'd never be found, did she?'

'What makes you so clever?' Dorothy was being sarcastic.

'Dealing with Charlie,' said Izzy.

Dorothy looked at her. She saw the glisten of tears in the younger woman's eyes and remembered all the awful things that'd happened to Izzy. No wonder Stevo had wanted her to have peace.

Izzy closed the wardrobe door on its secrets and took Dorothy's arm. 'Let's go downstairs. Everything looks better after a cup of tea, doesn't it?'

During the evening meal, Izzy tried her best to make conversation go with a swing. The wireless was belting out dance music, and May was chatty with the pair of them. She'd baked a few scones and they ate them with the last of the jam from the garden's small Victoria plum tree.

Maybe, Izzy thought, May was used to Dorothy's moodiness – after all, there were times on the boat when Dorothy was quiet and thoughtful. Of course she knew the reason for her friend's silence now. Izzy admired Dorothy for her patience.

May put Alfie to bed. When she returned, Dorothy gave Izzy a look that meant she was to make herself scarce.

'I'm going to bed as well. Think I'll read for a while. John Steinbeck's *The Moon Is Down* has me gripped.' As she passed Dorothy, she whispered, 'Be careful. Think about what your mother means to you.'

Izzy was reading when the raised voices floated upstairs. She prayed that, whatever the outcome between mother and daughter, the little time they had left before she and Dorothy visited Izzy's mum in Gosport would be peaceful.

After a while, the house became silent. Izzy eventually slept.

Izzy woke the next morning to breakfast in bed. Dorothy, already dressed, sat beside her.

'C'mon, wakey, wakey, we're going to Gosport today!'

'I thought that was tomorrow,' said Izzy, sleepily.

'No, and I want you up and dressed quickly, after you've eaten that.' It was a plate of fried potatoes, scrambled powdered egg and bread.

Izzy shifted herself into a sitting position. She remembered why she'd gone to bed early last night. It was obvious Dorothy hadn't come to bed at all. She wondered where and if she had slept.

With the warm plate now on her knees, Izzy asked, 'You're very chirpy. What happened when you confronted May?'

Just then May called up the stairs, 'We're off now. You'll be gone by the time we get back.'

Dorothy went to the top of the stairs. 'Bye,' she called. Then, coming back into the bedroom, she said, 'I blew a kiss from you to both of them.'

Izzy heard the front door open, heard the push-chair scrape over the step and then May called again: 'I did the ironing but leave it until you collect the rest of your stuff.'

Izzy heard the door slam. She put down her knife and fork. 'This is only the second time you've ever cooked me breakfast in bed and I'm not eating it until you tell me what happened.'

Dorothy sighed. 'Well, I started on her all blustery and wanting to know the ins and outs.'

Izzy looked expectantly at her.

'Mum said, "If Jakub was in a German prison camp, I doubt you'd ever hear from him. The prisoners' letters home are seldom posted." That's what she said. "You'd go on hoping and hoping. I didn't want that for you, love," she said. "I was shocked when after all that time of you having no replies to the letters you wrote one day an envelope arrived with several bits and pieces tucked inside. At first I was going to post it on to you. But I wanted you to live your life to the full, not go on hoping as I did, only to find your dad didn't come home after all."'

Dorothy's face crumpled. A tear made its way down one cheek. 'I waved the remains of the letters at her and said, "But it wasn't your decision to make."'

'And what happened next?'

'Mum told me she soon felt she'd made the wrong decision. But she didn't know how to tell me without me blowing up, storming away and taking Alfie with me.'

Dorothy got up and began pacing the bedroom. 'She was right. That's what I would have done yesterday until you told me to calm down and listen to her. I thought of how she'd stopped people pointing their fingers at me as an unmarried mother. She's always been there for me. She said maybe she hadn't been thinking straight after she'd lost her own baby. But after her decision to make me live every day as if it were my last, she found it harder to hand over the letters. But she kept them because, as you said...' Dorothy stopped pacing and stared at Izzy '...she intended to give them to me at some point.'

'The money?'

'She's put as much away for me as possible for a new start after the war when I'm not needed on the narrowboats and in case Jakub does, by some miracle, return.'

Izzy transferred the breakfast tray to the floor. 'How do you feel about that?'

Dorothy sat down again on the edge of the bed. 'Families do the strangest things in the name of love. You stopped me alienating myself from my mother, and I'll always be grateful for that. I don't think she knew my love for Jakub was so strong. Together she and I are going to try to discover his whereabouts.'

Izzy eyed the cup of tea on the bedside table. 'And where did you sleep last night?'

Dorothy coloured. 'With my mum, listening to

Alfie snoring,' she said. 'Look, I've got you to thank for your good advice. That's why I think we should go and see your mum a day earlier. She'll be missing you. Besides, a little space will do me and my mum a world of good.'

'What does May think about writing to the War Office? And what happens if Jakub is one of the lucky ones to survive and return home?'

'Mum said, "There's room enough within this family for us all to love Alfie. If his dad ever comes home, there'll be even more love."'

### Chapter Forty-one

*Oxfordshire, 1945*

Elsie glanced through the front window. She was keeping an eye open for the rest of her guests. Daffodils were in full bloom in the garden. A small bell hung from the branches of the little cherry tree. Though she couldn't hear it from where she stood, she knew it was jangling sweetly in the wind.

Her face lit with pleasure when she saw three figures nearing her front gate. The little boy's eyes focused on the bell and he turned excitedly to his mother, who bent and whispered something that made him laugh.

Elsie rushed to her front door, pulling it open. 'Hello,' she cried. 'It's so lovely to see you again.'

'I'd never have thought to do that,' May said, fingering the wild spring flowers fashioned into a welcome wreath on the door of Lock Cottage.

'I'll make you one to take home.' Elsie laughed.

She felt momentary guilt that she had only a box containing home-made gifts for everyone, instead of shop-bought presents, but it was 1945, and the local shops contained little that was worth spending money on for her dearest friends.

Make do and mend was still the theme. Shortages were acute. Christmas had been awful with provisions so scarce. There had been shops with five Christmas puddings and five hundred registered customers. Easter eggs were non-existent.

The birth of a baby remained magical. Especially her daughter, Ruby. A jewel for Jack and herself.

The christening was arranged for Sunday in the village church, its stained-glass windows still intact and lit now the blackout had finally been fully lifted.

Elsie thought of the vibrant colours that would shine through and her heart was filled once more with joy. She was longing to hear Dorothy's news.

'Come in, come in!' She threw her arms around Dorothy and practically dragged her, May and Alfie indoors. Matey, the Jack Russell, was jumping and barking with sheer exuberance. The wireless was playing a Bing Crosby song and his deep, melodic voice blended with the chatter coming from the living room.

'It's lovely and warm in here, and it smells heavenly,' gushed May. It was the scent of the applewood logs Jack had chopped for them to burn in the big open fireplace.

'Let's have your coats,' Elsie said, and hung them

on the hooks in the hallway.

'You look so well,' returned Dorothy.

'I'm happy, that's why,' said Elsie. She helped tug off Alfie's boots before he ran into the large living room, followed by the excited dog. 'Come in and meet the others.'

'Hello, Dorothy.' The slim dark-haired girl stepped forward and kissed her cheek, then threw her arms about her.

'Oh, my God! Tolly, where have you gone?'

Elsie watched as Dorothy pushed her away to arm's length and stared at the girl in the tight dress.

'She's been helping me with the decorating at the Currant Bun and works so hard I have to remind her to eat. I'll make sure she doesn't fade away though,' said Tommy.

Tolly gave a twirl to show off her slim figure.

With his now-broad shoulders emphasized by his grey suit, Elsie knew Dorothy would find it hard to recognize Tommy as the skinny young man who'd fallen for Tolly. She was right.

'Tommy? Is it really you?' Dorothy said.

'Who else would it be?' He laughed and swept her into a hug. Elsie could smell his sandalwood cologne.

'I'll put the kettle on.' Elsie went into the kitchen.

'I'll join you,' said Dorothy, disentangling herself from Tommy. May and Alfie had found a comfortable seat near the fire and were now talking animatedly to Tolly.

Elsie saw Dorothy look around the kitchen. 'You've made it so lovely here at the cottage.'

'Not just me,' Elsie said, as Matey jumped up on a stool and pawed at her. 'It's not just my doing, is it, Matey?' She tickled the dog's neck.

'Where's Izzy?' Dorothy asked.

'She'll be here soon. She's travelling along in her boat and Jack's walking up the towpath to meet her.' Elsie lit the gas beneath the kettle – it made a loud pop – and Dorothy watched the blue and orange flames.

Elsie began putting cups and saucers on a tray, taking them from a white-painted wall cupboard. 'It'll be lovely to see her,' she said, 'though she drops in when she's down this way.'

'She wrote and told me her business is doing well,' Dorothy said. 'She's been travelling around the canals selling the stuff she's made, hasn't she? I think she's content for the first time in her life.' Then Dorothy asked, 'Have you heard from Geoffrey recently?'

'He and Jack have got quite friendly. He's still living on his own in Western Way and trying to put right the damage Sandra inflicted on the house and garden.'

'Has she had her baby?'

'Oh, yes,' said Elsie. 'A little boy. Geoffrey said Sandra finally admitted the child's father is an American sailor she met in a Gosport pub.' She frowned before she continued, 'Anyone can see Geoffrey's not the father, but he settled some money on her and found her a rented flat in the town.'

'He wasn't so bad after all, was he?' said Dorothy.

'Jack doesn't think so. He's asked him to be

Ruby's godfather!'

'No!'

'Would I lie to you?' Elsie laughed. It took her a while to get her next words out. 'And you won't believe it – poor Geoffrey got left with Sandra's cat! Animals aren't allowed where she's living now. Fluffy and Geoffrey were sworn enemies, but apparently they've learned to tolerate each other. Fluffy even sleeps on Geoffrey's bed!'

'You couldn't make it up, could you?'

'I heard the Queen thanked all the women who had done men's jobs throughout the war. Makes me feel proud of you all,' Dorothy said. 'Of course my job won't last now the war's over.'

Tommy poked his head round the door. 'Jack won't be long. Izzy's boat's just gone through the lock. I had a sneaky peek out the front door and they're tying up. If it's all right with you, I'd sooner have a beer than tea.'

'And no doubt Jack'll join you,' agreed Elsie. 'Help yourself from that barrel.' She nodded towards a wooden cask on a stand by the kitchen's whitewashed wall. 'Jack's tapped it ready for when guests come after the christening.' She opened another cupboard and took out two glasses, handing them to Tommy.

'How are you getting on with your new recruits?' Elsie asked Dorothy.

'They're all right. Not a patch on you lot, life is certainly quieter than it was with you. If you remember, after you left, Izzy and Tolly signed on for another trip. Christmas we had extra rations. One and a half pounds of sugar each, eightpence-worth of meat and half a pound of sweets!' She

293

laughed. 'Remember the sugar that burst from the crate in Limehouse and Tolly made apple pies?'

Elsie wiped her eyes. 'Oh, that pie was lovely,' she said. 'I wrote and told you Sonny got married, didn't I?'

'I haven't come across them yet on the cut. You said his wife is a shy little thing.'

'Not so shy or little that she couldn't give him a black eye for staying out all night in Birmingham!'

Dorothy poured the boiling water into the brown teapot. 'Gypsy wives don't stand for any nonsense,' she said.

'Is this a private party or can anyone join in?'

'Izzy!'

Her red hair had grown longer and she had it tied back with a green ribbon that matched exactly the colour of her long skirt. Her knitted top was as cheerful as her wide grin. She held up a white lacy baby's dress, taken from a brown carrier bag. 'I finished it.'

Elsie couldn't help the tears that spilled from her eyes. 'Oh, it's beautiful. Just look at all that fine stitching. Jack!' she called. 'Come and see your daughter's christening gown.'

'No need to shout, love. I'm right here.' Jack pushed his spectacles up the bridge of his nose. He stood in the doorway and his smile was just for her. Elsie knew she was the luckiest woman alive. He touched the gown. 'Beautiful.' There was genuine awe in his voice and eyes.

'Where's that tea?'

'Just coming, Tolly! I'll take the tray through, shall I?' Tommy had filled two glasses with beer. He winked at Jack and added them to the tray, picked it up and disappeared into the living room.

'D'you think Tolly knows she's got a good bloke there?' Jack asked.

'Oh, I think so. They're talking about getting engaged.' Elsie put her hand over her mouth. 'Oh dear, I'm stealing their thunder. I think they're going to announce it tonight!'

'Jack,' called Tommy. 'What d'you reckon to ol' Adolf killing himself then?'

'Damn good show, if you're asking.' Jack walked into the living room where Izzy was now pouring tea. 'Started out painting and selling postcards and ended up being responsible for the deaths of some thirty million people.'

'What did Churchill call him? A bloodthirsty guttersnipe,' returned Tommy, taking a mouthful of beer. 'Ah, that's good.'

'Should be. The publican of the Black Cow owed me that,' Jack confided.

'I've got some news I'd like to share with you,' Dorothy broke in. 'Are we all together? But first I'd like to say how grateful I am for your support, friendship and understanding about my own problems that, finally, my friends, I shared with you.'

She had in her hand a letter and began to read to the hushed room.

*Darling,*
*The Germans have agreed to surrender Belsen to the British. One of the guards was at least human and has posted letters for us. He was severely reprimanded by the camp commandant. We have knowledge of evacuation, repatriation to rest camps in England.*

*I pray I live to see you again, Dorothy. So many dead, friends, women, children, so much sickness in mind and body. But now, so much hope, my darling.*
*Jakub*

The room was hushed, until May broke the silence, saying to Alfie, 'Your daddy's coming home, my love.'

But still the silence went on. Elsie knew every one of her friends in that room was filled with a great sadness. No matter how much they'd helped to win that terrible war, many, many people had paid the ultimate price. Forfeited their lives.

Again the silence was broken. This time by a lusty cry from upstairs.

'I'll go and bring her down,' said Jack. 'I expect my little girl is hungry.' He swallowed the last of his drink and left the glass on the table.

Elsie put her arm around Dorothy's shoulders. 'You've a lifetime to make up for with Jakub,' she said. 'You both deserve happiness.'

'I should say so,' said Tommy.

Izzy and Tolly agreed. Just then Jack came in with Ruby in his arms. Her long white nightgown was wet. 'Look around, my little one,' he said to the baby, holding her up so everyone could see her. 'There's your three godmothers, who are going to guide and love you. There's Tolly, there's Izzy and there's Dorothy. They were Idle Women, but not so idle at all.'

Elsie found his eyes now claiming hers, with the special look that was hers alone.

Ruby opened her eyes, blinked and began to cry.

## Acknowledgements

Writing is a lonely business. Sometimes you wake in the middle of the night worrying about characters you've created. After finishing the novel, if you are lucky enough, you get to pass it on to the people who make dreams come true. In my case these are Jane Wood, Therese Keating, Alainna Hadjigeorgiou, all of Quercus, and Juliet Burton, my agent. A huge thank you too to my readers for your loyalty: it is a pleasure to write for you.

Although this novel is based on the fantastic real-life Idle Women it is a work of fiction, and its events and characters exist only in the author's imagination.

The publishers hope that this book has given you enjoyable reading. Large Print Books are especially designed to be as easy to see and hold as possible. If you wish a catalogue please ask at your local library or write directly to:

**Magna Large Print Books**
Cawood House,
Asquith Industrial Estate,
Gargrave,
Nr Skipton, North Yorkshire.
BD23 3SE

This Large Print Book for the partially sighted, who cannot read normal print, is published under the auspices of

## THE ULVERSCROFT FOUNDATION